Captive Songbird

Book 2 in the Songbird Series

Ophelia Lockheart

Copyright

Table of Contents

Chapter 1

Roseanna

Copley's Revenge

On my last day in 1921, I stand on the steps of the Alderman Manor and wander down the dirt driveway with intention and curiosity but little by the way of excitement. Leaving the family, who I have come to love as my own, especially Danny—the love of my life—is like leaving behind my own heart.

Procrastinating from making the journey to return to 2021, which six months ago I wanted nothing more, I stand taller and stare down the structure that forced me back in time. The arched standing stones from the Emerald Isle that can move a person through time on the summer and winter solstices remain unchanged as the day I miraculously appeared here six months ago. I don't know yet if I am the sole person who has ever been transported by this power or if other people have travelled through time on these dates. Danny hasn't lived at the Alderman Manor long enough to know if people suddenly disappeared or appeared on the solstices and no one within the family's inner circle have ever mentioned it.

I still wonder if the jewellery or watch I was wearing had anything to do with the arch, or perhaps time wanted me here to find poor Benjamin's killer. It still makes me sad that I was unable to prevent the murder of Danny's younger stepbrother, but I am glad I was able to find his killer—and ensure he can never kill again. I would have preferred the law to administer the justice rather than for him to receive capital punishment at my own hands.

Nevertheless, the inner workings of the arch remain something of a mystery, though in theory, according to family lore, I should be able to pass forwards and backwards on the solstices.

Which might mean that, for the first time, I control my future. I can leave through the arch today, go and care for my beloved Nanna—who needs me more than anyone since her dementia has likely worsened in the six months that I have been gone—and tie up all the loose ends of my "old" life, until it is time for me to return to my "new" life in the past.

I wonder what items of use I can smuggle back through time with me. Some antibiotics perhaps and a support garment for Ida's sore hip; definitely some modern underwear, since I don't think pantaloons and I will ever get along.

Satisfied with what I must do, and in the absence of another way—where I get to have everything and everyone I want in the same time—I muster my courage for the hardest part of my day, saying goodbye to Danny. I put the picture he has drawn for me in the pocket of my knee-length, blue dress and am filled with longing to stay. If there were any other way I could take care of Nanna and remain with Danny, I would choose it in a heartbeat, but since travelling through time is a painful and physical challenge, I can't risk Nanna surviving it, and Danny has the children who depend on him. He can't just up and leave, and taking his whole family to the future isn't an option since it would pose too many questions. Neither of us want to invite those sorts of questions, so we're keeping our knowledge of time travel firmly under wraps.

I close my eyes and picture Nanna, for if I don't hold onto the thought of her, I fear my need for Danny will pull me under and I will never leave 1921. I picture her standing in the music room of our Victorian house, her soft skin wrinkling as she smiles, and her hands clapping as I play the piano. Nanna calling me by my mother's name, though doing so with utter love and admiration. Her encouraging my education and cheerleading my career as a paramedic. Nanna may not have given me life, but she has made sure my life was full of love and joy. And so, now I must return to her time and do the same for her.

It's not quite dawn, and the December wind blisters my cheeks and I feel the icy drops of rain start to fall. "It'll be raining. It always is." I remember Nanna's complaint and I chuckle to myself, knowing that the longing I have held onto and the sense of unrest inside of me will soon be over once I have Nanna safe beside me again. I try not to dwell that those feelings will be replaced by a different sort of longing and unrest. Danny knows I will return to him as soon as I am able and then our future will begin together, in the past.

I pull my lips into a smile, comforted that while it will hurt, it is the right thing to do. This way I get almost everything I ever dreamed of—romance, family and love, though not from all the people I love at the same time.

With those thoughts firmly in my mind, it's time to open my eyes and face the hardest day of my life. But something in the distance draws my eye. The silhouette of a wiry man in a dark suit.

Copley?

He's here, a dozen metres or so up ahead. Sizing me up as though he means me harm, he holds a gun in his hands and hatred on his face. Beside him,

Blundy stands watch. He nears quickly, my face screws itself into my most unwelcome of expressions.

"Had a visitor just after midnight. Claims he saw you shoot Eli Harris and dispose of the body. You're coming with me, and this time you ain't getting away with it."

"What?" Confusion hits me like a tonne truck. Okay, so I did shoot Eli Harris, and yes, he did die, but how does Copley know? Jimmy got rid of his body and no one there that night would have gone to the police, except... *Frank*. Danny's no-good father who conned the community and left with much of their money. He was supposed to leave town, never to darken the Alderman's doors again, but maybe he didn't. Maybe he went to the police instead.

Copley's lips smugly curve up at the edges and when he's close enough for me to smell the dried sweat on his uniform, I realise he's serious. I inch back, but he is prepared for my attempt at escape and rushes me. To evade his capture, I turn and race towards the house but his hand snatches my wrist. "Get off me—"

"I'll tear you and Danny apart if it kills me. Why should he have everything while I have nothin'?" He sneers through gritted teeth. I'm far enough from the house that it would be difficult for any of the sleeping residents to hear me. Still, I try but Copley is too soon dragging me away from the house. I kick and yell for help but Copley's cigarette-stained fingers clamp around my mouth. In the ruckus, Blundy rushes to help, bundling my legs and taking half my weight.

They drag me away and we pass the back of the house and head towards the road behind.

I am screaming.

No one can hear me.

When we reach the truck parked on the lane behind the house, they pause to catch their breaths.

I fight like an alley cat backed into a corner and wrestle my legs free of Blundy's grip. Copley grunts as he tries to hold me still and shouts at Blundy to, "Fucking grab her!"

In the tussle I scratch the length of Copley's face and kick Blundy hard enough in the balls that he crumples to the floor. Copley has one hand around my bicep. With his free arm, he elbows my face and my nose spits out blood.

"Fucking bitch! Let's see if you're as tough when you get to Holloway!" He laughs outrageously and secures my hands behind my back with heavy handcuffs and then he throws me face down onto the floor of the waiting police truck.

Chapter 2

Roseanna

Hello Holloway

During the thirty-minute drive, I yell, scream, and beg through the small window in the metal partition for Copley and Blundy to return me to Danny. Until, when he has had quite enough of my noise, Copley slides across the metal insert and closes the tiny window between us. I am left in darkness and consumed by both anger and regret.

I think of Nanna, and I wonder if she is safe or even still alive. I shelve that thought. In this time, Nanna won't be born for another twenty-four years. The mere notion of her being absent from the two timelines that I have somehow come to straddle sends me into a panic that I cannot afford to spiral down right now, so I think of Danny instead, who will believe I never said goodbye before leaving through the arch and returning to the future.

That thought alone crushes me even more than my fear of the 1920's prison that awaits me.

I'm thrown around as we move but can still hear Copley tell Blundy that "they got me good." He instructs Blundy to drive right up to Holloway without stopping, like he is afraid something will go wrong in his plan to incarcerate me. Blundy responds eagerly, asking questions which I do not want to know the answers to.

The ground steadies beneath me and with the absence of being jolted around in the back of the police truck, I notice how my body aches from the struggle of my altercation with Copley.

In the darkness, I don't need to strain my ears to hear Copley over the hum of the engine tell the guards of the jail to open the gates. Shortly after, I hear the grating sound of heavy metal in need of an oiling being wrenched open as though one inch at a time, then I am once again jerked around as we travel over uneven ground. My stomach stirs and not from the movement. With my hands still bound behind my back as I lie face down, I manoeuvre myself onto my back in time for when the truck's rear panels open and the back of the truck is flooded by the early morning December glow. Gripping the handle of the door and glancing down at the tangled state I am in, Copley smirks. "Comfortable enough for ya, was it?"

I use my heels to push myself back against the side of the van to an almost sitting position and tell him, "You need to let me go, now! I won't stand for this, Burt. You have no evidence and I have not even made a statement. You cannot throw me in jail. It's—"

A shriek is forced from my throat as Copley's hand forcibly snatches my ankle and I am yanked forward enough that he can grab the tops of my arms and pull me out of the truck. Blundy walks around the vehicle to stand beside me, his hands outstretched as though anticipating I will fight. Copley shoves me forward so I am sandwiched between the two men.

"You're in shit up to your ears, young lady," Blundy says without malice. It strikes me as odd that he calls me "young lady" even though he isn't very much older than me. He looks at Copley over my shoulder as though seeking approval in speaking with me.

"You two are going to be sacked for this!" I reply, as Copley jolts me forward for a step I was not expecting.

"I've got a concrete witness and a dead body. I've got the murder weapon and, thanks to a new piece of police equipment, I've unshakeable evidence that you did it! I'm getting you locked up before the Aldermans hide you somewhere. We'll get to statements later." Copley snatches my wrist, yanking me to a standstill. I flinch as he brings his palm towards me, but he doesn't hit me, he just twists his hand around in front of my face. "Fingerprints!" he says with a flourish. "I thought it'd all be a load of tosh and bloody useless like everything the department comes up with, but it turns out, they're quite nifty." He bends his hand in all directions and I notice a burn spanning from his index finger to the bow of his thumb. "Each one of those soft little pads is unique. No other man or woman in the world has the same pattern. Marvellous, isn't it?" He checks my reaction and seems peeved with the look of disgust I am throwing him and then carries on. "When you came to see me at the police station, I took your fingerprints from the cup of water I gave you. I didn't know at the time they'd come in handy, but I knew you were one to watch. All that hanging around with scum like Daniel Alderman, you had to be. And I was right! Murder, no less!" His moustache changes shape entirely with the brim of his grin. "Well, that was more than I could have hoped for. Utterly unique, they are," Copley says again while admiring his fingers.

"Yes, fingerprints are utterly unique. So identifiable that I'll be sure we remove yours before your bloody corpse is thrown in the river."

Copley stares at me blankly as he takes a moment to understand my conclusion.

"She means fingerprints can be used to identify dead bodies, too, boss," Blundy replies with a look of revelation.

"I'm not the one walking into Holloway," he counters. "And since I can't get justice from Daniel, try as I might, and even Frank is a free man now despite everything he has done. But you, having you hanged for murder, that will ease my annoyance."

"You don't give a damn about the murder of Eli Harris! You've looked the other way for worse crimes. You just want to get back at Danny. Well, you won't. He'll get me out of here and you'll just end up looking even more stupid than normal." I throw the insult at him knowing that he is a proud if not a bitter man and hoping it will give him enough of a jolt to want to avoid the path he is dragging us both down.

"This is justice for all the Aldermans have done." He grips the flesh of my bicep angrily and forces me forward towards the huge wooden doors of the prison.

"Oh yeah, and what about all the things you've done to him, huh? I know it was your lies that got him those beatings in the workhouse. This vendetta has to stop. Punishing me, punishing Danny… what's done is done." My legs scramble, and I dig my heels in as best I can to prevent us from going forwards.

Copley smiles as though my fate is inconsequential, so long as it hurts Danny.

"You're fucking crazy!" I spit.

His hand roughly snatches my face and he forces me to look up at the cold stone before us. "And you are a murdering bitch."

I don't reply. Instead, I stare up at the imposing greyness until it blends in with the sky and let his words infiltrate my soul.

Murderer.

I can't even argue with him, except to say that Eli Harris deserved it, and if Danny's life were in danger again, I'd do it once more in a heartbeat.

"Scary old prison, ain't it?" Copley says, bringing his face close enough that his moustache scrapes my chin.

I lean away, jutting my jaw towards the huge castle-like building that's as wide as it is tall. It's imposing and deeply intimidating. The enormous grey stones of the prison are darker than the sky that is threatening rain. It's suffocating, like the building has sucked the oxygen, along with the colour, right out of the sky.

I scan the rest of the space and see that beyond the main building is a grassed area leading to the walls that contain the tomb-like jail. They're at least fifteen-feet tall and impossible to climb. Back the way we came, a gravelled path leads back to the gatehouse with two uniformed guards standing watch.

Heavy foreboding weighs me down along with the sense that I am being watched.

"You terrified yet?" Copley asks with a smugness that has me wishing my hands weren't bound so I could wipe the smirk right from his face.

I answer indifferently, refusing to allow him to bask in the pleasure that my fear brings him. "It's Holloway prison, Burt. I've seen it before and it is nothing to be afraid of. Besides, I won't be here long."

I have seen Holloway prison before in my own time. It recently closed its doors to inmates and remains a London landmark. However, driving past the signs is nothing like becoming an inmate in 1921.

I push away thoughts of the horrors that are contained within the building, and instead I focus on getting myself out of this situation. "You, on the other hand, have much to be afraid of. Danny will tear you limb from limb once he hears of this and I will be powerless to stop him. Now, you've had your fun. I'll tell Danny it was all just a miserable joke and make sure you are not punished, but you must return me to him, now."

Copley combs his moustache with his fingers, then shakes his head. "Can't do that. I've got an eyewitness who made a police statement, a body, the murder weapon and fingerprints, too. Why, I wouldn't be doing my job properly if I didn't incarcerate a murderer."

I wonder why, of all the modern amenities that I have missed or wished for in the six months that I have lived in 1921, something so utterly benign would lead to my incarceration. It's a cruel twist of fate when I was so close to going home.

Blundy takes my other arm more lightly, lifting my weight so we travel faster. "Come on, let's get her inside. She won't be so full of herself once she goes through processing."

"Go to hell!" I spit my reply, but as we enter the heavy wooden doors that are flanked by evil-looking gargoyles, I realise it isn't Copley that's going to hell, it's me, and I am powerless to stop it from happening.

Chapter 3

Danny

Weathering the Storm

Beside me, the bed is cold, the sheets still wrinkled from use but I know—can feel it in the ache on my bones and the echo of my heart—that my Red, my captivating songbird, is gone.

Still, I must check. She promised not to leave without saying goodbye, though I knew it was a farewell neither of us could stomach. Too often I have strategised ways to keep her here. Ways in which I can force her not to leave me. From blowing the damned arch to smithereens to throwing myself down at her mercy and begging her to stay, all has crossed my mind, such is the calculated bastard that I am.

I walk to the window, not bothering to dress, and watch the rain batter the pane. The sun, completely concealed by a troubled sky, barely lights the view before me. Beyond is the damned arch—the source of my torment—yet I can't bring myself to destroy it, not yet. Not while my love requires it to fulfil her duties to her kin. But one day, one day it will be gone and I will rejoice that she is in my arms from now until forever.

Once I have gone through the motions of readying myself, I trudge downstairs and prepare for my first day without my darling Red.

"Tea is brewed." Ida nods her head to the cup and saucer on the counter without looking up, her bony hands wrist deep in dough. I take the cup and mutter a thank you. "Red gone, then?" Ida's steely gaze softens as she glances up to me and I nod. "Probably for the best. There's work to do at the factory and matters of the heart are best kept away from business."

I already searched the house and the grounds for Red, even though I knew she was gone—I could feel it in the bones of my soul. It would be like she never existed if it were not for the pain in my heart reminding me that she is no longer here. All I have left of her now, in this time, is a letter—written in her own hand, confessing her love for me and a vow that she will return, and also the dozens of drawings I have traced of her perfect profile. The letter, now in my chest pocket, warms my black heart. Meanwhile, until she returns, I vow to become the man she deserves.

"She'll be back once she has taken care of her grandmother," I reply with a firm conviction that overrides the whispers of the devil on my shoulder. Or perhaps it is an angel, my better self, urging me to listen and to do what is right and destroy the arch so she cannot return to this godforsaken place. As always the voice is steadfast with its ironclad argument that Red will enjoy a safer, better life in the future. It's just a shame for Red that I am far too selfish a man to listen to the voice.

I quieten the sound of doubt in my mind, blocking out the guilt and shame as I have become so used to doing when there is something that I want. I remind myself, as she has so often told me, that she wants me too. She has chosen this life. She chooses me, and I, despite vowing to never subjugate another to my lifestyle, choose her.

I put down the cup and saucer and straighten my tie. If I am to be the man she deserves, there is much to be done.

**

"The machines are salvageable. The engineers are on site and they'll have this place up and running by the end of January," the contractor tells me, and I know I'm damned lucky the fire didn't destroy all the machinery.

"Not soon enough. I'll pay all the men overtime if they have this place up and running before 1921 is out."

His furry brow tenses while he looks at the board that holds his papers. "But that's…. ten days."

"Problem?"

"Mr Alderman, I'd need extra men, orders—"

"I've already spoken to the suppliers. The goods will be delivered tomorrow, and the work will go ahead as planned even if I need to find new contractors."

I pause, allowing him to digest this information. I deliberately chose this man, a local contractor with a gang of hardworking family men. Good people who usually don't get a chance to work on large-scale commercial projects.

"Pull this off and I'll pay 40 percent more. I have big plans starting in the new year, including a new site I have just acquired in Dagenham. Get Alderman Inc. up and running by January and I will make sure Thomas Builders are hired for the new site."

His mouth pops open. "You're opening a new factory?"

"I intend to open several."

"Can you afford all that?"

I nod. "Business is thriving after the war. I have the insurance money that will cover many of these costs." He doesn't need to know I also sold my gun operations for a very handsome profit—the new Daniel Alderman has no use for illegal business if he is to provide Red and his family with a good life. Now, all my eggs are in the future of motorcar's basket, which Red assures me is the very future of the world. Thomas doesn't look convinced and it causes me to smile only partly at his reaction. I clap him on the back. "Mr Thomas, one day every man and his wife will own a motorcar. They'll be as common as the household cooking stove or the inside lavatory, and I want Alderman's at the forefront of manufacturing. There is no time to rest."

"That common, huh?"

I nod.

"Not sure I'd trust the wife in a ten-horse power lump of steel."

"So, we have a deal?"

"Same arrangement with Dagenham factory plot as we have here?"

I agree immediately. Thinking he was competing with the biggest building firms, Thomas gave me favourable terms. Still, his men will be well compensated for their work.

"Oh, and Thomas—"

"Yeah?"

"It won't just be your wife in one of my motorcars, it'll be your daughters too. The world's going to get a lot smaller and people will be travelling all of it."

Thomas looks at me like an eccentric fool but has the good grace not to voice his concerns and he holds out his hand to shake.

"I wish you luck. It's good to see an honest Alderman making his way in the world." The way his eyes hold mine denotes the bona fide authenticity of his statement, and I grip his hand tighter for the gesture.

"Good day, Mr Thomas. Remember, up and running before 1922. I have big plans!"

I walk away, back to my motorcar to go to my next appointment, to fulfil another promise—a school for the children. I feel a sense of pride and hope for the future that has alluded me since my feet touched the soil of Flanders Fields, and before the news broke that my father had deceived our community. It's a calm peace, a gentle tide filling my heart and rinsing away some of the stains of my past, and I immediately wish I could see Red's face as I tell her of our good news. But, even though her absence is only temporary, there's a stirring in my gut. A sense that all is not right, and it isn't. How can anything feel right when I have a Red-shaped hole in my life? Still, it won't be forever.

Chapter 4

Roseanna

From Bad to Worse

I'm pushed up the corridor, my legs floundering like a newly born bird's, Copley to my left, Blundy to my right. My heels click on the stone floor in a rat-a-tat-tat. The ceiling is so high the noise echoes off the beige, stained walls in a rhythm that's almost as fast as the beat of my heart.

There's an immediate absence of natural light. It induces a headache that worsens as we pass the caged yellow lights on the walls. We reach a side room with a desk that has a barred window looking out onto some kind of grassed courtyard. Women in white mop hats and brown oversized gowns lurk outside the window, walking in straight lines, each alone as though passing the time together is forbidden.

"Name?" the burly man at the desk says in an impatient tone; it's clear he has asked the same question a thousand times. He clutches a fountain pen in the fat of his hand like a pre-schooler just learning his first letters.

"Please, you have to help me. I shouldn't be in here. This is all a terrible mistake. This officer here," I gesture with my head towards Copley, "is the very worst of the London police. He has a grudge against my boyfriend, Danny Alderman. If you just call him, he'll prove all of this is nonsense, I'm certain. He'll do something—"

Copley interrupts. "Roseanna Chapman. An acquaintance of the infamous Danny Alderman, son of Frank Alderman. You'll want to pay particular attention to this one, Ned. Don't take any of her shit about Daniel Alderman. She's to have no contact with him. If I get my way, by the time he hears of this, she'll already be hanged for her crime."

The desk man's eyes glance upwards at me, lingering on the heave above my breasts before travelling to my face. "That right?" The look in his eyes darkens and I wonder how fearful I should be of this man as he scribbles down my name. "That Frank Alderman did a right number on a lot of folks round here. You won't be popular, princess." His tongue darts out of his mouth like the tongue of a lizard scenting the air. "But there are other ways to be popular in here, so you'll be all right."

"You're disgusting. Let me out of here now!" I thrust my hands against Copley's restraint. He and Blundy hold me tighter until the burn of their grip travels up my arms.

Ned ignores my protests. "Charge?" he asks Copley.

"Murder," Blundy interjects proudly, clearly wanting a piece of the action.

"It's all a big mistake," I reply, trying to ensure I am in some way heard and forcing stern authority into my voice, which waivers on the final syllable.

The men laugh, like I am joking, making me feel small and impotent. Still, I try again. "You must call Daniel Alderman. I can't go to jail. I don't belong here. Please!" My display of strength vanishes at the final hurdle and my voice leaves as a desperate beg.

The smugness in Copley's expression hits me like a physical assault and my legs shake of their own accord. "Ned, go and tell Ian that I'm here. He'll be interested in this new inmate."

Ian.

I remember the name.

His brother, the warden.

Fear shivers up my spine and makes my voice vibrate as it leaves my throat. "Ned, please. You have to help me."

"Yeah, yeah. You're innocent. It's all a mistake. Heard it all before." Ned stands and leaves the room. While he is gone, Copley taunts me about the terrors of Holloway Women's Prison, threatening that my treatment will be the worst of any inmate in its entire history thanks to my ties to the Alderman's.

"If you all hate Frank so much, why didn't you arrest him when he came to make a statement? He is a wanted man, after all. His escape from Wormwood Scrubs is well documented in all the newspapers, I've read it. You're going to look incompetent and I'm going to make sure, once I've seen my solicitor and gotten out of here, that the whole of London knows about it."

Copley tugs on my wrists, jarring my shoulders. "Frank got an honourable release. New evidence." His face turns up in an angry snarl. "Paid off the right man, I expect, or he blackmailed someone, the rotten bastard. Frank'll get what's coming to him eventually, but meanwhile, I've got you. You're as good as dead, and when Danny finds out, it'll destroy him." He's so close that when he grins, baring badly stained teeth and a missing incisor, I can smell last night's whisky on his breath. "Watching him lose everything, it'll be even better than watching him die."

"You utter bastard!" I struggle against him and use my shoulder to butt him away so that he crashes into Ned's desk. Copley lets out a hiss and cups his hand with his other. My eyes focus in on the puckered skin of a burn that's healing. It's serious enough that I can tell straightaway that he will always be scarred. A vision of the factory fire, me stuck behind a barricaded door while the unit burned… I remember the arsonist leaving me in there to burn. It takes me a moment, and then, sure that my accusation is right, I spit, "*You*. You set the fire at the Alderman factory. You did it!" I'm incensed when I think back to the devastation that the deliberate act of the vengeful man has caused. I tussle forward but Blundy has a hold of my wrists.

Copley's eyes cross to his partners then back to mine. "You're crazy, of course I didn't. Perhaps we should take you to the wing with the asylum." He looks momentarily concerned, and as a police officer who was responsible for an arson that almost killed a woman, I'm not surprised.

"You're going to pay for this. I'll see to it if it kills me!" I kick my foot out at his knee as hard as I can. If my hands were free I'd be hitting his face.

"You bitch!" He backhands me across my face just as his left knee gives way. For a moment the artificial light blinkers off and then on again and by the time my vision is clear, Copley has left the room, though I see him in the hallway outside.

"Look, love, piece of advice. You can make this time easy or hard on yourself. You can't go round assaulting police officers and think you won't get burned. You're on remand for the next few weeks until you make your plea and get your court date. Keep your head down or you'll get it knocked off," Blundy whispers in my ear, and I stop my futile struggling as Ned enters the room and reseats himself behind his desk.

"Address?" Ned asks.

I give him the Alderman's address, and while Ned takes his time scratching it down, I listen intently to Burt informing Ian that I have been charged with the murder of Eli Harris.

"Eli Harris?" his brother replies. "The world is probably a better place. His mother has been in and out of this place more often than a whore jumps into bed."

"Yeah, no one will miss Eli Harris, *but* she's Daniel Alderman's bit of skirt, Ian. Daniel Alderman!"

"I see. And you want me to do what with her? She'll stay here until she goes to court just like the other remand lags."

"Yeah, but you could make her time worse. Make her suffer. Ian, it's thanks to the Aldermans we're, you know… it's their fault!"

I'm no longer trying to slyly glance at the door, as I openly turn myself to watch the scene just six feet away. Copley, who is not much taller than I, looks at his brother beseechingly. Side by side, the two men look similar. Ian wears perfectly round, black-rimmed spectacles and unlike his brother, his black moustache is styled like Hitler's rectangle whereas Burt's is more of a handlebar. Ian, with his flecks of grey, looks to be in his forties compared to Burt's late twenties. What both men have most in common is their wiry frames, dark hair against white, sallow skin, and hollow cheeks that enhance their hate-filled eyes.

"Burty, you know her time will be terrible. As terrible as I can make it."

"Yeah, but I want that bitch to suffer. Take her out and give her the rod every day. In fact, let me know when you're doing it and I'll come watch."

Ian cups his brother's shoulder. "I'll see to her treatment. But you'll not come here again unless you have official business. I've got the press and the bloody cabinet on my back. The Duchess of Suffolk just came through my doors and now suddenly people are concerned with prison standards." He polishes the glass of his spectacles with his sleeve and then replaces them casually as though he is discussing dinner instead of my abuse. "Speak to

Ned and tell him she needs a careful eye. I've got a gala this week with the commissioner and a bloody report to write on rehabilitation! Like any of these good-for-nothing retches stand a chance at rehabilitation."

"Date of birth?" Ned asks loudly enough to make me jump. I lose part of the conversation I am eavesdropping on while I rethink the year that I was born ... eighteen-ninety-seven." Saying the year aloud makes me tremble, as though by voicing it, I have somehow made it true and now I will never return to my own time.

I was supposed to see Nanna today.

"I have to get out of here," I shriek and somehow, Blundy's loosened grip lets go and my legs move urgently, away from the desk and out of the room.

Copley catches my arm as I pass. "And where do you think you're going?" His fingers dig painfully into my flesh.

Ian looks down at me over his circular spectacles. "Escaping already? Why you haven't even been shown the ropes yet, my dear." He passes a small agreeing nod to Burt, then turns his attention to the guard behind the desk. "Ned, throw her in segregation. Let's see if we can't show her what's what."

Burt pushes me into Ned's suddenly waiting arms and I'm dragged back with such speed my legs can't keep up, and I wind up hanging from his grasp. Then Ned pulls me down the corridor and through a heavy door that he unlocks with an iron key fastened to his belt by a metal hoop.

I can't stop myself from screaming and struggling. Demands turn into pleas for freedom but Ned doesn't respond. I kick my legs and try to make us stop, but it's futile. I am restrained and barely half of Ned's weight and so he marches me along with no problem at all.

We pass a series of corridors and descend stairs until we reach the open door of the last cell in the barely lit space. He frees my restraints but holds both my hands in one of his, tightly until I can no longer feel them.

"You're lucky you're not dead for running off like that. Anyone who attempts escape is either shot on sight or they get the rope, then they're thrown in the ground around back with not so much as a stone to mark their names. Think about that next time your legs get the wind in them." He jolts me forward into the threshold of a tiny black cell. "When I come back for you—*if* I come back for you—you'll want to be on your best behaviour!"

"Please! Don't put me in—"

His thickset palm meets my temple and with force, I am thrust back until I land on the dirt floor of the cell.

Then the door slams shut.

Chapter 5

Danny

The Sun Still Rises

"Finest beef from the butcher's," Ida says, placing the cut steak in the centre of the table. Henry is already salivating, hopping up and down in his seat like Christmas came early. "Butcher says our Clifford was in there the day before, buying bacon. The cold store is full of the stuff. We've enough bacon to stuff a pig."

I don't answer. If Clifford wants to buy bacon or see Trevor that's his business.

"I don't mind having bacon for breakfast every day. Anything beats oats," Henry mumbles.

"Roseanna said it's important not to eat too much meat. She said five portions of fruit and veg a day," Alice interjects, ignoring the face Henry pulls at the mention of vegetables.

"Wise woman, is our Red." Thoughtful silence falls on the room and I stare at the empty chair opposite me. She's been gone just three days. I make sure to eat three meals a day and continue to breathe, but her absence still feels like I am starving and suffocating at the same time.

"She'll be back, though, won't she Danny?" Alice asks, her hand lets go of her fork and it slides across the table to hold mine. "It's Christmas Eve tomorrow. We've got the tree up now ready for Father Christmas and Henry and I have made all the paper chains. Do you think she might pop back, just to see us on Christmas Day?" Alice's face is lit with a hope that crushes my chest.

I force a smile. "She'll be back, Alice, but not in time for Christmas. Now, come on, let's eat this fine meal Ida has provided." I stand to serve the meat and Alice's hand moves back to her cutlery. "Where is Clifford, anyway?" I ask. What with endless meetings to win business, I haven't seen much of him. It seems since the Aldermans won the council contract for police vehicles, and the subsequent announcement in the newspapers, there are councils right across the country looking for vehicles, not to mention the private car sales market I am working on tapping into.

"He gave Harriet a ride into the city for those mints she likes... Fox's Glacier—bags full she's eating, but she'll still share some with me and Henry. Says she's been craving mint. It's the baby," Alice says, grinning. She grins every time the baby is mentioned. I suppose we all do. "Do you think Roseanna will be back before the baby is born? I hope so."

Ida speaks directly to me as she answers Alice's question. "The sun still rises every morning and falls every night, no matter when she's back, there's work to get on with. Still, nothing like a new baby to signify a fresh start," Ida says, slopping mashed potatoes onto my plate. "But spoil the mother, spoil the child. She'd do better to eat the liver I keep offering her. Iron, that's what a growing babe needs."

"Roseanna says no liver. It contains high levels of retinol," Alice says proudly.

"Retinol. And what's that?" Ida asks cynically.

"Um… well, I don't know. But Harriet believes her. She's not eating it." Alice's voice is righteous and it causes a smirk to rise up on my lips.

"Poppycock. Didn't do me any harm or Fra—" Ida stops before she says my father's name and instead drinks from the wine glass in front of her. Her expression abashed. She regrets mentioning Frank, and looking around the table, it hasn't escaped the children who look equally saddened by the memory of him. Thankfully, there has been no sightings of the man who tried to take what belongs to the children.

"How did your meetings go, Danny?" Henry asks, changing the subject and filling the silence.

"They went very well. Very well indeed, young Henry. We are now looking at contracts for the whole of London and the south from Brighton to Dorset. If the orders keep coming like this, we'll need ten factories."

"Ten factories." Henry's eyebrows rise up into his hairline. "Roseanna'll surely come back if we've got ten."

"She'll come back because she loves us, Henry. Roseanna doesn't care for factories and such things. 'Tis love that will return her to us," Alice says admonishingly to Henry.

I put my fork down, suddenly not feeling much in the mood for beef. For even if Alice is right and Roseanna cares not for factories and riches, I owe it to her, for all that she is giving up, to give her the very best life here. I vow to.

"The girl is right," Ida says, placing her cutlery in the centre of her plate. "She'll return, and when she does, mark my words, she'll be very proud of what you are achieving. Now, less talk of people we can't see and more effort on cleaning those plates before you. I'll not have good food going to waste."

At Ida's comments, I glance at Henry, who is licking his plate clean, and then turn back to Ida and grin.

"Can take the boy out of the workhouse but you can't take the workhouse out of the boy," Ida huffs, and I consider she is right. The Aldermans are on the uppers, but it's a slippery path and there's always a risk of sinking back down, so I retreat to the office, passing the newspapers I still buy but cannot face reading. Every day Red is away, I'll work so hard she'll want for nothing when she comes back to me.

Chapter 6

Roseanna

Isolation

I scream. I scream until my throat burns and no sound comes out. The small space is terrifying. Panic sets in like an electrical current beneath my skin. Terrified and unable to rationalise events, my thoughts become dark and irrational.

Is that burning I smell?

Thick smoke from smouldering flesh chokes my airways.

If there's a fire, will they come for me?

I doubt they have a risk assessment or any such plan to respond to fire, it's even more doubtful the so-called guards would risk themselves for an inmate.

Even less so for one that is hated so much by the warden and his brother.

I tune into each sound individually. A cough from far away... the sound of a bell ringing... the jingling of keys... the scuttle of a rodent. Then I isolate the smells: dirt mixed with the ammonia of urine... stagnant mildew and mould... stale body odour gradually being diluted by cold air coming through a draft in the too-small-to-get-my-hand-through vent that leads to the outside. I cling to any such things that will distract me from absorbing the mania inside that is trying desperately to claw its way out. Time, I am certain, passes; how much time, I do not know.

Without night and day or a clock as a marker, other rhythms of life beat louder. When my stomach begins to painfully ache, I wonder if it is lunchtime. When my tongue begins to feel thick and furry, and I notice the stench of body odour closer to my nose than that which infiltrates the air, I wonder if it is approaching bedtime.

The width of my cell is reachable from the span of the tips of my fingers and only slightly longer in length. There is no furniture. No bed or even a blanket to keep out the draft that passes from the vent and beneath the door. On my tiptoes, I can feel the rough concrete of the ceiling and, apart from the cracks in the brick, there are no gaps for windows or any hope of an escape.

I sit in the corner and an overhead pipe drips water on my head. Slow and rhythmic, I focus on the torture of that instead of my incarceration.

My bladder bursting, and with no one answering my calls for help, I've no choice but to relieve myself in the corner farthest from the door. Part of me hopes the guards don't see it. Part of me wishes I could throw it at them in protest.

Anger comes in waves, often followed by self-pity. Nanna, Danny, all of the Aldermans.

Will I ever see them again?

Will I be hanged for the murder of Eli Harris?

Ophelia Lockheart

I could die and no one may ever find out what happened to me; my remains will be dumped in the unnamed graves planted behind the prison grounds. But at the heart of it all is the knowledge that I did, in fact, murder Eli Harris, and for that I am guilty as charged.

Captive Songbird

**

When the guard comes for me, I have no idea if it has been a week or a day. I've had no offers of food or water and I feel weak—perhaps that was their intention in throwing me in this hole, to destroy my resolve. But I suppose if it had been a week, then I would be dead by now. One thing I know for sure is that I've missed my one shot at seeing Nanna, and by hook or by crook, I'm going to get out of here, then I'm going to see Copley pay. If that means playing nice and doing as I am told for a while, then so be it, but Copley WILL pay.

The door unlocks like thunder—the reverberating sound of metal-on-metal echoing through the air—and suddenly warm light is cast into the void.

"Get up. You're going to be late for today's processing." The voice is hard and clipped but decidedly female for which I am glad; at least it is not meathead Ned.

It takes my eyes a few moments to adjust to the light and for my limbs to follow the orders I have been given.

The guard wears a thick, floor-length garment that neither identifies as a coat nor a dress. Brass buttons fasten it up the middle and the chain of a pocket watch swings from the central fastening of the waist. Between the join of the material, it is parted in protest at the expanse beneath and reveals the thin cotton of a white shift.

"You want me to bash that thick head of yours?" Her hand reaches for the baton that swings from her hip. "I said, get up!" I stand despite the protests of my aching limbs and she rough handles me out of the space. "Filthy pig," she mutters, noticing the wet patch in the corner. "You'll learn cleanliness is next to godliness in here. Among other things…"

I protest. I need her to phone Danny. I need legal representation. I need a drink of water. My treatment has been barbaric and shocking and heads must roll.

"Shut ya cakehole or I'll fill it with me fist!" she spits back.

I bite my lip, too tired to argue and hope that there will be opportunity to fulfil my requests soon along with some offering of food and water once "processing" is done.

I try to remember the paths that we take, in case there is opportunity to escape, but one wing looks much like another. The guard leads me up the concrete stairs and down a few corridors until we reach a hole in the wall. An office space with some shelving set back from the corridor, it's contained by a window and there's a queue of four women being handed bundles of rags with a pair of shoes placed on top by the female guard behind the glass. She's dressed identically to the guard pressing me forwards and just as sturdily built making me wonder if the prerequisite to be beefy is a part of the prison guards' job description.

I stand in the queue as directed and look to the burn of my wrists where the handcuffs were previously. Angry and sore welts darken my skin and I say a silent prayer that the skin doesn't get infected. The guard notices my watch and snatches it from my wrist. "Fancy. I'll take that so ye can't hurt yeself with it." She puts it in her pocket and taps the baton at her waist when I take a step forward to retrieve it. I allow her to have it for now and delicately finger the pocket of my dress to check my earrings are still there. They are, for now.

"Verity, not surprised you're back," the guard, now holding my shoulder says to the woman before me. She's a similar age to me, I notice.

"I ain't done nuffin' this time, Mo. I wasn't selling to him; I was just giving directions to the bloke. Coppers got nuffin' better to do," the attractive bobbed brunette replies. "Anyway, they can't keep me long this time. I'm telling the judge the second I get on the stand I've got a bairn on the way and we all know what happens to women with child in this shithole." I immediately look down at her tummy and then look away quickly as she tells me earnestly, "I ain't lying this time so you can all think what you want. There's a babe inside of me and I ain't having it in here!"

I nod and open my mouth to congratulate her as one might usually but then clamp it shut as the guard speaks over me. "You'll have that babe wherever the judge says and ain't nothing you can do about it now."

The guard behind the screen hands Verity her uniform and she moves aside so I can get mine. The brown material is pushed across the well-worn desk and I freeze, reluctant to take my uniform and submit to this place.

"Go on then, take it. I haven't got all pissing day."

"I… I can't stay here. You need to contact Daniel Alderman for me, please. Tell him that I am here. I'm not meant to be here."

The words that spirt from my mouth are met with an eye roll from the prison officer before me. Only Verity, beside me, appears in anyway sorry for me as her eyes widen and she speaks. "Daniel Alderman? You're Danny's new bit of skirt? I heard he was off the market, but I didn't think he'd go with a lag."

"I'm not a lag. It's all a big mis—"

"Take the bastard rags and go!" the guard orders but I don't move. Instead, I am thinking that maybe, just maybe if Verity knows Danny, she can get word to him.

Verity quickly takes the rags for me and tucks them beneath my arm, pulling me away so the person behind me can get theirs. "What you in for anyway?"

"Murder," I choke out.

**

After processing, Mo shoves me into a cell and pointed to a piece of rope dangling from the ceiling. "It attaches to a bell for emergencies and it'll snap if you try and hang from it," she says, followed by a warning never to ring the bell or risk a beating and to follow orders or I'll definitely take a beating. Then the door slams shut with the heavy grating sound of a key churning inside a lock.

The new cell is only marginally bigger than the hole I was put in when Copley first brought me here, and I wonder what happens next and when I will see a solicitor or if I might be allowed to make a phone call.

Furnished with a small bed made of planks with no mattress, only the thin sheet and blanket that covers it stops it being mistaken for a short-legged table. A metal jug and bowl are provided atop the desk for what I assume is washing and a bucket sits in the corner for toileting. In among the pile of clothes I was ordered to change into is a small pile of handkerchief-sized worn-out rags that I have no idea what their use is so I leave them beside my pillow. Tucked beneath the desk is a chair that wobbles uncomfortably when I sit on it. Also on the desk is a copy of the Old Testament. It has pages ripped from it and a joyfully pressed message carved into the pages— probably by someone's fingernail, in the absence of ink—that reads, *you will die here and God won't save you!*

The book lands with a thud as I toss it onto the bed, then move to the only sanctuary in the room: the window. Framed with thick black bars, the single, cracked pain of glass opens inward just enough that I can press my face through the bars at the top and inhale the now icy, December breeze.

"You're like me. First thought is to crank open the window and get some air on your face." I quickly turn back to my empty cell then realise that the familiar voice is coming from outside, which is strange because we are at least three floors up. "Looks like we're neighbours for now at least."

I crane my eyes to the left and see a small hand waving from the window of Verity's cell, perhaps only ten feet from mine.

"Are all the rooms so small?" I ask while watching the women in the exercise yard beneath us walk swiftly to keep warm. Some are grouped, others alone, and all are dressed in the same rags we were given in processing: a brown burlap-like materialled dress that finishes at the calf and itches as you walk, and black, scuffed shoes worn in enough that they don't rub.

Verity laughs. "This ain't the Savoy. The cells are all titchy but up here we get the better view and a lot less bleedin' rats!"

"I see," I reply and gaze out at the view beyond the walls of Holloway. 1920s London stares back at me beneath the darkening grey sky. A few rows of houses to my left are the only markers of normal life outside the prison. They're close enough that I can see children playing on the road between the terraced houses. Beyond that, a few high-rise buildings mark the hustle and bustle of North London and to my right lies the green grass of Richmond Park and the promise of freedom. So close, but also so impossibly out of reach.

"I'm Verity, by the way, but my friends call me Titty—not like boobs. My boyfriend Sammy has a stammer and can't say Verity so he calls me Titty— it caught on." She giggles loudly though I suppose she has told this story many times.

The introduction makes me almost chuckle despite my solemn mood. "I'm Roseanna. My friends call me... well, they call me Roseanna." She laughs again and I wonder how she can laugh so often in this place of sadness and misery. But then, I suppose if a person were here long enough, they'd have no choice but to make the best of it. I hope I'm not here long enough to find that out.

"You know, it's Christmas Day tomorrow. Of all the bleedin' places to spend it. There won't be no goose on the table, that's for sure."

I calculate the date. I was supposed to go home to Nanna on the twenty-first of December. It's now the twenty-fourth and I've been here four days. Four days already! Time is slipping by and I'm impotent to stop it.

"You still there?" Verity asks breaking me out of my reverie.

"Yeah," I reply, glad of the distraction. I wonder if Verity can supply any information that will help me. "Nice to meet you, Titty," I say and try to conjure some enthusiasm. It's not her fault that I'm broken by this place, and I suppose she needs to talk to someone just as much as I do. "Do you know Daniel Alderman?"

"Well sure," she says, which makes my heart beat faster with the knowledge that she can contact Danny as soon as the judge lets her out of here. With her being pregnant, surely she will be freed soon.

"Could you get word to him that I'm in here? I've asked the guards but they don't seem all that inclined to help me."

Verity takes her time before she answers and I find myself crossing my fingers. "I know *of* Daniel Alderman. Not many people actually know him. Like old Saint Nicholas or the king, I suppose. *If* you're his girlfriend, how in God's name doesn't he know you're here? You sure he hasn't chucked you?"

"No. Nothing like that, we're very much together. I was supposed to be leaving to look after my grandmother, but I was taken by the police on the morning I was supposed to go. Could you ask one of your visitors if they might go to him and tell him I am here?"

"Visitors!" Verity cackles a sound that pains my ears. "Ain't no visitors in here, love. Besides, murder… you'll be in here 'til they push you off the block. Ain't no point in visitors."

A whelp escapes my lips and my stomach spins. I grip the bars, pushing my face into them as though it might be possible to squeeze through them and run home—to Danny.

"Hey. Don't upset yourself, Roseanna. I'm sorry, that was uncalled for. You might not get the rope. Stranger things have happened. I heard people were starting to call for women not to get hanged no more. You might just get life…" I try to tune her out but she waffles, trying to make me feel better, until she comes up with an idea that might actually help me. "I could tell my boyfriend Sammy you're here in a letter. He'd go find your Danny if his mum went with him."

I hold onto this glimmer of hope. "We can write letters? How soon until I can write a letter to Danny?"

"Well, we ain't supposed to write nothin'. I only just got here. I got to find some paper, a pen, and someone to write it for me. Then I got to find out who will be released soon *and* be willing to sneak the letter out with them." It occurs to me that privileges such as writing letters probably don't apply to inmates in circa 1920s prisons. "Sometimes the guard might send you one, sometimes they won't. But I reckon we'll have your letter with Danny in the next few months."

Few months.

Hopeless.

I don't know if Danny could get me out of this situation even if he did know I was here. Perhaps he would blame himself or be consumed with legal fees when he is trying so desperately hard to get his business back up and running. I shake my head and say anything, anything at all that will change the subject and keep me from drowning.

"What are you in here for?"

"Turning tricks." Her voice is quiet, tinged with shame but it quickly turns defensive. "I was only doing it one last time to keep from losing mine and Sammy's room at the inn. Sammy says by the time the baby comes along, he'll have a job and we'll be able to afford a little house down at Stratford and Bow. He means it this time."

Verity's account is a powerful distraction. I doubt she wants to hear that Sammy sounds like a lowlife—and since he is possibly my only way of getting word to Danny—I don't upset her by saying so. Instead, I ask another question. "How far along are you in your pregnancy?"

"Last bleed was bonfire night. I reckon she'll be here in the summer." There's a whimsical lilt to her tone that's soothing. The promise and possibility of a new baby is about as freeing as I can imagine—especially if said baby will be born outside of Holloway prison, something that Verity seemed quite certain of before.

I calculate her as about seven weeks into her pregnancy though she could be more. There'll be no access to marmite or even proper sanitation. If she gets six months jail time, then she'll be cutting it fine to have her baby in a proper hospital.

"That's lovely. A summer baby…" My voice trails off and I watch a fight break out between the women beneath us. A blonde older woman, perhaps fifty, smacks the face of a brunette until she falls to the dirt before running back inside before the blonde can deliver any more of her punishing blows.

"That's Bet down there with the brassy blonde hair. She's as rough as assholes and likes to pick on the new ones. You'll want to keep an eye out for her. And over there…." Verity's finger points to the right where part of the wall meets the building. A small rotund woman with a short mop of white hair stands alone, rubbing her arms to keep warm while smoking a cigarette. "That's Mag's. She's probably in for bootlegging again. If you want some moonshine to take the edge off, she's your woman."

"Chang?" I wonder aloud. That's where, in some ways, all of this started.

"You don't seem the type for chang—"

"I'm not," I immediately correct.

"Well, she won't get you that. You'd have to go to Bet for that, but you don't want to wind up owing to her. She'll finish you off soon as look at you."

I mentally mark the women's faces down as a warning to stay away.

As though she senses my apprehension, Verity continues. "You'll get out of here in no time once you get your court date, you'll see."

Court.

"When will that be?" I ask.

"You'll get a date in the next few days or weeks—"

"Few weeks?! I can't stay here until… I have to get home to my nanna and Danny will be wondering where I am. He's going to think I…"

"Shhh. It's okay. The weeks fly by, you'll see. Come on, we'd better get ready for lunch. You'll want to get changed into the dress and shoes you were given. Mo's on shift and she's a right bleedin' cow if we make her wait."

I close the window and change quickly, then tuck my earrings into the bible, close it and hide it beneath the sheet on my bed. I stand and wait for the door to open. Even though my stomach is entirely empty of sustenance and I should be starving, it cramps and I heave air into the bowl meant for washing.

Then the door opens and Mo motions for me to get up and out. This time I follow her orders obediently.

Chapter 7

Roseanna

Allies and Enemies

Before I am allowed to join the others and go to the food hall, I am taken
to Dr. Hadfield, an unremarkable man in his fifties, who wears a white coat
and seems thoroughly bored of his job. He inspects my wrists and applies
an ointment to the open wounds though doesn't dress them stating that "air
and clean living will see them right," even though the air is stagnant and the
place filthy and rampant with rats. He remarks on the bruising to my face
but he stops me when I try to tell him how I suffered them, reminding me
that his is the job of healer, not legal assistance, and that according to policy,
all women must receive an evaluation of fitness before they begin their
sentences. So, I endure the process hoping that I manage to get something
to eat before the canteen closes. His examination is light in the most literal
sense of the word, and he makes it very clear that he has no interest in the

circumstances of my incarceration and will not pass on messages to my boyfriend. He scratches down on paper my name and date of birth, and asks me if I have any venereal diseases. Then he asks the date of my last period and being unable to explain the details of the Depo contraceptive injection, since it won't be invented for quite some time, I make up a random date and assure him I'm not pregnant.

The guard posted outside the room takes me to the canteen and I fill my bowl as quickly as I can after I am warned that anything not finished in five minutes will be discarded. Heavy stew pans rest on the counter and another inmate slops watery grey liquid with a few lumps of brown and green into my bowl. I move along the line but there are only empty serving dishes. A cook unapologetically tells me that the bread is gone and I'll have to make do with stew. I nod and take a spoon, grateful that there is at least something to fill my belly. I'm so hungry surely anything will taste good, though after I sit down and take just one bite, I realise that even one of Ida's tongue sandwiches would be preferable to the tasteless, barely tepid water with overcooked carrots and chewy beef still attached to what resembles part of a hoof.

With the canteen mostly empty, I sit alone. Famished, I pick up the bowl to drink directly from it but before I can take a sip, it is whipped from my hands.

"What you gonna do 'bout it?" says Bet, the woman Titty earlier pointed out, as she holds the bowl out of my reach. She's older and has a face worn by hardship. Looking around to see if she has supporters, I wonder if I should fight her. A guard stands in the corner of the room watching, and I raise a brow to her to question if she is going to do anything to help me but she just shrugs. "Exactly what I thought. You ain't gonna do nothin'. Fool," she spits and walks away with my bowl to the sink at the back of the room and tips the entire contents in.

Tears of fury burn at the back of my eyes but I refuse to allow them to spread. I have just enough time to chug some water that's warm and tastes of rust from a metal bowl before the guard calls me to go to the exercise yard.

I file out of the room as instructed behind a woman with long blonde curls that bounce as she walks. As I follow her down the corridor, I get a waft of perfume so perfectly proportioned with sweet notes of jasmine that I'm sure it must have been expensive. She must only have recently arrived to still smell so good. It's then that I see the shoes on her feet are not the standard issue leather pumps with a worn heel. She has her own shoes, with a delicate heel at the back. As my own shoes slob off my heels and I scuttle to keep them afoot, I wonder what it must take to obtain your own shoes and if someone brought them in for her.

I catch up to her and introduce myself since she has a friendlier appearance than the likes of Bet or the guards.

The blonde snootily looks away and continues walking, only faster now.

Bitch, I mutter internally before the door to the outside is thrust open and a tide of crispy leaves are blown inside, and the glory of the sun glows my cheeks before I am even level with the threshold. Like a beacon, I rush forward, accidentally brushing Blondie and earning myself an annoyed hiss, but the excitement of clean air and a somewhat open space are too much temptation and my legs continue to propel me forward.

Then I am tripped and fall face first into the dirt.

"Don't walk on the grass. You'll get a beating for that," the blonde woman says and dangles her polished fingers towards mine. I ignore the offer of assistance and glare at her, standing quickly, brushing remnants of my assault from my dress.

Behind me, the guard has turned her attention to one of the other women and seems to have missed Blondie tripping me up.

She throws me a look of indifference when I ignore her hand and then she continues walking a sharp right along the path. "Exercise: walking this rectangle until you go mad with frustration. Twice per day after eating no matter the weather for twenty minutes. It's in the prison manifest." I ignore her hoity tone and the fact that she tripped me up since she seems to want to talk to me now and she might say something of value. "I had to stop you from walking right out into the middle of the grass. My accommodation overlooks the exercise yard and I saw a woman viciously beaten this morning with a bat, no less, for rushing to the middle like you were about to."

"Oh. Thank you," I quickly reply, feeling suddenly grateful she tripped me. "Why won't they let us use the whole yard?"

"Power. And control. They want us meek and pliable, and rules are rules."

I nod my head and then remember seeing the women earlier standing alone. "Are we allowed to walk together and talk?"

"Yes. For now. They don't care about the remand section mixing but once we're sentenced, no talking." She brings her index finger to her lips and I notice how flawlessly pretty she is. A young woman, perhaps midtwenties like me, she has a delicate bone structure, and a small, straight nose frames hazel eyes so wide they're almost cartoon-like. "Not that I'll miss the talking." She pokes her chin in the air with an air of being too good for this place. "I'm Beatrice," she provides with a huff as though I pressed her for the revelation.

"Roseanna," I reply and continue to walk beside her while scouting out the area. All together there are probably fifty women walking in a vast rectangular loop, all looking miserable. The walls are more than twice my height and stand firm on all sides against the fortress of Holloway. Four guards: two men, two women, which doesn't seem much muscle to keep us all contained, but the guards all carry batons that swing by their hips and they wear an expression like they're keen to use them.

"Stop it!" She hisses and then, provoked by my unaware expression provides, "If you keep looking around in that way, the guards will think you're looking for means of escape."

"What if I were? Has anyone ever managed to escape?"

Beatrice laughs. "No. No one has ever gotten out of here illegally, though if you can pay the right people, then you stand a chance of getting out sooner." She looks me up and down then returns her eyeline to my bruised face. A flash of care is quickly replaced with self-preservation. "If you're planning to attempt escape then I can't be seen in your company. I for one very much intend to get out of here alive." She walks ahead to widen the gap between us and I allow her to so I can focus my thoughts on remembering the TV episode I watched with Katie during a slow night shift where a guy was trying to break his brother out of jail.

**

Later that day, I endured a full bowl of barely edible slop at the canteen that once again had barely any food left, and after watching another fight break out, I was returned with a line of other inmates, one by one, to my cell. I learned that Beatrice was in the other cell beside mine.

During dinner, I learned that Verity seems to know a lot of the other inmates. She pointed them out like I might know them with references like

"Lil from Up West" and "Deb's from down the common." And after I told her my first meal was taken, she warned me to stick up for myself and fight anyone who tries to take what is mine or I'll get labelled as easy prey. "You're in for murder, aren't you? I'll help you put the fear of God into 'em, don't you worry." I hope I won't be here long enough to have to deploy such methods.

As the sky outside my cell darkens to a deathly shade of midnight, and despite surviving my first day, I still feel bereft. Then, with the moon high in the sky and still no nearer to speaking to Danny or seeing a solicitor, I lay down to sleep and I am alone again with my thoughts.

There are no distractions except the haggle of women communicating to each other outside the windows and I dread a return of the nightmares that have gone away for a short while. So, I lay alone on the wooden planked bed, holding my own hand and imagining Danny is beside me. And somewhere between the hollers of the inmates as they pass contraband—moonshine and cigarettes—between their rooms via the windows using DIY rope, I persuade myself that he is with me and it comforts me even though sleep is elusive. It doesn't escape me that while Danny believes we are separated through space and time, the reason is much less scientific. Hate, cruelty and violence are what has separated us and I can't help but wonder if this is my punishment for the part I've played.

I hear a woman singing. It's a song that's so lovely it feels familiar, and the voice is as beautiful and sweet as the comforting scent of roses in the rain. A vision of my mother's face comes to me and I wonder if my psyche is calling up the sound to get me through the darkness. It startles me at first since it has been so long since she abandoned me, but strangely the concept of her watching over me is so comforting I decide it doesn't matter if the sound is imagined or real. I am drifting away to a nicer place where my

Ophelia Lockheart

mother cares deeply for me, Danny has my hand and Nanna is right around the corner.

Chapter 8

Danny

Full Steam Ahead

Thomas made good on his promise to have the factory up and running, and by the new year, the assembly line is full steam ahead. Still, I can't shake the feeling that there is something I am missing. Something is wrong.

"Danny, another load has been shipped to the warehouse. Counsellor Edwards put in another order for twelve dozen motorcars and we've had more orders from Dorset and Wiltshire." Clifford hands me the paperwork and waits for my approval. He's cut his hair short and now looks less like Benny. Part of me wants to tell him to grow it back, but since Benny's murder, perhaps it is even more important for him to become his own man, even more so now that he has stepped away from selling chang and is solely focused on the business, though I doubt even that focus will help him get used to the loss of his twin.

"Great job, Clifford. That's just grand." I throw him a congratulatory smile. "You've worked very hard for these orders. We all have. Now, do we have enough men to cover the work?"

"Already thought of that. June's telephoning *The Daily Herald* to place an advert. We'll need to employ two more dozen men."

I pat Clifford on the back. "At this rate, we'll be the biggest car manufacturer in all of London."

"That we will."

Clifford and I walk up the stairs together to the office and I force the smile to remain on my face. This is good. Life is good. Alderman Inc. is going places. Finally. After all our work and dodgy dealings, we have the orders we need to help the business grow. We have turned a corner. Folk seem to have short memories and the gossip regarding my father conning the folk of East London out of all they had seems to be fading from time, and a new, respectable Alderman name is taking root.

After the disaster Red and I faced with Eli and Frank, I can't say I'm not thrilled one is dead and the other is long gone. My father was the noose around my neck for far too long. Making this change and taking the right side of life has never felt better. And while I should be happy, all I think of is Red and if she'll approve of the changes I'm making—and if she will come back to me. I know in my gut we are connected, but since the morning of her departure, I've had the gnawing feeling like something with her is wrong, which deepens my fear that she'll decide this life is far too difficult when compared to the one she'll be leaving behind in the future.

Clifford stops me, gripping my arm to get my attention before we reach the office. "Jimmy's in there. He said he has urgent news."

I pull out my pocket watch. "He'll have to make it quick. I have Detective Scott coming at nine."

"Scott? What does he want?" Clifford's face pulls down in disgust.

"Says he wants to talk about the fire."

"They got new leads?"

"I doubt it, Clifford. Man just wants to make sure I'm not planning to run off with all the money like Frank." I grin jovially but Clifford doesn't return the gesture.

"You ain't like Frank. And if Scott even dares suggest it, he'll have me to deal with." He pulls his suit jacket aside to reveal his pistol.

I shake my head, trying to keep the angered look from my face. "Going straight, Clifford. No shooting. Alderman men keep their cool. Besides, I deal with the cops. You stay far away. Go deal with all these orders you keep taking." I throw my arm towards the factory floor that was empty of workers just a few short months ago. Now there are teams of men taking all the overtime we can offer them. The sight sends the heat of pride straight to my heart.

I leave Clifford, taking the papers he has handed me and I stop at my secretary's desk. "June, can you make sure these orders are filed, please? With the rate they are coming in, I want to make sure we have accurate accountings." June nods at my request, but I don't miss the doe-eyed look she's giving me.

Ignoring her is my best option, so I open the door to my office. Inside I find Jimmy sitting on my chair with his feet propped up on my desk. My decanter of brandy and an almost empty glass in his hand, a cigarette in the other.

He stands when he notices me, vacating the seat so I can sit at my desk.

"You'll need to make this quick, Jimmy. I've Detective Scott coming at nine."

"Fucking Scott. What does he want?"

"Nothing of importance, but I'll need you gone before he comes." Jimmy's mouth turns up bitterly. He knows he's not supposed to be here at the factory. It sends the wrong message to have known criminals frequenting the business when I am trying my very hardest to go straight.

"Came to tell you the Murphy's want a meeting. They want guns. A lot of guns."

"And did you tell them we are no longer in the gun business?"

Jimmy shrugs then puts his cigarette in the empty glass.

"For fucks sake, Jimmy, not in the glass. There's an ashtray right on the desk." My voice is an angry hiss. Jimmy's face scrunches as he is abashed.

"Full of heirs 'nd graces now, ain't ya. A legitimate business man." He rolls his eyes as though that is the very worst of things to be. "What about the men who work for us. What about them? Huh? You're all smug up here in your ivory tower but there are men, good men, who rely on the earnings from the guns. What you plan to do about them—"

"Jimmy, you knew the guns were only temporary. They all knew."

"They knew they had money coming in. They thought they could trust you. I thought I could trust you. There's a pittance from the racket and were still fending off the other scallywags after a cut." He shakes his head and slams his glass on the desk. "You've changed."

"I haven't changed. I—"

At that moment, June knocks briefly before walking in. "Detective Scott to see you, sir."

Behind her, Scott walks straight in, removing his bowler hat as he passes June.

"I'll be off then," Jimmy says, not before jutting his shoulders at Scott, his head coming dangerously close to headbutting the man in a show of defiance at the law.

I eye Jimmy with contempt but he just smiles back at me like he doesn't give a shit. I light up a cigarette and on my exhale I try to let my anger go. Jimmy is just angry. He feels like I'm veering down a path that doesn't include him, but that couldn't be further from the case. We're like brothers and he has had my back more times than I can count. He's also fucked up too many times to count and gotten me almost killed just as many times, but he is family. And I take care of family.

The meeting with Scott is another pointless waste of my time. He doesn't know who torched the factory and has no leads to find out. He mentions my enemies, as he always does, but I don't give him any names, and then just as he is about to leave June enters again and announces that the accountant will be here momentarily, as she knows to do whenever there is a police visit. It doesn't do to make them overly welcome, after all.

"I'll bid you good day then and be in touch if I should get any further with the arson case. Still baffles me, though." He lifts his hat onto his head. "I hope I will not find out you had anything to do with it."

My tone turns icy immediately and any warmth I just had fades. "I would never incinerate the children's inheritance. I am not like Frank."

Scott nods and the fat cheeks of his face relax. "No. You're not. I've always known that. I hope you continue doing well." His hand sweeps the room. "This life suits you better." And with that parting statement, he leaves the room.

"He's right, you know."

I glance up, I'd forgotten June was still in the room. She sits on the desk opposite me and crosses one leg over the other in a manner that might appear seductive—if I had any inclination to be interested in such things.

I raise my eyebrow, waiting for her to continue, hoping she doesn't cross a line.

"This life, all you've achieved... It's something."

I brush off her comment. The business might be in the early phases of thriving, but a lot can go wrong. Finally, though, the place holds promise and for that I am grateful. "All I ever wanted was a chance."

She nods.

"Can you get me the accounts. I've work to do." June ignores my attempt to dismiss her and remains perched on the desk, holding a pen in her hands, twirling it around.

"Will Roseanna be gone long?"

She's asked this before. Lately, people seem to ask it every damn day. None of them know there is no possible chance for her to try to return until summer solstice and even then, it's doubtful. Her nanna could live another twenty years, but I'll wait for her. Living without her is like living without air, it's painful and it might kill me but I'll not take a breath or another woman into my bed while there is a chance I could have her. Right now, the thought of her returning is all that is keeping me putting one leg in front of the other.

"She'll be back." I leave it at that.

June stands.

"But will she definitely, though? It's odd, her leaving so suddenly."

I feel my jaw tense. June may be good at her job, but her constant game of seduction is beginning to cause umbrage.

"'Tis none of your business. Now, is that the postman? Go check if there are any letters. You'd do better to focus on your job than my love life." I raise my brows at her to hammer the point home. I have no interest in her. Nor will I ever.

She saunters to the door and through the window. I see the postman and raise my hand to him, wishing that my beautiful Red were a mere letter away.

Chapter 9

Roseanna

No Such Thing as a Free Lunch

I am woken abruptly by the terrific sound of doors slamming and orders being yelled to fill our jugs from a communal faucet, to get washed and dressed for breakfast. Once our doors have been unlocked and I leave my cell to clean up, I notice Ned carrying a mattress into Beatrice's cell and I pause at her doorway.

"I just cannot sleep a wink on that wood," she says to him, quickly followed by, "Don't drag it on the floor, man. Pick it up!"

Ned drops the mattress and his fists tighten. Beatrice's throat bobs like she has had the good sense to realise that he is not one of her minions and he might just bite back.

"You'll get the back of my hand if you don't shut ya' bleedin' mouth. You ain't a lady in here, you're an old slag just like the rest." His tone and sheer size should make Beatrice shrink back, but instead she stands taller like she plans to argue back. Ned drops the mattress on the bed. "Think I'm one of your servants, do ya?" He laughs manically then fumbles with his trousers. "You want a nice clean bed? I'll show you what you fucking deserve." Bile springs up into my mouth as I realise what Ned is about to do. He's taken his penis out and is about to urinate on Beatrice's bed.

"Might I get one of those mattresses, too, please. These beds are awfully uncomfortable," I interject to distract Ned from what I am sure he is about to do.

Ned tucks his penis away with a grunt and turns around to face me. "You again," he growls and stares at me menacingly as though deciding what to do with me. The sound of a bell ringing from the tower outside pauses him in his intention and he pulls out his pocket watch. "Get back to ye cell before I put ye in the infirmary. I know Burt Copley would be glad to see you put in there. Keeps asking me if you're suffering enough."

"Burt Copley is a snake and a coward and when Danny hears of this you and he will—"

Verity pulls me by my arm and then pushes me inside my cell. I poke my head back out and see Ned muttering something in the corridor drinking from a flask he tucks in his belt.

"You ain't getting any luxury items in here and you do not want to provoke Ned. Man is as nasty as a rat and twice as rancid." I turn back to Verity and give her a perplexed look. *Beatrice has them, why not the rest of us?* As if she knows just what I'm thinking, she says, "She's a Duchess. They'll bring her anything she wants 'cos she's got money. A lot of money, I heard. Like thousands and thousands of pounds!" Her eyebrows raise up in exclamation. I must still look confused, so she sits on my bed to explain while I sit on the chair. "They say she's in here for fraud. Took a load of money that should've gone to her husband, the duke, and now they can't find it. But she must have some rich friends outside and they're making sure she's comfortable in here. Must be bleedin' nice, ay? To have people like that. She's got books and changes of clothes and proper nightwear—"

"He was about to urinate on her bed!"

"Ned's a sadistic bastard. Watch out for him as that ain't the half of what he's capable. Keep your head down, okay?"

I nod, then another thought occurs to me. "Has Beatrice got writing materials?"

"Maybe. She's got the bleedin' kitchen sink by the look of it."

"Do you think they'll let me make a telephone call today or speak to a solicitor? No one has told me what's happening." I throw my hands up in frustration.

"Telephone? They ain't going to let you use that—costs a bleedin' fortune and the likes of us ain't worth the operator's time. Last time I was in here two weeks before Mamma found out where I was and then she only found out 'cos Poppy Wheeler got out early and saw Mamma at the market. These things take time."

My temper spikes. If I am likely to be hanged for murder, time is one thing I don't have. "Everything in this godforsaken time takes so damn long," I complain, then shake my head because not so long ago, I felt a fondness for the slower pace of this time, particularly as it passed with Danny at my side.

"This time?" She smirks. "Whatever other time is there?" She chuckles good naturedly enough that I don't think she is questioning my word choices then continues, "Time is always against us. Mamma always says." Verity shuffles on the bed until her back is against the brick of the wall. "That's weird."

"What is?"

"You keep your lady rags next to where you lay your head." She turns up her button nose distastefully.

"Lady rags…" I let my voice trail off. I've no idea what she is talking about.

Verity points her finger at the small pile of rags that look to have been washed so many times they are no longer of any discerning colour. "Lady rags… you know, for your monthlies. I always keep mine out of sight, you know, for privacy," she adds with a frown.

The pile of rags lay crumpled at the head of my bed. I had no idea of their intended use but the reality makes me squirm a little inside. When Ida had taken me shopping, she had bought me a pack of Kotex and told me to make them last. Make them last I did, since I haven't had a period for years thanks to modern medicine and the introduction of the contraceptive injection. Which I am glad of, sanitary wear circa 1920s looks too long and thick and uncomfortable to be compared to modern designs. It hadn't occurred to me what women might do in the absence of such basics, and now I know. Then I wonder, how many other women have worn those rags before me. "Gross." I shudder.

"Perils of womanhood, Mamma says." She stands up and cheerfully smiles. "Right, I better go dress before Ned comes back to take us to breakfast or one of the others brings up a load more luxuries for Her Bleedin' Ladyship and finds me where I ain't meant to be."

**

With the morning sky still a deep shade of navy, we dress and are funnelled to a breakfast of dry bread and watered-down milk and Mo, who I am furious to see is wearing my watch, warns that we have ten minutes to eat before we are sent to our relative occupational activities. Not that I need ten minutes to eat. My bowl is less than half full and Bet swipes it out of my hand before I can so much as lift it to my mouth. With my stomach so empty, the aches holler loudly, and I stand ready to fight when Titty grabs my hand and tells me she'll share hers, whispering in my ear that Bet *is not* the person to try and stand up to. Of course, I don't take Verity's food since she is pregnant and needs all the calories she can get. I tell her I'm not actually very hungry. But I do wonder, if Bet is too dangerous to stand up to, who does she think I should fight since she is the one who mostly takes my food. Then I watch everyone eat and wonder if I'll die of hunger while I wait to find out if I will be hanged.

Work, as it turns out, is one of three tasks: sewing coal bags and mailbags, laundry, or housekeeping, which consists of either cooking or cleaning.

Verity, Beatrice, and I are all sent to sew mailbags. It turns out that I do have something in common with Beatrice—neither of us know how to sew—and as we stand around perplexed, I whisper to her, "Do you have any writing materials I can borrow?" Before she can answer, my temple is met with a heavy blow by the dull end of a baton. "You're here to repent and to work, not idle your sinful chatter," Mo booms. I rub my temple furiously and face her. "When will I see a lawyer or get to make a phone call or write a letter? There must be laws against you keeping me here without so much as a trial to prove my guilt!"

The baton hits my shoulder, narrowly missing my head as I duck out of its way. "I see we have a troublemaker." Her meaty hands grapple for me but I inch away.

Palms up to show her I do not mean her harm, I tell her, "I just want to tell my boyfriend where I am. He'll be worried." Lead fills my stomach. He thinks I am safe in 2022 and will not know to look for me.

Mo's face squishes up. "Should've thought of that before you murdered a man in his prime. Filthy murderer, you'll do your work or I'll throw you in isolation!" Her words send the thrum of the room into silence and I feel everyone's eyes turn my way. I suppose now that word has gotten out that I am in for murder, I expect to be vilified and treated accordingly. So I keep my head down and listen to my instructions then spend twelve hours sewing mailbags until my hands are blistered and my back is aching.

In the coming days, I am surprised to find that I am not vilified as a man murderer, quite the opposite in fact.

**

"'Ere, watch that one. She killed a bloke with her bare hands," I hear the woman behind me in the lunch queue say. I look around, wondering who she's referring to.

"Ripped his tongue right out his mouth. So's, I heard," the woman next to her replies.

"Next," the kitchen assistant says, spoon in hand.

"Do you have any bread left?" I ask, though every day this week, the answer has been the same.

She looks away from me, her attention caught by the woman behind me. She seems to register something and then looks at me again, her expression softening towards me when usually she barely notices me. "I'll go out back and check." A moment later, she returns with a full loaf and hands me two slices. "They're dry and probably only fit for the birds, but here, take 'em." I grab them with both hands and insert one of them into the soup to moisten, thanking her with a wide smile and then shuffling to the seat Verity has saved beside her.

I pass Verity a slice of bread then eat quickly before anyone notices my spoils. Once my stomach is heavy, I recount what just happened.

Verity throws me a culpable grin.

"Why are you smiling like that?"

She giggles uncomfortably. "I only meant for a few of them to listen and think twice about taking your food."

I force down the last piece of gravy-soaked bread. Around me, women are watching me and whispering to their neighbours. "What did you do?"

Verity shrugs like it's no big deal until I urge her to tell me. Finally, she relents. "Few of the girls were saying you were soft and wasn't cut out for lag-life, so I told them. That Roseanna Chapman, she's Danny Alderman's girlfriend and she killed that bastard Eli Harris."

I'd told Verity snippets of what happened while she sat at the sewing machine next to mine. I needed to tell someone but I hadn't thought at the time she was paying much attention.

I look around and notice the women still watching me suspiciously over their soup bowls. Being noticed in this way makes me feel self-conscious, but I wonder if perhaps there are upsides to this information being in the public forum—after all, it's not like a jury can convict me on prison hearsay, and I am still very much hoping I can somehow escape paying for my crime because the alternative doesn't bear thinking about.

"Do you think anyone might mention me when they get out so Danny knows I'm here?" The excitement this tiny piece of hope brings me has me sitting up straight and caring less about all the watchful glances.

By the time Verity answers, that hope is crushed.

"Maybe." She fingers her bowl nervously. "But we may have a more urgent problem than that." Verity pushes her fingers through her bob and thanks to its unwashed state, it holds its shape right from her hairline to her crown.

"What is it?"

The colour drains right out of Verity's face.

"What?" I repeat.

"I wasn't to know, I never even heard of him."

"What weren't you to know?"

"Him. His mum. I never knew."

"What didn't you know?"

"Eli Harris. Bet Harris. I didn't make the connection; I swear I didn't."

I look at her utterly baffled but a stirring feeling in my gut is building pace.

"Bet *Harris,* she's Eli Harris's mother."

I vault from the canteen before I am in danger of losing my lunch.

The man I murdered: Eli Harris. His mother is an inmate in Holloway prison. And not just any inmate but the hardest lag inside the jail.

Chapter 10

Danny

Let Sleeping Dogs Lie

"There's Juniper!" Alice sings, hopping up and down from the back seat of my motorcar.

"Juniper?" I turn to the backseat to face Alice. My tone is mocking and I roll my eyes even though I know it irks Alice, who couldn't be happier to be attending school. The action earns me a disapproving stare.

All the children at this private school for the rich seem to have grand names and grand ideas, inherited from parents who have little idea of life's struggles.

"She sits beside me in class. Reckons her father will one day be Prime Minister and her mother is so beautiful she will be pictured on the newspapers. But I told her, no chance she is more beautiful than Roseanna. She's the most beautiful of all. Isn't she Danny? She will come back soon, won't she, Danny?"

I roll the car up to the grand entrance of Ellwood School—a school for the rich and affluent of East London and then lean behind and unlatch Alice's door. "Go on, you'll be late for your learning."

I had hoped all the goings on of education would distract Alice but it's now been weeks and she has asked me every day since Red left if I have heard when she will be back. Henry, who hops out the door and follows Alice, only asks every other day. Still, it makes me wonder if she will come back. Surely, once she reacclimatises to her modern life, with all her fancy foibles and protective surroundings, her sense of self-preservation will override any misplaced hankerings for a life best not lived.

Alice loiters at the open door of the motorcar, in no hurry to leave without an answer. Henry looks on over her shoulder, his eyes pleading though his stance is insouciant.

"She will," Alice supplies, tiring of waiting for my reply. "Roseanna promised and I just know we can all rely on her certitude, even you, Daniel." Alice smiles reassuringly, probing me with her eyes as though to transfer this sense of belief.

Always so ready to believe the best in everyone, I wish I had Alice's certainness. All I have to cling to is a letter from Red and the knowledge that she left without saying goodbye. Still, I suppose goodbyes are the hardest part of living, even if our parting is supposed to be temporary.

"The headmaster is waiting, Alice. Best to get on your way."

The children turn and walk towards the entrance and I make my way to the newly built factory to oversee another day of manufacturing cars for the council.

**

A few nights later, I am in the King's Head, enjoying a drink and going over the profits with Jimmy, when I spot Copley in the bar. I stand, but before I can take a step, Jimmy grabs my arm. "He's not causing any trouble and since Red stopped singing, well, I need the drinkers."

I don't sit back down. The last time I saw him, Copley threatened my woman. He's lucky all he had to suffer was a dislocated shoulder.

Copley sees me standing and approaches. "Daniel," he starts.

"Get out, Copley. You've no right to be in here, and if you don't leave, I shall break your arm this time."

He's still in his police uniform, but that doesn't scare me.

"I came to ask your pardon. I meant no harm. You know me, after all. We go way back, right to the workhouse and even before that. I never should have said what I said to Roseanna, it was the drink talking."

He's right in some respects. We do go way back. Right to when his father mortgaged their house and invested in my father's company. Then Frank did what he does best and took Burt Copley's father's money, along with a lot of other peoples', and scarpered. Not long after that, Burt's father took a pistol to his own head, and that's how both Burt and I ended up in the workhouse together. It's a circumstance I will always feel some measure of guilt for. A man died and two sons ended up without their father, thanks to the actions of mine.

"Come on, let me buy you a drink. I'll get Roseanna one, too, if she's here, show her I'm truly sorry."

Burt gets out his wallet, something that is quite rare in these parts, and I hold my hand out to stop him. I don't want his money and I'll never be interested in sharing a drink. I'm still undecided if I will break his face for his past misdemeanours.

"Come on, Daniel. Let's not be bitter. Where is the beauty? Let me tell her I mean her no harm."

"Roseanna is away." I leave it at that but Burt fills the gap in the silence.

"Oh?" He raises his thick brows, and his moustache make him look quite ridiculous. "Thought you two were quite taken with one another."

I don't like his expression. Verging on smug, I want to wipe it off his face.

"Now, now. I'm sorry, I didn't realise…" He seems oddly apologetic and afraid but I don't know why, other than the anger wafting off me. Burt knows I could end him in a heartbeat, and my scowling expression is probably making him behave even more weasel-like than normal.

He palms his hands up like a white flag. "I hope she's well, wherever she is." Burt's a war defector and a coward; his behaviour doesn't surprise me.

"Copley, sit your ass down." Jimmy has come over, more than likely to stop me from attacking the weasel. "Danny and I have business to discuss."

"So I can stay?" Burt checks with Jimmy.

"So long as your spending money and keeping your gob shut, there's a seat for you at the back, away from the fucking bar and away from me." Jimmy bares his teeth and Burt backs away.

"Fucking sleeveen," I mutter under my breath.

"Red can handle him. She nearly floored 'im last time she seen him, and she can do it again. I'd put my money on her in a fight between the two. She's got bigger balls than Burt Copley, that's for sure."

His comment makes me chuckle and I smile in fondness. She's certainly got fighting spirit. It's one of the things that immediately drew me to her.

"You shouldn't feel guilty about his father either, Danny." I turn to the sound of the voice and notice Agnes at the end of the bar. I quirk a brow, urging her to continue.

"What his father did, well, despite it being terrible and all, leaving two boys without no parents, it wasn't you what pulled the trigger and it wasn't you who could have stopped it."

My stare turns curious so Agnes continues, "Been servicing the needs of Burt Copley for more than five years now." I check Jimmy's expression and see that it has soured and I wonder if Red's assumption that Jimmy was developing a likening to Agnes was correct. "Okay, so that's not new information, but what might be is that he likes to talk as well as, you know…"

"Next you'll be telling me he likes to hug and wear your favourite bloomers." Jimmy lights a cigarette and tops up both our ales.

"No, well not really." She giggles lightly as though reliving a private joke. "But he does like to dwell on the past. One night, he was so drunk he could barely stand up let alone get it up and he was telling me what a bastard he thought you were, Danny—sorry—but he was."

I shrug. "Ain't like I didn't know Burt Copley hates me."

"Anyway, he was sobbing. Got himself in a right state. I was going to fetch the doctor but he emptied his pockets and told me to stay, so I did."

"You did the right thing." Jimmy nods.

"He was rambling but then wot he was saying started making sense. He said he coulda stopped his old man from doing it. Course I told him no ways he could have. If a man's intent on taking his own life, then ain't no one going to stop him. But that's when he said, 'Me old man said the money was all gone. And that's when I went and fetched him me pistol.'" I couldn't believe what he was saying. I thought I got it wrong but he said it. He said as much, 'I gave him the gun, emptied out all but one bullet and told him he was a disgrace.'" Agnes shakes her head disgustedly. "His old man was in a terrible place and his own son told him to do away with himself, and then he went and bleeding done it." We all look around to Burt who has seated himself at someone's table and seems to be boring them senseless. "I can't look at Burt Copley the same ever since." Right after she's said it, Burt beckons Agnes over and she goes to him.

I spend the rest of the night going over the accounts with Jimmy and ignoring Copley. Jimmy bitches about everything. He's overly concerned the Irish are taking over rackets in London and shipping booze to the United

States, who are currently in the Prohibition Era as Red calls it. I, on the other hand, couldn't give a shit about that and I tell him as much, reminding him once again that we are moving away from the criminal side of the organisation. I would have handed it to Jimmy willingly, if I didn't know he'd start a war he couldn't finish with the wrong people and he'd end up reeling me in to sort it out. No, I decided that I wanted criminal activity away from every person I love, especially Red, but also Jimmy, Tommy and all the rest of my men—who are good people at heart. They just need showing a different way—if only they'd just take the jobs I keep offering them at the factory and stop fighting me about getting back into guns and continuing the racket, the latter of which I'm still trying to wind down.

We finish by discussing the pub that always reminds me of Benny since it was like a second home to him and he loved helping out. Jimmy makes out like it's a step down for him, but despite what he says, he stands proudly behind the bar like he was born to be there. He breaks up punch-ups, even though I know he's quite partial to a wrestle, and he's quick to defend the girls who work here should he need to. The bar is paying its way, and under Jimmy's watchful eye, it's running along nicely without too much need for my input—which sparks an idea....

Chapter 11

Roseanna

The Cat's Out of the Bag

In the workroom Beatrice is sitting at the end of the long row of desks with a stack of material before her. Not working and absentmindedly picking a piece of lint from the fabric of her dress, she's startled as I pull out the chair beside her and sit on it.

"You look a million miles from here. Anywhere nice?" I ask, desperate to take my mind away from the bleakness of my current predicament.

Beatrice's eyes regain focus and fix on mine. "I was just thinking of my husband."

"You miss him?"

Her nose crinkles. "No. No, I don't miss him at all. I was hoping his haemorrhoids had returned, actually." She laughs lightly at my expression and then pierces me with an examining gaze. "Surely, you've heard?"

I shake my head.

"He's the reason I'm in here."

"What happened?"

"He had me arrested for taking back what was mine. He was going to divorce me; he sold my ma and pa's house in exchange for gold he could hide. This way once we reached settlement, my marriage maintenance would be less."

"You're a duchess, surely there's still a lot of money to be divided in the divorce?" I ask, only half focused on her plight. Her problems with the divorce settlement seem trivial, considering she's an inmate at Holloway women's prison.

"Divided money. Are you mad, woman?" She straightens the neck of her dress and sits taller as though realising she allowed her impeccable behaviour to slip. "Ex-wives don't get dividends. They get a monthly allowance and are told to keep out of the way. Dennis told me he wouldn't even allow me the manor house in Hampshire. He was going to stick me in a cottage next to nowhere to keep me out of sight while he remarried Lady Harlington!"

"I suppose divorces in 1922 remain in favour of the husband," I muse aloud.

"You suppose right. Ma and Pa passed last year, and now I've no one to help me." I do feel sorry for Beatrice, though I can see from her face she doesn't appreciate my sympathy.

I change the subject, leaning forwards and placing my hands on the desk in front as I plead my case. "I wondered if you might have some writing supplies I could borrow? I need to send an urgent letter to my boyfriend."

Her tone becomes suspicious. "But they're mine. Why would I give them to you? Is that why you came to me, to ask a favour?" She deliberately turns her attention to the sewing supplies in front of her, pulling the fabric tightly as though inspecting it. "You should go sit on the other side of the room. I've heard you're not one to be seen mixing with in here."

"I just wanted to borrow a damn sheet of paper and a pen!" I huff, just as Ned leads a queue of women into the workroom. They file in noisily and most take seats behind desks, while others fetch equipment and begin barking commands as though the pecking order has been well established much before my time here.

At the helm is Bet, and she deliberately walks along the row of desks I am seated at, her movement quiet amongst the rabble of women gossiping to their neighbours. She turfs out fabric from the box she holds onto the desks of the women. When she gets to me, she pulls a pair of scissors out of her apron. "So, you're the one who killed my Eli," Bet hisses. She's blonde, tall and full in figure, her face lined with wrinkles as deep as the ocean. "You're dead. Mark my words, I will get you back for what you did to my boy." She brings the scissors down in a stabbing motion, and I only just manage to slide my hands out of the way in time for them not to pierce my flesh.

"Move along, Bet. You can settle your scores in your own time," Ned says from behind her and she sneers menacingly at me before walking to her seat. Then Ned turns to me. "Made enemies already, I see. I shall be sure to pass it on to Burt. He'll be glad to know you're settling in so well."

Beatrice, who kept her head down while Bet was threatening me, glances up at Ned. "Isn't your job to ensure that the women here are kept safe?" She asks him in a voice that sounds innocent enough, but her delicately drawn eyes are steely and unrelenting.

Ned's jaw twitches and he narrows his stare to Beatrice. "It's my job to keep you rotten bitches in line and make sure you pay adequately for your crimes, *Duchess*." He puts his hand atop of hers and pushes down until her face contorts uncomfortably. "Men in the tavern have been asking me if a duchess cunt is better. I shall have to find out so I can let them know."

Beatrice winces as Ned stands and turns to face the warden who is entering the room. He claps his hands for everyone's attention.

"Silence, now!" The women immediately quieten their tongues while Ian Copley stands behind the guard's desk at the front of the room. In a smarter suit than the last time I saw him, he straightens his tie and clears his throat. Meanwhile, Ned releases Beatrice's hand and walks up to the head of the room to join him. "I don't make a habit of addressing you directly, but I have something of importance to share with you all." He turns his face up distastefully. "You are here at Holloway to repent for your sins. We work you hard and we expect the rules to be followed at all times. And in the foreseeable future, we will require those rules to be followed much more closely. There will be no chatter. No loosening your mouths and talking of anything except repentance and rehabilitation. You will attend chapel for two hours instead of the standard one on Sundays, and you will be sure to wash your stinking bodies every morning." The women turn to each other and high-pitched whispers fill the quiet. "I said, no talking. No gossiping!" Ian slams his hand on the desk in front of him and the whispers are replaced by silence. "Anyone who flouts this rule will receive twenty lashes of the cane." The reactions of the women descend to shock as mouths fall open and their eyes crease with concern.

Ian's stance relaxes. "We are to have a visitor wandering about the place. A reporter from *The Daily Herald*." As the news is absorbed by the inmates, Ian moves to the front of the desk and perches his hip on it. His glare sweeps the room, an obvious look of distaste for his audience seeping onto his face—until his eyes rest on mine. "There will be no mercy for those who break the rules." His jaw twitches hatefully before he turns his sights to my neighbour. "We have a celebrity among us, and the public are eager to see justice administered in its most hostile of manners."

"But the people all love Duchess Beatrice. I can't believe they'd want it to be harder for her. She's the diamond of the normal folk, they want her to get away with the stealing. That's what I heard, anyway," Mags, the older woman Verity had mentioned could supply moonshine, calls out—clearly without thought. Ned marches to her side and pulls the woman, who is old enough to be his mother, up and out of her seat. He looks to Ian as if for permission and Ian nods.

She can barely keep up as he drags her to the front of the room and pulls up her dress until it is hunched around her shoulders. The woman tries to object, to apologise for her outburst, but it falls on deaf ears as Ned snatches a cane from the table and whips it against her back so hard the cane breaks on the third lash. He strikes the broken cane against the old lady's wrinkled skin until blood oozes down her back and soaks into the white cotton of her briefs.

Inside I am screaming.

I stare at Ian as if I can hurt him with the power of my glare and notice that instead of watching the beating he has ordered, he diverts his attention to the papers he clutches in his hands, looking away like a coward who can't face the power of his own orders.

When the sound of whipping is over, and Mag's is crumpled on the floor while Ned is straightening his uniform, Ian looks up from his papers and continues to address the inmates, dutifully ignoring the sight of the injured woman on the dirty floor.

"Parliament want a tight ship and that is what the reporter will write in his newspaper… or else every one of you will pay. The journalist will be watching what goes on here. No one will speak of unfairness and no one will complain. You will speak only when spoken to and you will present Holloway prison as the finest justice establishment in England or mark my words, you will rue the day you stepped out of line!"

The women silently watch Mag's face contort in pain as she tries not to cry.

"As you were," Ian instructs as he turns to leave the workroom, not meeting the eyes of the seething women before him as though it is just another day at the office.

**

It's been a week and a half since Ian's threat and not much changes, except at night—the nights are very different. Most nights I can fall asleep to the lovely songs I hear from the talented voice that sings out over the night air. Each and every evening it is the sound I crave, the voice so comforting, and the only solace I get in this hellhole.

The only other sound I hear after we are placed back in our cells after supper is the quiet chant from the women that Bet "is going to get me." I live with the constant fear that Bet will come for me soon.

Titty does her best to distract me. She tells me anything and everything— a constant flow of chatter to keep my mind away from the threats. Despite the darkness of our predicaments, at times, Titty can be upbeat. She expects we will both receive positive news at our trials and suspects since she is pregnant, her sentence will be cut quite a bit shorter from the usual six months for soliciting. When I run out of questions to ask her, she talks over the cackling women and regales me with whimsical tales of the places and people she will take her baby to see, and it cheers me up—if that's possible— and gives me hope.

Beatrice, I notice, keeps her window open but doesn't attempt to engage in any chat. I wonder what it must be like in her cell with her plush blankets and supply of books. For her, at least, her stay doesn't seem so bad.

At lunch, while eating fast and sitting as close to Mo as humanly possible, I spot Mags looking grey and weak and, after checking no one is watching, I follow her out to the bathroom.

"You okay?" I ask casually, pulling the door so that I can hear if anyone comes in.

Mags looks me up and down as though deciding whether to reply, then grimaces and tells me defeatedly, "It's me back. It's bleeding killing me."

It troubles me to see the hardened older lady in such discomfort and so close to tears. "Let me take a look." I move slowly, hands outreached, and she nods and lifts her dress.

The door opens and my heart pounds wondering if Bet or one of her cronies have come to get me, but I am glad to see that it is just Beatrice.

"Holy—" I stare my warning at Beatrice to quiet her. Mags' back is weeping green discharge and it smells faintly of decay.

"Have you bathed since the… your beating?" I ask gently.

Mags hisses and her cough catches in her throat as I touch the edge of her back. The unbroken skin is heated and I am certain an infection is well set in. "You know those cold strip washes don't clean as much as the warden would like to think, and besides, even if I could have a proper bath, my bones can't stand the cold like they used to," she replies, and I can't help but agree that no woman of any age should be forced to bathe in the cold water issued here. And honestly, it would be difficult for a woman half her age to tend to her back without help. Feeling the heated skin, I can't imagine how she has managed this long without falling critically ill.

I rub my arms to warm them, just talking of the temperature sends chills through me. "Always so frigid here, isn't it? The air, all of the rooms, the food… there is no warmth to be found anywhere."

"Bit colder indoors than it is out. Always the way."

"Must be January by now but I couldn't tell you the date."

"Every day is the same except Sunday," she replies.

"Will the doctor see you at the infirmary?"

"Asked Ned only yesterday. He said the infirmary is only for those with the sickness and I ain't one of them."

"The sickness?" I wonder just how unwell one needs to be to see a doctor.

"She means diphtheria and three-day measles. Dr. Hadfield says the infirmary is filling up with cases."

I studied a measles module during my paramedic training. Rubella—which I think Beatrice is referring to—can be serious for pregnant women, and I wonder if any effort is being taken to lessen the spread. It won't affect me; I was vaccinated against it as a child. Nanna marched me right into the doctor's office the same day the letter came, like it was a matter of life and death. I still remember the doctor's amused confusion at her insistence I be vaccinated there and then. However, Titty could be severely at risk if there are cases here, and that concerns me.

"Beatrice, go and get salt, a bowl, some cloths and something I can use to bind these contusions. Tell the kitchen staff the cloths have to be spotlessly clean and dry." I'm not sure anything is clean in this place and mostly everything is damp, but with no alternatives I cross my fingers and hope they can come up with something.

"I can't—"

"Go!" I demand. "They'll not give it to me and you are after all, the Diamond Duchess!"

Beatrice inspects Mags's back again and recoils. Then she does as she is asked and leaves the bathroom while I help Mags remove her dress. "You sure you know what you're doing?"

"I'm a nurse, of sorts, Mags," I reassure her while washing my hands as best I can from the only working faucet in the bathroom. "No hot water." I shake my head.

"No ale taps either," she jokes.

I pluck lint from the lacerations, and when Beatrice returns I sanitise Mags's back and allow it to air dry before dressing the wounds.

"You sure you know what you're doing? I was told fresh air is the best thing for cuts."

"Fresh air helps. But Mags, your back is becoming infected and that dirty dress with its rough material is making things worse. We need to clean, then wrap the wound with fresh bandages each day to protect them while your body fights off the infection. Can you get clean muslin each day and meet us here?" She nods. "Mags, infection can become sepsis… and well, you really don't want that." I'm pretty sure Mags has no idea what sepsis is and that kind of blood infection can kill her, but I want to emphasise how urgent this is. "Do you understand?"

"I'll be all right. Managed to live sixty-something years, nearly twenty of 'em in this place. And I'll ask Ruth when I see her if she can help me get some bandages."

I don't know who this Ruth is but the sound of the name alone gives me hope. *My mother was named Ruth.* Keeping these wounds clean and wrapped could be life or death for Mags. I know damn well they aren't going to be sending her to the hospital and treating her with any IV antibiotics.

"It's serious, Mags. You could die from this," Beatrice warns.

A flash of concern is quickly replaced by an apathetic nod of Mags's pitted face. "Well, if you say I got to."

"You got to," I confirm.

"Well, I'll be buggered. I thought it was this cough that was going to kill me, not me damn weeping back."

Beatrice helps me wrap Mags's frail body with clean muslin and then we help her pull on her work uniform. I worry for the very real possibility that my help won't be enough. In lieu of antibiotics, Mags's only hope is to keep the wound clean and pray her body fights the infection.

Beatrice reminds me we need to hurry; we are all now late for the workroom.

Once dressed, Mags stands straight and heaves a sigh. "Feels better wrapped up. That dress was chaffing me something rotten." I dispose of the used cloths in the steel cannister that is used for a bin and we file out.

"Just remember, keep your wounds clean."

"All right, I'm old not deaf. Stop your mithering," she tells me, but it's in a friendly tone.

When we get to the workroom, Mo is talking to a suited man in the hallway. She casts a look at my watch and then glares at the three of us.

"Tardiness will be punished," she spits.

"Oh, and what is the punishment for tardiness?" the man asks, pulling the lid off his fountain pen and taking out a notebook from his leather satchel.

Beatrice, Mags, and I hover in the doorway, waiting for Mo's answer. A glance exchanges between the reporter and Beatrice, like they recognise each other. Though, I assume given Beatrice's background, it wouldn't be surprising she would know those of the press.

A smile hovers at the corner of Beatrice's lips and her sultry gaze lingers on the man who is probably in his late twenties. He is good-looking in a studious, smart yet unkempt way, as though he was in too much of a rush this morning to style the wiry mop of mousy-brown hair on top of his head.

Mo's hand idly taps her baton as though she intends to use it, but instead she answers the man, "They'll be punished. They'll do without supper."

"No supper," he repeats, scratching her words down in his book. "Seems a hefty price for a few minutes late." He tucks his notepad beneath the crutch of his arm and clicks the lid on his pen, then looks directly at Beatrice. "I'm Valentine. I'm reporting for *The Daily Herald* on prison conditions."

Beatrice holds her hand out to the reporter and introduces herself. She bats her lashes and smiles alluringly, and there's a moment between them as he takes her hand—an exchange like they are both in on a private joke. Mo looks at them both suspiciously, so I fill the quiet and distract Mo.

"We were tending to Mags's wounds. They're becoming infected and she should see a doctor." I point to Mags who shrugs like it's nothing while I wonder if the reporter's presence will spur Mo to act.

Mo points her thumb in the direction of the workroom. "And I'm in need of a sit down and a cup of tea, but I doubt I'll get one. IN. NOW!" she orders and we all shuffle into the workroom hopeful that missed supper is all the punishment we receive.

**

It's easy to know when Valentine is reporting at the prison on any given day. His presence has a shifting effect on the professionality of the guards like they have, too, been warned to present the image the warden wants. Where the guards might normally shout or hit first, in the presence of Valentine they order firmly, though it is often combined with a threatening stare that reminds us that violence will follow if we do not immediately act on their orders. The response is the same: orders are followed and everyone is on their best behaviour, thanks to the frequent reminders that anyone caught flouting the rules—which are either known or newly imposed without warning as though thought up on the spot—is dealt with immediately and harshly, though never in view of the reporter.

At lunch, and with Valentine and Beatrice both absent, the canteen is unruly. Verity informs me that she will attend her plea hearing on Friday. "I'll plead guilty. No point going not guilty and getting longer on me sentence." She taps her tummy. "He or she will be born in my mam's sitting room with the midwife if we can get one just like me and all me sisters were." I try not to let it show that the image she presents of the baby's delivery horrifies me, so I distract myself by taking a long slurp of the broth that tastes only a little like dishwater today.

"How will you plead?" Verity asks.

"I haven't decided yet," I reply. "I thought Danny would have found me by now and well, he's the only one I can talk to about it."

"—Oops," a clod of a woman cackles as she knocks my bowl sideways off the table. Broth spills across the scummy floor and my stomach squeals. "Better clear that up." She laughs right in my face and waddles back to her bench to sit beside Bet.

Over her shoulder, Ned watches on and does nothing. To my side, Mo orders that I clean up *my* mess. My jaw juts in the direction of the woman and I stand slowly, narrowing my eyes on her as she and Bet snigger.

The kitchen server hands me some dirty cloths and a bucket of water and then I set to washing my lunch off the floor. Verity bends to help me but I tell her I can do it. Then I stand, holding the bucket of water and hating this damn place so much my hands shake.

Suddenly, Bet is before me.

"They buried my boy with no name plate and no one to stand over him." Her face is crunched with anger and her tone more spiteful than I've ever heard.

My response is formed automatically thanks to my years in public health. "I'm sorry—"

"Sorry?!" she shrieks, and before I have had chance to brace myself for her attack, she snatches the bucket from my arms and drenches me in the cold, stolid water. The steel bucket then ricochets off my head. "My Eli was a good boy! A good boy! And you, ya rotten bitch, you took him from me. My only son!"

Her outburst has the whole canteen staring, and Mo rushes towards us.

"Your son was a child killer and a monster!" I screech. "He murdered a child right in front of me with no remorse. No feeling! And he would've killed Danny too." Even though I am soaked to my underwear in frigid water, it is not the cold that makes my hands shake; it is utter fury. "Your son deserved death."

Bet's mouth is agape, though I'm not sure if it's from my statement or if it's because she wasn't expecting my retaliation. Either way, I hold my fists higher so that she is clear that I will fight back.

"Now, now. We'll not have any fisticuffs today," Mo says as she marches right up to Bet and puts her hand on her bicep.

"I'll kill her. I'll bloody kill her!" Bet screams as she is pulled from the room and I am left where I am standing, soaking and overwhelmed by my emotions.

Verity stands and pulls me back to my seat. She's speaking but I don't hear her as I question once again whether I did the right thing. Was murdering Eli the only way? He had a shotgun pointed right beneath Danny's jaw. If I hadn't shot him when I did, he would have killed Danny and I couldn't risk that. I wouldn't. Yet still, guilt prickles beneath my skin.

He was her son.

A mother lost her child the night I fired the gun.

Surely there must be consequences to such an action? Then I wonder ultimately what it was all for. Me time travelling and leaving Nanna vulnerable and to suffer, and Benny dying anyway. Me loving Danny only to be ripped away from him....

What was the point of it all if it ends with me getting snuffed out by Bet or executed and left swinging from a noose?

Chapter 12

Danny

Too Soon

As January creeps into February, snow softens the harsh lines of the stone arch in the bleak morning sun. I find myself standing on the steps to the Alderman Manor, immune to the blistering winds, imagining the snow melting and bluebells springing up through the grass, only to fade and be replaced by the tall grasses of early summer that last year we couldn't afford to have felled by the cutters. I visualise the climates changing at speed, like the very ticking of time is a motorcar that can outpace the seasons. And with the brightening of the sun, I imagine marvelling at the sudden appearance of Red beneath the dusty arch as though delivered to me by God himself through a bolt of lightning. She raises to her feet and despite seeming confused, she looks for me. A vision of flowing amber locks that glow like flames beneath the sun, and suddenly a heat passes through my bones and I can no longer feel the chill of her absence.

However, a constant niggling that I have grown used to plagues me and ruins the vision. For although I know she is not near, something inside of me screams that she has not left. Within my soul a war rages with an irrational desire to search—to rip apart the world until I find her—and another undeniable feeling lingers; permitting Red's return is wrong, yet I allow the fates to fight their own battle and hope success falls in my favour.

I indulge the notion that if I can become a good man, an honest man, that I may deserve her and the light she will return to our lives, and so I continue my precision focus on creating an empire built on good, so that one day, when she is returned to me, I will be able to live a righteous and just life—and deserve the gift time has given me.

"What you standing out here for? You'll catch your bleeding death," Jimmy says, throwing a cigarette butt down on the ground as he hops out of his motorcar.

"Taking in the view, Jimbob."

"Ain't nowt out here but a shitload of the white stuff and a chance of frost bite." He marches past me, opening the door to the manor and calling to Ida that he hopes she's making a brew, earning him a furious glare as she throws another log on the fire.

"Cliff coming with us?" Jimmy asks.

"No. Just you and me today," I reply, leaving out that Clifford never came home last night. He was with Trevor. I've been keeping an eye on him since discovering his participation in dealing chang, but I believe he has kept true to his word and is done with crime. This late-night activity I suspect has more to do with a developing relationship, since their cars are often parked within twenty feet and our cold store has never been more stocked with meat, despite Clifford rarely being here to eat it.

Jimmy walks to the fire and warms his hands. "Can tell you've gone up in the world now that there's a fire lit in every hearth in the house," Jimmy says and I detect just a hint of his anger flaring.

"Are the fires not lit in your own house?" I check. Jimmy is paid handsomely for his work at the Kings Head and for collecting the remaining racket money. He should want for nothing.

"They are indeed. Though doubt you'll have need for me for much longer."

"Jimbob, I've never had need for you, but here you stand, like a shadow that still spits on the ground beside me long after the sun has gone down."

Jimmy appears slighted, so I clap his back to let him know that I am joking.

"There's always a place for you at my side. Now, come on. Let's go tell the good people of London that we are winding down the racket."

I grab my coat and call to Ida that I shall be late, and then Jimmy and I head out the door to do the first good deed of many.

**

When I return to the house, something seems different. No one is downstairs, but the fires are blazing like they've been kept in wood all night and there's an absence of the usual smells of a dinner polished off. The house is quietly calm, yet there's an undercurrent of activity.

I take the steps two at a time, eager to check each and every one in the household is safe when I spy Henry and Alice sitting on the wooden floorboards of the landing, marbles before them like they started a game that was quickly abandoned.

"Everything all right?" I check.

Alice looks deathly pale and she is fighting back tears.

"Henry, tell me, what is it?"

He looks up then nods his head to the bedroom Harriet has been sleeping in since she moved in with us. Then Henry looks back down at the floor; he looks scared to death. "It's the baby. Ida says it's coming."

I shake my head. "You must be mistaken; the baby isn't due for another—"

I stop talking.

The baby isn't due for another month.

Chapter 13

Roseanna

Apples and Oranges

I'm escorted to the workroom with the others.

Around thirty minutes into our afternoon work shift, Beatrice arrives and seats herself in the only vacant seat next to me. Valentine trails in behind her, and neither Mo nor Ned so much as raise an eyebrow.

"I'm late because Valentine interviewed me for *The Daily Herald*. He says he is going to make sure it's a feature on the front page. Valentine says my fans are worrying how I am fairing; they're sending letters into the newspaper to ask after me. Apparently, there has been an uproar in Westminster too," Beatrice tells me in a smiling voice that she cups beneath her hand.

I nod and look around, wondering how much public support there is for the plights of the rest of the women here.

"Valentine says they always sell more papers when my name is mentioned. He wants to see if they can get a picture printed of me—to draw more support. Of course, I'll have to get Fanny to bring me in some better clothes."

I finish the bag I am sewing and add it to the pile.

"Still vexed I won't share my writing paper with you?"

I bite down on some thread to snap it and continue sewing when I notice Valentine to my side, looking admiringly to Beatrice.

"Can I help you?"

He looks abashed at my interruption of him gazing at Beatrice. "Oh. And who might you be? What's your story?" he asks with little interest.

I remember the reporter who turned up on my doorstep in 2021 and wonder if they are all as self-serving. Then I give my head a wobble. I have an opportunity that I must not waste.

"My name is Roseanna Chapman." I tap my finger on his notebook. "You'll want to write that down if you are to print my story." He unclips his pen at my instruction and writes down my name.

Ned is talking to Mo but still in earshot, so I lower my voice. "Treatment inside Holloway's walls is not what it seems," I hiss and point my thumb at Beatrice. "How she is treated is not the norm, but *I'm sure Beatrice has mentioned this.*" I throw Beatrice a sideways glare and hope that she realises how self-serving she is. "We don't all have comfortable beds, clean clothes and books. There's an infestation of rats. No hot running water or a place to bathe. There is no adequate healthcare or maternity programme. Some of the women have rashes that are contagious and could become diseased, and there are cases of diphtheria and rubella. The woman over there," I point at Mags, "has an infection on her back, thanks to a beating from a guard—" Ned turns around and glances at me before talking to another guard who has entered the room. "There's little to no food and the women, they're not protected from each other." I have his interest now and he is scribbling down all I say. "I haven't seen a lawyer or even given a police statement. I haven't even been charged. They just threw me in here and I have no idea when I'll get out…" Valentine's face is serious and he pushes his spectacles up the bridge of his nose.

"What are you accused of?"

"Murder," I reply.

A disparaging expression reaches his eyes and he averts them down to his notebook. I try to reengage him before his doubt can take root. "I didn't murder anyone."

He looks up from his notebook. "Oh?"

I flounder and wonder if killing Eli Harris was self-defence or maybe it was manslaughter, it certainly wasn't a premeditated killing—not by me at least.

"It was self-defence, to stop him from killing someone else—"

"Roseanna Chapman," a guard who I am not familiar with says, "come with me. You got a visitor."

The beat of my heart stops and a glorious image of Danny replaces the miserable sight before me.

Has Danny come for me?

Chapter 14

Danny

A Baby is Born

"We'll take her to the hospital."

I'm cut off by Ida who walks to the threshold of the room and pierces me with a glare. "No time for that. The head is engaged and the baby wants to be born now." I hear Harriet squeal in pain, quickly followed by the sound of Clifford comforting her. "The boy is in with her—she won't release his hand. I gave her some brandy to take the edge off and now she's gripping onto our Cliffy like he's the reincarnation of Benny."

"Is she… hallucinating?"

"Harriet's about to become a mother. She's doing whatever she needs to get through it and in enough pain to summon Jesus himself. All I know is it's not right to have a man except the doctor in the room while a babe is born. It's not proper and it's not right, but it'd take a woman with bigger balls than me to prise the want and need from a birthing mother's hands. If what she wants is Clifford's hand to hold, then that's what she'll have. Now, tell the doctor to be quick. I've delivered more than a dozen bairns but not one as early as this."

Ida's steel voice is a warning but beneath it is the shaken tone of a woman afraid.

I know nothing of pregnant women or babies being born, but the mere reminder that this is Benny's child bolsters my resolve that everything that can be done must be done. The survival of this family hinges on the survival of the child—our family cannot sustain another loss. We won't.

I take a step back. "I'll fetch Jenkins. He saved that baby in the news, the one caught up in the tyre factory explosion. He'll know what to do."

"He better had."

**

"It was nothing short of miraculous, Danny." Clifford paces the room, the smile on his face not leaving even when he pauses talking to gulp down his brandy. "The pain, though. Jesus, Danny, the pain was hard to watch, but Harriet, she swallowed it down, gritted her teeth and grunted like a pig in a paddock, pushing right from her heels until she pushed the baby all the way into the light." Clifford's shaking his head in disbelief and amazement. I'm not even sure if he is talking to me anymore or revisiting the experience again purely to etch it into his memory the way one does when there is something so precious you fear you might one day forget it. I know the feeling well. I do it when I try to remember the first time I heard Red sing. The voice of an angel playing only to my heart.

"And Ida, Jesus Danny, she knew what to do. We couldn't have got it through it without her. Ida was mopping her brow and when Harriet said she couldn't bleeding stand it no more, Ida told her, 'You'll stand it and you'll push because if you don't, so help me Lord, you'll not ever get over it.' And Harriet listened. She took in a big breath and she pushed and pushed until the baby plopped out on the bed and sucked in its first breath." He pauses for air and a deep swig of the brandy and then I refill his glass, clapping him on the back because I'm not sure any words will properly convey just how proud I am of him and Harriet.

"Danny, the baby will not want for anything, I'll see to it. I'm going to make Benny proud."

"I know you will, Cliff."

Clifford stops pacing, peering down at me, I can see that the process has changed him somehow. He looks older, wiser if that's even possible.

"I mean it. I can't change the past but I will make sure that going forward, Ellen Alderman has the best life that anyone dared even dream of."

"That she will." I find myself grinning. It's remarkable how a family can go through the absolute worst of times, plunged in the depths of devastation and destruction, only to find themselves buoyant in strength and solace through healing and the care of family.

Clifford sits beside me, his gaze settling on mine. "She'll come back you know."

I nod. "'Course she will." Only even as I say the words, I'm not sure I believe them. For my Red, she seems further away than ever.

Chapter 15

Roseanna

The Devil's in the Details

I am too excited to remember to learn the paths of the prison as I usually try to do whenever I end up in a different part of the vast structure. Thoughts of escape are long behind me, since for now seeing Danny's face and hearing his voice is all that matters to me.

I tuck escaped tendrils back into my hair tie and wipe beneath my eyes. I suddenly feel warmer and my clothes chaffing in their wetness doesn't bother me as much as it did.

I wonder if he'll have good news or bad but decide it doesn't matter. I just need to see him. Breathe him in. I wonder if I am allowed to touch him or if we will be separated by glass. I hope not since I have missed the earthy, spicy scent of him. I'm suddenly filled with yearning to know about his kin, the family I wish were my own. How Clifford is following Eli's revelation that it was his order that killed his twin. If Ida is managing without my help, and if Alice and Henry have started their new schools yet, like Danny promised they would. Harriet will be in the late stages of her pregnancy now and I try to imagine her with a swollen belly, smiling.

So much I want to know that the missing information imbeds a hole in my head and causes an ache.

The guard unlocks another door and we pass through it into a corridor that is only slightly nicer than the grim reality of the rest of the prison. He stops outside a closed door and informs me, "You've got fifteen minutes and that's your lot." Then he swings the door open to a square room with a barless window overlooking the front gates. Sitting in the rooms middle at a table and chairs for two is not Danny. It's Detective Scott.

**

"Well, you look rather different from the lady who came to my station to report a murder not two months ago," Detective Scott says, kicking a chair out from beneath the table with his toe and indicating for me to sit.

My hopes are crushed and my fears return.

I lower myself into the chair and the guard closes the door, leaving us alone.

The man before me is large and wears a smart suit. His face is weathered with age and suggestive of a hard life, but there's something paternal about Detective Scott. He alludes a calm aura of safety and it's a feeling I wonder if I should trust.

"What are you doing here… I mean, I wasn't expecting to see you." My voice is barely-there, eaten with disappointment.

"Someone had to come and take a statement from you, and I wasn't leaving it to Burt. Crown Court announce a trial date for murder, and I only just saw the paperwork." He shakes his head in a pissed-off manner. "Anyway, it was the first time I'd heard anything of it, and on the paperwork

I noticed your name—I never forget a name. So I found out you're in here—on grounds of murder no less." His shovel-like hands pull notepaper out of his briefcase and the puniness of the pen he holds looks almost comical if it weren't for the seriousness of what he is about to write. He scribbles my name and the date at the top of the page. I'm curious to learn it is Wednesday, February eleventh.

"Let me tell you, this is not how we usually do things. I would normally have seen you at the station for this, but Burt thought it was urgent you were incarcerated immediately—so you couldn't escape or abscond and then he lost the paperwork and forgot to mention it to me." The way he says this and the expression he pulls suggests that he does not believe for one moment that Burt accidentally neglected to tell him any of these details.

"I need you to contact my boyfriend, Daniel Alderman. He doesn't even know I'm in here. He'll be worried."

Scott looks at me curiously. "Where does he believe you to be?"

"I…" I clear my throat. Saying that he believes me to be in the future will not wash well. "He doesn't know where I am."

"Yet he has not reported you missing." Scott now looks suspicious, though maybe that is my paranoid belief. I dare not mention our story that I would be away looking after my grandmother, in case Scott looks into my grandmother's whereabouts.

"Please, can you just get word to Danny." His eyes pause on mine and I detect enough sympathy that for a moment I think he will grant my request. Then he shakes his head.

"We have statements on file linking you to criminal gangs and organised crime. The prosecution service has approved your incarceration to be kept confidential. No press release and no informing anyone of your whereabouts in case the trial is compromised." He raises his eyebrows at me over his glasses.

The dejection I feel is so enormous, I stand abruptly. "And this is justice?! Clandestine trials and withheld information. I don't... who said such things about me having links to organised crime?" And then I realise who would have reported such things. "Burt Copley? Frank Alderman? They are both bloody corrupt and you cannot take their word for this!"

Scott, at least, has the decency to look sheepish as I make such claims. He knows I am right. I glance at the paper where he has written my charge. "Don't I get a lawyer?"

"Can you afford one?"

I shake my head. Danny can't afford one either—he's putting every last penny into Alderman Inc. Besides, in no way do I want to bring Danny's name into this. He's had too many negative dealings with the law, and the last thing I would ever do is focus the police with a murder case on him.

Although dejected and weighed down by the hopelessness of my situation, I focus on self-preservation. "I didn't kill Eli... Well, I did, but it wasn't murder."

Detective Scott nods his head sympathetically. "Start from the beginning, don't leave anything out."

"Well, you see..." My voice trails off as I sift through the information that I can disclose without entangling Danny and his killing of Lorenzo, which led to us not only knowing Eli killed Benjamin, but that his twin, Clifford, was dealing drugs and working with Eli. It suddenly occurs to me, there doesn't seem much truth I can say without implicating the Aldermans.

"Where were you when you fired the gun?" he asks as though sensing I need a starting point.

"Mile End Road," I reply, which is, in fact, true.

"Good." He writes Mile End Road on his sheet of paper. "And this was on the twentieth of December, 1921." I nod and he writes the date beside the location. "So, you shot Eli Harris in the belief that he killed Benjamin Alderman?"

"Yes, well, no. I wasn't seeking vengeance… I wanted the police to arrest him for Benny's death—"

"I remember. You wanted us to arrest him." He stops writing and looks at me. "Then why didn't you come back to the station like I told you to?" After a few seconds without my answer, he qualifies, "Look, love. Eli Harris will not be missed. I looked into him after you left the station all those weeks ago. Nasty piece of work he was, with plenty of officers on my beat telling me tales of just how rotten an apple he was. I won't go into it with a lady present, but he would have seen the rope before long. However you pulled the trigger and now a man is dead. It needs proper investigation and the law needs to be applied correctly, despite what Burt Copley may think. Now, if you want any hope of not living a miserable life in this place, you got to give me something." He puts down his pen and runs his finger and thumb over his perfectly groomed moustache. His voice is fatherly and reassuring, pleading if only for my own sake.

"He was going to kill someone I love."

"Who?" He picks his fountain pen back up.

I can't tell him the truth, so I tell him the version that is as close to the truth as I can. "It was self-defence. He threatened to kill me. I knew he was capable of it, so, to stop him, I shot him."

The detective writes "self-defence" on his sheet of paper. "And what was Eli's motive? And what of the person you love?"

I can't disclose that Eli wanted to kill Danny and everyone associated with him so he could take over the illegal side of Alderman Inc.; instead, I recall an ugly threat he made against me in hopes it would distract him from anything to do with Danny. "He said he wanted to take me to the brothel to work for him until my face was wrinkled and my fanny was ripped." Detective Scott winces as though truly offended on my behalf. "Naturally, I declined his offer," I add and Detective Scott chuckles, though it doesn't reach his eyes.

"Was there a struggle before you shot him?"

I remember how my heart stopped as I watched Eli press the shotgun into the underside of Danny's jaw. "Yes. There was a struggle."

The detective's smile straightens as though he disappointed. "Eli Harris was shot, and from the state of his body and by my reckoning it was a distance of around ten feet by a pistol we have in custody."

I think back to the night of the murder, wondering how the police ended up with the gun I used. After I shot Eli, Danny took it from me and put it on the table. Frank must have picked it up as he left the King's Head.

"We have your fingerprints on the pistol and an eyewitness who says he saw you shoot Eli Harris for no good reason."

I'm shaking my head, imploring him to believe me that his witness is a liar. I think a part of him believes he is too.

"Roseanna, all I have is that you were in an argument about… employment, let's say… and then you shot him. Is there anything else you can tell me that defends what you did?"

I shake my head. There is nothing else that I can use to defend myself without bringing any of the Aldermans into the narrative.

"Then I'm sorry. I have no choice. We're charging you with murder." He stands slowly, his face remorseful. "You'll make your plea to the court Friday. I strongly suggest you plead guilty to murder for if you plead not guilty and are indeed found guilty by the jury, the penalty will be death by hanging."

**

Following my visit from Scott, I soon find myself inside the court house for the first time. Some say negative connotations of Friday the 13th is superstitious nonsense, and before today, I would have been inclined to agree with them. But standing here in front of a judge in a full gown and a wig, he's looking at me with complete and utter contempt and I wonder if the date is a bad omen.

"Miss Chapman, how do you plead?"

I look around the courtroom for Danny. Even though he has no way of knowing I am here, a part of me hoped he would somehow discover my whereabouts, but he's not here. Then I look for some kind of sign. Writing on the wall, an encouraging glance from the audience, anything that might identify if what I am about to say is the right thing or utter madness.

There's no sign and no hint of what I should do.

A bunch of other inmates are in the cells below the deck, including Verity and Beatrice. They're waiting to announce their pleas to the charges they are accused of and I wonder if they are as torn in how to plead as me.

The judge lowers his half-moon spectacles and eyes me over them impatiently and then he passes a message to the scribe below him and I wonder if it is his lunch order as he has a hangry kind of look about his face.

"Young lady," he addresses me, "I am sure you have already been told this but 'no' plea is a 'guilty' plea. And if you plead that you are innocent of the crimes you stand accused of, and are indeed found by a court of law to be guilty, then the sentence for murder is death by hanging. Please take me seriously when I say I will not allow you to hold up proceedings." He looks down at the paper in front of him. "Now, you have sought council. You are charged with murder in the first degree. How do you plead?"

Sought council?

If by this he means the ten-minute interview before I was led up here to plead with a thoroughly harassed—barely out of university—little swot who could not care less about my fate, advising me to plead guilty to murder and receive life in prison to escape hanging by a rope, then yes, I have sought council. And it was bloody useless!

Captive Songbird

The solicitor, pro bono and only here for legal experience before he starts his own legal practice, did not clarify how I might prove my innocence, as though that was for paying customers only.

The judge clears his throat in a manner that implies further impatience and a shortening of his temper.

I search one last time for Danny but am met with only the peasant stares of the gallery, who are eager for me to hurry up and plead so they can see the actual star of today's reality show—Beatrice.

"Not guilty, Your Honour." The words expel from my lungs louder and prouder than I feel. Against Detective Scott's advice, I'm pleading my innocence. Living here for the rest of my life would be equal to death. I'd rather take my chances with proving my innocence.

The judge nods and writes on his piece of paper and then dismisses me with little interest. A guard pulls me by the heavy metal handcuffs at my front. "Wait! What about parole? I shouldn't be in jail."

A smirk turns the fossil-like man's mouth up at the edges. "Parole? You're a woman of no means who is a flight risk. There is no parole. Court date set May thirtieth." He shuffles his papers and then announces, "Next!"

The guard yanks my cuffs and I stumble down two steps until I can only just see the top of the judge's head. Realising I am soon to be returned to Holloway prison, I call out to anyone in the audience who may hear or be able to help, "You have to get word to my boyfriend. Daniel Alderman. Please, tell him I am here!"

The judge doesn't answer my pleas and there is no indication that anyone else heard either. No one gives a damn and my plight is lessened even more as the crowd cheers when the Diamond Duchess is lead past me up the stairs to her waiting fans.

Down below I'm thrown back behind the bars of the cockroach and rat-infested communal jail.

Chapter 16

Danny

Make Hay While the Sun's Shining

I wake early to the sound of a screaming baby. Since Harriet moved in and gave birth to little Ellen, early mornings have become a regularity.

I go to the child, picking her up and comforting her while ordering Harriet to rest awhile longer. She protests but the promise of sleep wins out, and I take Ellen back to the room that I shared with Roseanna and coo the baby while I stare at the arch marking the entrance to our property. The same arch that wields the power to return my love to me.

I've wondered a million times if one day, the strength of our love will be enough to pull one of us through it and into the waiting arms of the other. I guess that's just fairy-tale talk, though Norma, who grew up in this house, believes the tales of lovers cursed and women scorned marking the arch as some kind of relic to be feared. I suppose it's not too farfetched when I consider that time travel is possible.

I place little Ellen on the bed I shared with Roseanna and remember how her hair would fall across her face as she slept, and how, the first thing I would do each morning was comb it back so I could admire her face. And when I say admire, I mean take in every freckle, memorising every dip and pout so I could draw her later in the day with my pencils. I must have over one hundred drawings of Roseanna, but no stroke of a pencil can come even close to her beauty.

I carry Ellen downstairs where Ida is waiting, holding a cup of tea for me in her hand. Lately, Ida seems older, frailer in her presentation. Something about having a new baby in the house and the passing of time makes everything seem more fragile, even my relationship with Roseanna.

The night before she left, I was certain she would come back to me. I would have bet my life on it. Our love grew slowly, though I knew it was there from the moment I'd laid eyes on her, and like a limb or an organ, you only realise it is there when it hurts.

She wrote me a letter, and I assume it was too hard that morning to come back upstairs to wake me for a final goodbye—well, at least for six months. Though that nagging feeling like something is wrong and she will decide to stay in her time still plagues me.

"She'll be back. A fine man like you doesn't come around too often and your life is on the uppers," Ida reminds me as though she can tell I am thinking of Roseanna.

"She'd better," I muse, "since I intend on making her my wife." I throw the comment out there not knowing where it comes from though knowing it to be true nonetheless.

I wait for Ida to complain or to tell me I am mad, but she doesn't. Ida hasn't always liked Roseanna or approved of our relationship, but like everyone else, Ida has become quite fond of her, even if she will never admit it.

"Doubt there'll be need for an old lady around the place once she comes back," Ida says and I'm about to interrupt, to tell her we'll always want her around the place, but she doesn't give me the chance. "Give me that baby. It'll want changing and that's not a job for a man," she says, changing the subject.

I pass Ellen to Ida's outstretched hands and chuckle. Roseanna often told me that modern men change baby's arses, bathe and feed them. I like the picture she painted of a man so involved with his family that he shares all of the care, and I find myself imagining such a life with Roseanna.

"There's bacon on a plate in the morning room. You'll want to get it before it goes cold."

"Trevor been here?" I ask casually.

"Yeah. Wanted to see our Clifford but Clifford said he's no time for the butcher's boy. Think they've been going to the jazz clubs up west, probably to meet women, but since Harriet had the baby Clifford has no interest in meeting women at all."

"Indeed." My reply is noncommittal, but I find myself wondering what Clifford is up to. I was sure he and the butcher's boy were developing some kind of friendship… at the very least.

**

Walking in the house after a day working at the factory, I find the family in the sitting room. Henry clutches his copy of *Comics Monthly*—a new publication that I picked up from a street vendor that has proved popular, while Alice's reading has come on so well that she's now getting to the end of *The Story of Doctor Dolittle*, and I make a note to buy them some more reading materials—after all, business is booming and these children have gone without for too long.

"There's a plate of cold meats and boiled eggs in the cold store for supper," Ida informs me, still concentrating on the bonnet she is knitting for Ellen. With all Ida's weaving and sewing, the child has more clothes than the rest of the household, but I suppose children grow fast. The notion makes me wonder how old the child will be before Red returns.

I sit beside Clifford on the new settee I purchased last month.

"Harriet's taken the baby for a walk," Clifford says, putting the papers he is skimming down on the coffee table. "Orders are on track, brother."

"You're doing a grand job at the factory, Clifford. Everyone thinks so."

Clifford nods stoically but then I notice the corners of his mouth tip up at the edges.

At the back of the room Ida puts down her knitting, stands, and is checking the mantle for dust.

"Do you think Roseanna will be back soon?" Alice asks probably for the millionth time.

Just the mention of her conjures an aching in my chest. "It'll take as long as it takes, Alice. Red loves her nanna and giving her the very best care is at the centre of what's right. She'll be back when the time is right." While I've given Alice the confidence that Roseanna will be joining us, there is a pain in the pit of my stomach caused by the wait. I need her back with me. I need her to choose us and this life that we can make together. The confidence I have in us will need to carry me until she returns, but I'd be lying to myself if I didn't acknowledge my fears that time has taken her away from me and perhaps she is gone for good.

The constant feeling I now get that something is not right is hard for me to elude, but I still try to stay chipper for the sake of the children.

Ida walks to the window and fingers one of the drapes. "I don't suppose I'll be needed round here for long once your woman comes back." I recall our earlier conversation where I mentioned marrying Red and wonder if Ida has been stewing on what this may mean for her. Ida juts her jaw, as though she is too proud to show that she cares whether she will remain needed.

"Is that what's worrying you?" I ask, shaking my head at the ridiculousness of her comment. "Ida, how many times do I have to tell you? You will always be needed around here. You're the children's grandmother. My grandmother. You are the head of our family."

"I'm the head of nothing." She blinks and dismissively shakes her head.

"You know that's not true."

"A glorified floor scrubber, that's all I am."

"We'll get a maid to help you around the place and you can finally start enjoying your retirement."

"Retirement," she *tsks* beneath her breath.

"It's time you started to take things easier. We'll employ a maid. Now things are on the uppers, it's time we had some extra help in this big old house. We'll need you to show her what's what."

"Well, yes. You'll need me for that. Place will fall to rack and ruin in no time if someone isn't overseeing things. It's all well and good to fall in love, but you didn't pick a homemaker, Danny. Your Roseanna knows now't about keeping a house."

"Exactly," I reply, keeping the smile from my lips—I could not care less whether Roseanna knows how to keep house. The only person in this room bothered by the standard of our home is Ida. And while we all adore Ida and her bullheaded and uptight ways, I know the rest of us have no interest in the cleanliness of our mantles.

Ida walks the room, seemingly coming around to the idea of a maid.

I'm beginning to realise Ida is feeling less central to the family's needs. She doesn't seem to feel wanted—and to Ida, nothing means more than being needed and also fulfilling her sense of duty. I tuck the thought away for now and hope her trepidation passes.

"No one, and I mean no one, cooks bacon quite like you," Henry adds, seemingly feeling the need to inflate Ida's ego further, and it works because Ida's thin lips rise by at least a millimetre.

"That too." I wink at Henry to thank him for lightening the mood while also hoping Ida will finally understand how much she means to us all.

"Old lady like me taking up space in a big grand house like this…" Ida kneads the hip that gives her trouble when it's damp outside. "No, I'll not fit in round here once you're married and after you finish up with all your fancy decoratin'. I'll see if there's any board and lodgings down at Compton Street."

I change tact.

"I hear they're opening a new bakery in town. You could stop making the dough every morning to get the loaves in the oven for lunch, and ride that old nag of yours to buy a loaf or you could take up my offer of teaching you to drive. The baker's boy even says they will bake cakes on Fridays."

"I'm not eating cakes made by another hand, never know what they put in those cakes in this day and I've no need for a motorcar. An old woman like me, driving around like she thinks she's something she's not, whatever will people think."

She turns to us all, her worried expression evidence of her love for us. "Since you've been going to all these fancy dinner parties, there's an air of fancy about you, Daniel. Mind my words, it'll not rub off on me." She looks at me disapprovingly and I return an innocent smile.

"Come on, Ida. Stay here with us. And besides, Danny needs to go to all the dinner parties and the business meetings. It's what gets us the rubber stamp on the new orders for the factory," Clifford says. "Without him going to those things, we would still be living here with barely a stick of furniture and oats for breakfast every day." Henry pulls a sickened face while Clifford goes to Ida's side. "He's not changed and you won't either, no matter how rich we become. We need you. Harriet too. You're helping her with the baby and she'd be lost without you."

"I suppose the babe does need another helping hand." The point of her chin begins to rise and fall and then she folds her arms as though a decision has been made. "I'm very proud. I'm proud of every single one of ye. But you'll not shine me up like a new penny. I'm an old lady."

"Come on," I say. "You're just grand as you are. None of us want to change ye, we like you just as ye are." I tap my nose. "Stop worrying. Everything is in hand and you're going nowhere."

"You're going to marry Roseanna. You said as much. You can't go on living over the brush with her. Once you're married, there won't even be room for me once the babes start coming."

A house full of children and my Red beside me, it's a wonderful image she paints.

"There'll always be room for you, Ida," I tell her.

She shakes her head, trying to find another angle to prove she's right, that we're trying to get rid of her. Her fight is unnecessary though. We do want her to live with us. If only she'd stop with her stubbornness.

"You'll both want to start having children straightaway—Roseanna's not getting any younger—and if you wait 'til she's older she'll end up with a babe that's sickly and only half of what it should be. Everyone knows the youngsters make the healthiest, strongest babes." I shake my head at the nonsense Ida believes. "So, it won't leave room for me, will it? Unless you're thinking I'll be dead before then."

I pinch my eyes closed and take a deep breath.

Ida can be such a pain.

I explain, in my most patient of tones, "When we are married, and if we have children, we will find room. Or we will buy a bigger house." I sigh exasperated.

Ida still doesn't look convinced.

"Good times are ahead," I assure them all despite my inner turmoil.

Clifford's nodding his head firmly and pride heats the blood in my veins for the boy who has been through more than any boy ought. "There is one other thing, something I need to tell you all," Clifford says. "While we're all here together and talking of marriage…." I look at him studiously and wait for him to continue. Clifford is gay. Marriage to another man is illegal so I wonder why he's got thoughts of marriage in his head. I urge him to continue. "I've decided I'm going to ask Harriet to marry me."

The news almost knocks me off my feet.

"Marry Harriet?"

Clifford nods.

"You're going to marry Harriet?"

He nods again.

"Your deceased twin brother's girl," I check.

Clifford's expression turns sour. Hurt, even. "Yes. That's what I'm going to do. To make things right." His expression is so fierce. He's so sure of his decision that I blink away all trace of doubt from my face. "I've been thinking about it a lot. Benny's daughter is a bastard at the moment and Harriet is getting sideways looks from the people in the city. I can only threaten so many of them to pack it in and I can't be with her all the time. We can't allow it. Benny was my twin brother and my best friend. I love his child as though she is my own. I like Harriet very much. She's a good mother and she is becoming a good friend of mine. Something could bloom eventually. We could build a life together. And it'll make room here because once Harriet and I are married, we'll want to get a little house of our own."

I try to keep the shock from my face.

"And what does Harriet think about this? You know she gets a say too," Ida says, having moved across the room to Clifford's side.

"I haven't asked her yet, but we're together every day playing with little Ellen and caring for her. It seems the logical next step, I think."

I take a step towards Cliff. It's obvious from his face he is indeed serious.

"Clifford, a relationship, it doesn't work like that. Feelings do grow, but if there is not that immediate spark then it won't ignite. Love needs roots to survive over time." It makes me think of Roseanna and how strong our roots are. When we're together, it feels like not even a storm can make us weak, but apart, it feels like every piece of us is delicate and vulnerable to even the slightest of winds.

Clifford's face has gone from defiant to hurt. I grip his shoulder to remind him I care for him very much.

His eyes land on mine, vulnerable and scared. "Not everybody gets to find the love of their life like you did, Danny. This might be mine and Harriet's only opportunity to have a life that people approve of. It'll help Harriet and Ellen gain some respect from people, that's got to be worth something. No one deserves a life where people think they're nothing just 'cos they didn't marry and do things the proper way."

I nod as his words choke me. Clifford still hasn't told me that he's gay and this revelation has me thinking I should bring it up. Another part of me thinks he isn't ready to have that conversation yet. Maybe marrying a woman would help him. It'd certainly stop anyone believing he is gay and keep him safer, for now at least. But it makes me wonder how long he can hide his true self. And will hiding himself cause even more harm than has already been done to him? He's practically running the factory floor with only some help from me. Eventually, he will be more than capable of taking the factory over. Clifford has worked night and day to learn the industry, from importing the metal through to driving it off the end of the production line. He wants to know everything and he is learning fast. It's helping him not dwell on the death of his twin brother—a matter that he was unknowingly involved in. A death I hope he can one day be at peace with. But marrying a woman he doesn't love, surely that can only end in disaster.

"We are marrying, so long as Harriet agrees, and that is final," Clifford says.

I wish Roseanna were here. She'd know what to do and say to help. But she's not, so I'm left to wonder if Harriet and Clifford marrying will can help them both to heal or will their marriage be doomed from the start?

Chapter 17

Roseanna

Time Flies

Beatrice pleaded not guilty and was silent in the truck the whole way back to Holloway, even though Verity tried her damnedest via nervous chatter to get her to spill what happened. I didn't question her as I could tell from the look in her eyes her hope had been dashed, much like my own.

Verity pleaded guilty to soliciting. The judge sentenced her to a mandatory six months—not the three that she had hoped for on account of her pregnancy. She, too, is dejected though perks up a little when I help her work out her pregnancy dates and surmise that if all goes to plan there is a chance she could have the baby in her mum's sitting room, if she goes a day or two over—which, with a first baby, would be entirely possible if she weren't an inmate of Holloway prison in 1922.

"It's like you said, Roseanna. If I can reduce my stress, avoid the sickness, get plenty of rest and eat well, there's no reason Mamma and Mrs Clark won't bring the babe out nice and safe." She repeats this three times on the walk to the workroom and her nerves are starting to penetrate.

I focus on the things she can control. "Wash your hands with soap and hot water when you can get it, and put your feet up every moment you can," I remind her though the list of complications is spiralling inside my mind.

"I think your Danny will find out where you are soon enough. Even I could hear you screaming his name from the gallows."

I turn into the workroom behind Beatrice and bump into her as she walks right into Ned.

"Watch where you're going ya stupid bint!" His comment reminds me of Jimmy and I can't help but miss even him and his cranky moods.

"Sorry," Beatrice apologises, and instead of behaving with her usual affront at Ned's crassness, she pulls her heart-shaped face down to her chin and sidesteps him. Before she can pass, Ned's hand lurches out and he grabs her chin. A stomach-churning stench of stale whisky and tobacco emanates from him. "No parole for the Diamond Duchess, then?" He looks utterly smug.

Beatrice raises her chin and delicately meets his glare. "The trial will come soon enough. My lawyer assures me worse-case scenario I'll be living under her Majesty's pleasure for six months. Just six months." She speaks as though reassuring herself rather than Ned.

"Six months can be a lonely long time in a place such as this." His finger trails her jaw and she takes a step back.

"I enjoy solitude." She narrowly passes beneath his arm and hurriedly slinks to her work desk.

"What you looking at, ginger?" he asks. I, too, try to pass but he stands in my way. I realise he is drunk and shudder disgustedly, rushing by him, pulling Verity behind me.

As I sit in what has become my usual place in the workroom, I watch as Ned stares at Beatrice while taking a drink from his flask and then lighting a cigarette. And it's like I can see his disgusting thoughts and I fear for Beatrice. If she doesn't get out of here fast, Ned will get to her somehow, I'm sure of it.

**

"You takin' this bowl of slop, or what?"

I hold my hands out and accept the bowl from the server while watching cockroaches scuttle along the concrete floor until they disappear behind an industrial-sized bag of flour. Beyond that is a door that leads to the outside— probably used to accept deliveries and such. It's surely kept locked, but still, I wonder if it has possibility to help me escape this godforsaken place.

I follow Verity to our usual seats, near to the exit and close to where Mo stands, but today she is not here. Another guard stands watch instead.

"What do you think about Beatrice for a name if it's a girl?" Verity asks and then takes a slurp of her broth.

I look at Beatrice and grin.

"God awful name that was bestowed on me upon the death of my old, spinster great-aunt who was a rancorous old harridan who hated me on sight. I sometimes wonder if my namesake will turn out to be an omen." Beatrice stirs her bowl listlessly while Verity and I gape at this revelation, but we manage to hold our tongues still and she continues. "I have not been blessed as a mother, most likely why my husband has found another, but if I were to be, I would choose a name with vibrancy and promise." Her tone is almost scornful to Verity and she raises a well-placed eyebrow to hammer her point. "Something like… Cordelia or Miranda…"

Titty hangs off Beatrice's every word.

Her suggestion of other Shakespearian names doesn't escape me. I wonder why, if Beatrice dislikes her name so much, she would choose others in

William's plays. A well-bread woman such as her, I imagine she knows of Beatrice's feistiness in the play *Much Ado About Nothing* and if she actually honours the name she has been given despite her misgivings about her great-aunt. Either way, it is a distraction I cling to.

"I want a name that's… charitable. Like you, Bea." Beatrice gawks at Verity for her shortening of her name. "You did that thing what was in the newspaper. You took all those children at the orphanage baby clothes and books and toys."

Beatrice's eyes mist over. "I couldn't stand to look at it all any longer." She pushes her bowl away and then shakes her head dismissively. "Verity, must you always chatter? Whenever you are around your incessant blathering is like pins to my ears."

"I was just trying to…" Titty pierces her with a hardened stare. "You're right up yourself sometimes, know that?"

"And you bore me." Beatrice stands and with the meal finished, we filter silently into the line to disperse of our bowls when I'm suddenly knocked sideways and pinned against the wall by my neck.

Bet is holding a broken mop handle in both hands and using it to crush my windpipe. Around me, women are pushing Verity and Beatrice aside, providing a blanket for what is going on to be hidden from view should the guard, who has stepped outside, return.

"I told her she'd pay for doing what she done to my Eli!" Bet talks to the women, not me. "I got her good now." She pushes harder and my arms flail out trying to push her shoulders back. She's bigger than me by more than six inches and wider too. It's impossible to breathe, and I kick my leg out and make purchase against her crotch. Bet hisses inwardly and her face scrunches up. I'd be glad I hurt her if it weren't for the complete lack of oxygen to my brain. I try and try again to lunge my arms and legs, to get her in some kind of hold but her arms are forcibly holding me against the wall

111

by my neck, and my only allies, Beatrice and Verity, are being held back by the force of Bet's supporters.

I jerk and wrestle again, but my neck is pinned solidly to the wall. My reason is floundering and my hope dissipating. Eye to eye with the vicious perpetrator of my impending murder, I see her likeness to Eli. The same bulbous nose. Half her teeth missing—though that is not hereditary. Corn-coloured hair and muddy skin... and despite my depleted oxygen, I again wonder what the point of it all was. For fate to bring me back to kill Eli only to be murdered by his mother... the only possible reason was to save Danny, who is good, whose family need him. And I'm okay with that I realise. He must live.

"Watchers are a' coming!" Mags, not a moment too soon, screeches from the doorway and as suddenly as it was pressed against my airway, the broken broom handle is released and clatters to the floor. The condensed flux of women disperses until half are casually seated, innocently chatting to their neighbours and the other half filtering out of the room.

Before she walks away, Bet warns me, "Next time you're dead!" Then she, too, filters out through the canteen door while I drop to the floor and gasp for air.

Beatrice is the first to lift me, then flanked by Verity. They hold me up while I try to pull air into my lungs. The guard enters the room and the remaining women point at me with a scornful warning not to snitch, and so Beatrice and Titty help me walk back towards our cells

With Bet's net casting closer, I wonder if I will live long enough to attend my trial.

And I vow to fight back, even if it kills me.

Chapter 18

Roseanna

The Devil isn't in Hell

Danny is never away from my thoughts, and on his birthday I say a prayer that we will find our paths back to one another.

With Titty likely not getting released before my trial, and probably after my death, I am on the hunt for someone who can speak to Danny, so I try to befriend every new inmate who arrives on my wing. I question them about Alderman Inc. and hang off every scrap of information they throw me. "I hear they're throwing out cars as though every man and woman can afford them," one such new inmate tells me. "Bleedin' loaded, so's I hear," another says. "My old man got a job building them a new factory," another says and I delight in hearing that the Aldermans are opening a new site in Dagenham. But the information I really crave, none of them can provide. I want to know if Danny is well and if he misses me. The mere thought of him makes me crave him like I imagine a junkie craves their drug of choice. I feel the magnitude of every symptom of withdrawal amplified to the point of excruciating pain. When a woman describes having seen Danny in a bar, I cling to the details and make her describe him in considerable detail only to notice that she is mistaken. It wasn't Danny she saw, for he is neither greying or with a paunch. Hopes dashed, a despair hits me that I try desperately to keep from enveloping me.

I also crave knowledge about the rest of the family. I am desperate to know if Harriet's baby was delivered safely. If she is cradling a son or a daughter and if the child has the Alderman aesthetics and their temper. I wonder if Ida is in less pain with her hip now that the season is warming and if the children settled in well to their school. Concern over Clifford and his feelings of guilt plague me and I pray he has found solace and peace. Mostly, my beliefs are positive in their Alderman focus and I imagine them happy and thriving, but without much firm evidence of such things I often worry.

Mostly the women of Holloway are poor and mix in small circles, but I make it my business to befriend anyone who is getting out soon, begging them to go tell Danny I am incarcerated. But as a small fish in this enormous sink hole, my opportunities are limited and there have only been two women so far who I have asked to find Danny and tell him I am here upon their release. But with little means to pay them upfront for their efforts, I don't hold out much hope they will follow through. I even considered parting with one of my earrings as payment for their time; they're still encapsulated in the Old Testament and are of little use to me if I am dead, but with no guarantees the women will fulfil their ends of the bargain, I'm holding out for now.

Prison life is hard and terrifying at times and I keep my head down but am always on the lookout for Bet. I'm not looking for a fight but I won't shy away from one either.

Mo gets sick of me asking her when I will see the solicitor and warns she'll belt me if I continue. So, I concentrate on other things. I learn that following Valentine's press coverage the government is reviewing the role of rehabilitation in prisons and reports are being written, which may account for Ian looking so incredibly stressed each time I see him. He's so preoccupied, he doesn't seem to be too interested in my stay, which can only be a blessing. Left to Burt Copley, I imagine I would be dead already.

I learn most things from Mags, who has taken to sitting with us for meals, and Titty whose stomach is protruding more as her pregnancy progresses. They know I'm keen to escape by any means possible and humour me with my questions, if only to fill the time that seems endless yet passes quickly.

The kitchen receives a delivery each Thursday from the butcher and grocer. There is no bakery delivery, all the bread is made in the kitchen by the women. Knives are given out at the start of meal prep and then taken away once used. Inmates are watched the whole time they prepare the food and jobs aren't shared. So, if I am caught in the kitchen, I will be beaten if found.

"No one. And I mean, no one, has ever escaped Holloway prison," Mags tells me.

"You'll never get out of here. You need a legal team and if you haven't got one then you'll die in here. It's as simple and as complicated as that," Beatrice tells me, earning her an annoyed glare.

"It's not so bad once you learn the ropes. A bunch of us have spent most of our lives in here and there's even more in the asylum wing that's been here even longer. Ruth down in the infirmary and I have been here getting on for twenty years years," Mags reassures. "For the most part, we've done just fine. You should have pleaded guilty and then you'd just get life. There are worse places you could be."

I glance around the dingy walls and can barely imagine a worse place.

"Mags, why didn't you get this Ruth woman in the infirmary to help you with your back?" I've been helping Mags to clean her back when I can but opportunities are few. I'm nearly furious at both women. How could this so-called friend not have helped her?

"She did. It's hows I was able to get some of those clean wrappings you used but getting to see her to get treatment isn't so easy. You gotta learn to keep your head down and keep quiet. Ruth coulda got a beatin' for taking those supplies for me."

As we file out, I watch Bet and she watches me. Both of us waiting for something to happen, but with Ned escorting my queue back to the remand wing and Mo taking Bet's, she is powerless to start something, for now.

The usual mundane routine of filling bowls to wash before changing into night clothes extends before me and I know soon I will be locked in my cell for another sleepless night.

Ned watches us all coming and going from our cells while sitting on a stool in the corridor and drinking whisky from a flask. His appearance is angry as usual, as though hunting an excuse to exert his power over the tired and beaten-down women. We skirt around him, moving quietly and making our tasks quick to avoid poking the beast.

I'm in my nightgown and loitering in my doorway, making the most of the short time before isolation when Beatrice leaves her cell to fill her cup from the faucet on the wall.

Ned stands, leery and unstable, he walks towards her.

"Get in ya cells, ya old bitches," he yells for the benefit of everyone, though his gaze is fixed on Beatrice in a manner that turns my stomach.

Beatrice ducks out of his way, into her cell and closes the door behind her. I sigh with relief.

Ned locks Titty in her cell and then me in mine. I listen carefully and expel a held-in breath as he locks Beatrice's door and then his footsteps disappear down the hallway and the sound of other doors being locked echoes within my earshot.

I race to open the window and hear Titty already rattling off the parenting advice she heard today and the sound is comforting. And then, above the rabble of over a hundred women all sharing conversations out of open windows, I hear the deepness of a man's voice, calling loudly, "Listen here. Listen up!"

Through the gap in the window, over the wall, is a row of houses close enough that I can see the rooftops and a man standing atop. Just to see a person that is not a prison guard is exciting and my imagination runs wild. My heart gallops and for a moment, I imagine the shadow of the man is Danny even though his voice is not the same. There are others standing behind him too. I allow myself to hope that he is among them.

The women's chatter quietens.

Hope threatens to burst from my chest. I remember Verity telling me weeks ago that the rooftop from which this man calls from was once used to get messages to the suffragettes when they were incarcerated for protesting. At the time I wondered if this could be of use to me to send my own message, but since there has never been a man atop the roof before, it seemed moot.

"Beatrice. Diamond Duchess! Can you hear me?" the man calls.

"Yes, I can hear you!" Beatrice shouts back using that sing-song voice of hers.

Hope shattered, shameful resentment licks at my gut and I'm tempted to close the window.

"The people love you! We are petitioning to get you out. Holding placards and demonstrations, we WILL get you out of there."

"Thank you!" she calls back. "I can't wait to leave this place and meet all of my fans. Please, act quickly!"

She rallies her fans using a charm saved only for those who can aid her, and I find myself cynically judging her. But in her position, I would do the same—any woman here would, such is the need for freedom.

So, I yell above Beatrice's voice, shouting that my name is Roseanna Chapman and they must go to Alderman Inc. and tell Daniel Alderman that I am incarcerated here. The other women hastily become excited and they, too, yell announcements of their own until all that can be heard is a white noise of desperate pleas with no single voice of any discernible message.

The ruckus creates a retaliation by the establishment and a bell in the watch tower starts to ring. At the edge of my viewpoint is the pitter-patter of footsteps and the ringing of the bell is soon replaced with guards blowing whistles.

The man on the roof is helped to climb down through a window and suddenly the quiet is booming. I wonder if the man has committed a crime by communicating to Beatrice. My earlier resentment softens and I hope their petitions help Beatrice to get out, realising that just because the situation seems easier for Beatrice doesn't mean that she should be held in here. The system is punitive and unrelentingly cruel to the men and woman faced with it. It makes me wonder if perhaps Beatrice's public support and the will of the people could also aid the innocent inmates here, if only she will use this newfound power to help them.

I decide to make it my purpose to persuade Beatrice of this but then something happens that shatters my plan and has bile surfacing in my mouth.

The door to the cell next to mine opens with a creak then slams shut, followed by Beatrice's helplessly high-pitched shriek for Ned to get out.

"Quit your screaming. I've come to see if the Duchess's fanny is any better than a peasant's, and there ain't nothing you can do that's going to stop me!"

Chapter 19

Roseanna

A Perfect Storm

"You must leave my room at once!" Beatrice's voice is stern and foreboding.

I stand on my bed and crane my ear to the window, praying Ned listens and leaves her cell.

"Got men calling to you over the walls now. Bet they all want a taste of your clout now you're in the papers."

"I did not ask that man to come. I don't even know who he is, so if you've come here to punish me, you can save your time."

"I don't give a shit about the bloke. Leave it to the watch tower men to deal with that. I got more important things to worry about."

The chatter of the inmates increases as the show of the man over the wall is over and none of them can hear what is about to take place in the cell beside mine.

"Lovely nightdress. You look proper, not like the others. Must be nice, having friends in high places," Ned says, his voice spasmodic with inebriation.

"I don't know what you mean. Out. Come along, you shouldn't be in here." Beatrice's voice suddenly sounds younger, less sure.

"You don't tell me what to do. I tell you! Take off your nightdress. I want to see your titled cunt."

"Get off—get off me! Ned, I will see that the warden—"

SMACK!

"Others have tried. The warden ain't going to give a shit about this. He doesn't give a damn and he won't save you."

Beatrice lets out a yelp.

"We've got to do something," Verity calls to me.

I bang the bars of the window.

"Stop! Ned STOP!" I scream and Verity calls out too.

Beside my cell, I can hear the indefinite sounds of thuds and clattering, muffled protests and broken screams. Verity and I bang and scream louder, waiting for the unmistakable sound of Beatrice's door being opened with Ned leaving.

That sound doesn't come and the absence of it sickens me and tears prick my eyes. I pick up the heavy-set bible and thump it against my door, screaming for someone to come help.

Anyone.

I'm screaming to the Gods themselves to intervene.

And then screeching with sounds drawn from the pit of my gut at the unfairness for powers unknown to move me to this time only to render me helpless over and over again in the most punishing, agonising ways.

No one comes.

And then I do the only thing I have left to do.

I ring the rope for the bell, leveraging my swing with everything I have in me to make the sound as loud as it can be and I continue to scream until someone comes.

The door swings open so hard it cracks the wall when it smashes against it.

Standing before me is Mo and her face is wrinkled with sleep, her feet in some kind of comfortable slipper. Her hand lurches into my cell and grabs me by my shoulder, forcing me forwards into the corridor. "This better be good."

My stare fixes on Beatrice's door.

"It is. I swear. I think Beatrice is in trouble. You have to open the door. She's—"

I lurch forwards but before I can get to her door, Ned is already out in the corridor, looking dishevelled with a claw mark right down the side of his face. I have a strong feeling the moment he heard the bell, he pulled himself together.

I peer behind him and see Beatrice drawn in on herself at the head of her bed, still clothed, thankfully.

"What exactly has been going on here?" Mo asks.

Ned stumbles towards me, his finger pointing in a jabbing motion.

"You!" He jabs his finger in my chest and then snatches my forearm and spins me around as he pins it behind my back. He tells Mo, who looks at us both reproachfully, "These women been causing a right ruckus." He takes out his baton and beats it against my thigh and I yelp. "You'd have heard if ya weren't catching ya winks, ya lazy old bint," he tells Mo and then thrashes the baton down again, this time hitting the side of my knee and my leg gives out in the pain.

Mo peers beyond us, right at Beatrice. Ned twists us both around to face the same way. Beatrice looks pale and her body is shaking violently. Her hair, lacking its usual elegant style, is in a state of complete disarray. Her usually perfectly dressed bed is adrift with tangled sheets and the pillow torn and on the floor beside her feet.

I hear Ned sneer and feel his body tense with anger. There's no way Mo won't guess what was about to happen and I hope the bastard is made to suffer for it.

Beatrice lifts her chin just enough to see me through her tears.

"He was about to ra—"

The baton smacks down on the top of my head with such force that Ned loses his grip on my arm and I plummet to the floor.

I roll onto my side and cover my face with my hands while yelling, "He was, Mo, he was in—"

Ned's boot connects with my abdomen and the wind is knocked straight out of me. Gasping for air, I hear Verity's voice right before the blow of the baton beats down on my cranium. I scrunch my body into the foetal position, making myself as small as I can while holding my hands over my face but the blows keep hammering down.

One, two, three… I lose count.

Mo, at least I think it is Mo who speaks sharply, saying something like, "That's enough now. You'll kill her." He replies something inaudible and Mo booms at him. "Ye'll leave the girl be now or I'll stop ye meself with the bat!" I register the fury in her voice just a second before the bat comes harder and faster until I can't pinpoint where the blows are landing.

My hands are the only thing partially saving me from death, though I can no longer see or hear. The agony becomes a global, stabbing sensation all over my body until, as suddenly as pushing the off switch, the pain stops and all sense of life is extinguished.

Chapter 20

Roseanna

The Arms of an Angel

I hear sounds first. The pitter-patter of footsteps, the squeaky wheel of a trolley, the light moans of a woman in pain. Regaining the sense of smell takes more effort. My nostrils are filled with hard matter, like someone pumped them full of concrete but through the fullness is a mild scent of detergent and it reminds me of the sanitiser we used to use to disinfect the ambulance between patients. There is the sweetness of soap and also the unmistakable smell of fresh coffee.

My eyes feel too heavy to open, like they are pried shut and tremors of panic shoot through me which alights other discomforts. My entire body, from the tip of my toenails to the ends of my eyelashes feel tender and heavy. A sudden flinch or a twitch through the stiffness is like a physical blow, and what brought me here resurfaces in my mind like a horror movie on repeat.

"It's okay. You're safe now." The voice is tender and warm and makes me think of Nanna.

I try to ask where I am but my vocal cords won't comply.

"I'm Ruth. An inmate, unpaid nurse, friend…" She stops talking and I feel her fingers against the skin of my temple, adjusting my hair. "You've got bandages over your eyes." Her tone lifts to suggest she is mildly amused. "Dr. Hadfield believes darkness is best for a brain injury." I feel a hand clasp my finger and I flinch. The woman lets go and I suddenly wish her hand was still there. "We can take those off when he finishes his shift later. You've been in here a little over two weeks. Dr. Hadfield didn't think you'd make it at first, but I was sure you would."

Two weeks.

"I've never seen such a sight. Unrecognisable. But don't worry, you're looking better now. Still as beautiful as ever and healing very well."

I try to speak again but the sound won't come.

"Rest now, my love. We'll talk soon enough."

Lassitude overtakes me and time ceases to hold me to account. I sleep and wake in waves, remembering where I am and what brought me to this place during the crest, only to lose my thoughts and memories of the attack during the crash.

What stays with me throughout, whether awake or asleep, is visions of Danny that are so visceral, I can feel him holding me, hear him telling me everything is going to be okay, and smell the sweetness of his scent.

**

I stir to consciousness in the warm glow of sunshine. It takes my eyes time to adjust to see beyond the phosphenes that float before me. The iron bars against the window are the first things I notice. Beyond those, the tiny carpark out front, not that I can escape. My body is still so weak and sore I doubt I can even stand.

"You're awake." The lovely voice is back and I attempt to smile though it hurts my eyes. "Don't worry. That cut above your eye is almost fused now. It's right in your eyebrow, so with any luck the scar won't even show." She puts an empty bedpan on the table beside my bed and I remember faintly her holding me while I toileted.

"Sorry." My voice sounds raw and gravelly, a testament to its disuse.

"What, that?" She crouches at my bedside so I can see her and thumbs the bowl. "Don't be. Absolutely no bother at all compared to a certain Mrs and her bowels." She winks and nods her head to the corner where an elderly lady snores loudly and I muster a chuckle.

"How are you feeling, Roseanna?" she asks, and I notice it is not only her voice that is lovely, so is her face. Her hair is a faint shade of amber, like it bleached in the sun and her face is weathered around her smiling eyes and full lips as though age marked her in just the right places.

I clear the build-up of phlegm in my throat rather ungracefully, and she helps me to sit up by plumping my pillows and cupping me beneath my arms to lift me.

"I feel like I've been hit by a tonne truck," I reply before realising that tonne trucks may not even be a thing yet. The nurse doesn't seem to notice as she lets out an uneasy chuckle.

"You might ought to have been." Her smile flattens. "It'll be a little while until you're running about the place. I'm quite sure you have a few broken ribs, though without access to an X-ray it's impossible to say. You had a brain injury, that we know—you've been unconscious, but every now and then you'd speak. Who's Danny?" She pauses and waits for me to respond, her eyes lit with affection.

"Daniel Alderman, the man I love," I say automatically, but something she said is nagging at me. *Are X-ray machines in use in this time?*

Her face breaks out in a smile. "Nothing is better than the promise of love to speed healing."

A hiss of pain escapes as I try to reposition myself on the bed. In my head I'm doing a quick analysis of what is wrong with me.

"You're covered in bruises. Your knee was definitely dislocated. A reduction popped it back into place, so I'm hoping by now it is feeling a bit better. Unfortunately, we've only been able to give you aspirin—there's no adequate pain relief available to prison inmates I'm afraid—apparently they're not worth the expense." She hisses disgustedly. "Still, you're a strong one, make no mistake about that. We should probably try and get you up and moving around soon. Some physiotherapy and movement and you'll be right as rain in no time." She pushes a tendril of my hair away from my face and her bottle green eyes fix on mine in such a caring manner that an ache shoots directly to my heart.

"Physiotherapy, huh? We do physiotherapy now?" Dr. Hadfield says entering the room and the nurse picks up the bedpan and takes a step away from me.

"Tony."

"Dr. Hadfield," he asserts.

"Of course. Miss Chapman is awake."

"So, I see." He glances in my direction and then stares pointedly at the nurse. "She'll be fit to go back to the general population soon. Ruth, a word in my office, please."

The nurse follows him out the door and I feel the onset of a headache around the edges of my brain.

Ruth.

I've heard it said before but hearing her name, right as I am looking at her, sparks a gnawing sense of recognition.

Surely not.

No. It's impossible.

The thought is too much but I don't get the chance to dwell on it as I suddenly collapse into unconsciousness.

Chapter 21

Roseanna

Every Cloud

I don't see Ruth for the rest of the day which gives me ample time to dwell on my current state of mind… my first thought being, *have I finally gone mad or have I been mad all along? Travelling through time and finding my one true love and my mother? It certainly seems like madness.*

I'm left in a state of shock and wondering if I hallucinated the entire situation.

I go over what I know to be the facts. Facts that seem unreliable and open to interpretation.

Ruth mentioned X-rays and while they have been invented already, they are not yet common. If Ruth has spent most of her life in Holloway like Mags told me, then how would she have any knowledge of them? She wouldn't, surely.

I haven't seen my mother since I was five, but Ruth seemed familiar in the sense you get when looking at a photograph of a relative you never met but one you know living facts and nuances about.

The song I heard during my first night in my cell and have heard since, it felt familiar but could it be more than that? My memory is telling me it is the theme tune to my childhood—a song about a little girl lost. I can't decide if it was sung to me or if I am now only convincing myself that it is.

The fallibility of memory is so frustrating, I find my fists clenching despite the pain it causes to shoot up my arms. Then I wonder if I died during Ned's beating.

But everything feels too real for this to be purgatory, and so I am left waiting and wondering thoughts that are too big with each creating another set of questions like a maze that just goes round and round, never arriving at a destination I can find peace in.

At dinner time Verity arrives with a bowl of soup for me, and she's flanked by Mo, who doesn't come near, instead she lights a cigarette and stands in the hall with the door ajar.

Verity runs right inside the infirmary, past the row of beds and up to mine, sloshing soup everywhere. "You're alive!"

She puts the bowl on the nightstand and throws her arms around me. I pull her close with all the strength I can muster and delight in the joy of human contact. Tears spring to my eyes and I blink them away.

She leans back, leaving one arm looped around me and says, "It's so good to see you. We thought you were dead for sure. Even Mo said, 'I doubt we'll be seeing her again,' and I thought she was right."

A tear spills over my lashes and my muscles protest as I wipe it away.

"Sorry. I didn't mean to upset you. It's just… I'm glad you're not dead."

"It's okay." I laugh. "I'm glad I'm not dead too. How is Beatrice?"

Titty nods. "She's... well, haven't you heard?"

I shake my head.

"The reporter printed a story about the attack in *The Daily Herald*. Couldn't name Ned—the bastard—since he's not been convicted and it won't go to court, but a load of people went loopy and I swear half of 'em turned up right at the gates shouting. Ned got suspended for two weeks and he got told he mustn't do it again and Beatrice, well, she's okay, I think. Determined to get the hell out of here, but who isn't?" She places her hand over mine and stares at the bruising that marks my arms; her expression turns sallow for a few moments until another fleeting thought lifts her spirits. "They printed your name in the paper. Valentine brought it in and showed Bea. Your Danny will definitely see now, won't he? He'll finally know where to find you!"

"They printed my name in the paper?" After months of nothing and being beaten almost within an inch of my life, it finally feels like there has been some point to it all. Something positive to hold onto.

Verity lifts the spoonful of broth to my lips and I swallow.

"They did!" She grins.

"When? When was it in the newspaper?"

Verity looks down and stirs the soup. "Well, it was a week ago now. But it's something, right?"

A week ago.

"Have I had any letters? Has anyone visited?" I ask Mo. I've been unconscious for weeks. Maybe he came while I was out cold.

"No. No letters and no one's come," Mo replies in a pitiful voice.

Verity looks upset for me, so I change the subject and we talk for a while about how much more comfortable the beds are in the infirmary, but as she feeds me the broth I find myself sickened by the sensation of sustenance as it hits my stomach. Then I look down at my legs from the top of the blanket and notice how thin and spindly they look.

"You've looked better if I'm honest, but you'll get yeself back to yeself in no time. And Beatrice said to say thank you and she meant it too, I could see she did." She lifts another spoonful of broth to my lips and continues. "'Ere, never guess what?" She doesn't wait for me to answer. "Bet got a ruddy good hiding from Mags, no less! Couldn't believe it. Bet said something or other, probably about you since Mags likes ya so much, and Mags went spare, she did! Should've seen it! Was like a night at the Foundry with old Mrs Castle and Brenda going ten to the dozen…"

She chatters on about everything I have missed—which isn't much but Verity manages to make every bit of it sound fun and exciting while feeding me a few more spoons of broth until I put my hand up to stop her. "My stomach can't take any more."

Verity frowns. "You need your strength."

I assure her I'll eat again later and then she looks at the bowl with a wanting stare. I smile at her and tell her to finish it so she drinks it down in one— straight from the bowl—then Mo coughs and drops her cigarette on the floor, putting it out with her toe. "Verity, times up. You're not meant to be in here and it was good of me to bring ye. Say goodbye."

Verity stands and stretches her back. "It's good to see you."

My cheeks warm and my grin widens slightly. "Verity, you're blooming!"

She looks down and cups her stomach and her smile beams. "I know. Not long to go now, just hope the poor mite ain't born in here."

Mo coughs loudly and begins to look as though she is losing her patience. "You'd better go."

Her face tightens in a grump. "Will you be okay?"

"I'll be fine. There's a nurse here and she's taking care of me."

Mo orders Verity to leave but before she does, she replies, "Nurse? Ain't no nurses here. Only the doctor, and he ain't even here half the time."

Chapter 22

Roseanna

Just a Dream?

The twelve beds—six on each side of the room—are revolving doors for mostly older women with various complaints, though I suspect most have rubella. Passed to one another through coughing and sneezing, the guards seem to believe isolating them in the infirmary will stop the spread.

Having been vaccinated as a child, I don't worry for myself, but I do worry for the frail and of course, Verity, who's in the late stages of her pregnancy and could become very ill indeed as well as her unborn child.

Dr. Hadfield visits two or three times a week. The rest of the time, the sick are tended to by inmates, who are mostly unskilled, while under the watch of an equally unqualified guard.

There's a sense of unworthiness that absorbs into almost all the souls touched by Holloway. An absence of care for life or death is the norm, and when it is challenged there is genuine surprise that any person would value the lives of the women here.

During one of his few visits to the infirmary, I try to mitigate some of the risks of the rubella epidemic. I suggest to Dr. Hadfield that if the women had access to hygiene supplies, and if the communal facilities were appropriately disinfected, then there might be at least some hope of stemming the epidemic and saving lives.

"Good God, woman. You spend a few nights in the infirmary and now you think you're a doctor?"

Even though I want to, I don't mention to the pompous asshole that in my time, every member of staff in the hospital, whether a cleaner or a consultant, are trained in infection control. And it works!

"I've worked in healthcare, and doing these things reduced the spread of illness and infection. Isn't it worth a try?" I plead to his better nature, hoping he has one. "Imagine how quiet things would be around here if there were less patients…" This seems to get his attention.

"And you think Warden Copley is going to front the money for all these resources?" he asks cynically.

I make my tone casual, hoping that if I can convince him it is his idea, he might run with the suggestion. "Warden Copley might find the money if he thought it would look good in the report he is writing for Westminster. Raising standards includes keeping the women alive, after all. There is no maternity care for the women here—they aren't even given adequate food. There's a woman on my wing of the prison who looks as thin as a child despite being midway through her pregnancy, and women are only brought to the infirmary when they're at the very gates of death. And well, infection control… it's the most basic of care. I hear even Florence Nightingale herself advocates for it."

Hadfield nods his head in a manner that makes me believe he is taking me seriously so I continue, "Of course, if the women all wore masks over their mouths until the spread is contained, then it'd be all the more effective—"

Dr. Hadfield starts to laugh. "Ha! Good one!"

I quirk my now healed brow at him, I had to take the stitches out myself since I haven't seen Ruth. I'm beginning to wonder if I conjured her out of my imagination.

"April Fools has passed already, you know!"

I'm reminded that time seems to be speeding so forcibly towards my trial date and also wonder if Danny saw my name printed in the newspaper.

"I can tell you're ready to return to your cell. You got your sense of humour back."

"No, Dr. Hadfield, you don't understand. I'm serious—"

"I'll have none of that nonsense wasting my time. Now, let's see you get up and move around."

I pull my legs from the bed and stand. Still thinner than a child's, they wobble with my upright position.

"You remind me of the suffragettes and their ludicrous starvation strikes. Still, we got them eating in the end."

"Oh?"

Dr. Hadfield sits on the stool beneath the window and examines my knee, pulling it this way and that. "A tube, inserted down their gullet, and pure cream poured straight to the stomach. I'll not have women starving themselves to death on my watch."

"You did that?" My tone is milder than the heat bursting through my veins.

He smiles. "Not by myself. Ha! Feisty bunch they were and needed holding down. All in the name of women's rights." He shakes his head. "Women will be just fine when they stop all this nonsense about rights and go home and take proper care of their children." He stands and takes my arm in his hands and rotates it around my shoulder, and then does the same to the other. "Take Katherine, over there. Six children and ends up in here leaving her mother to care for them. You tell me what is right about that?"

I snatch back my arm.

The tales of unfairness that so many of the women have shared poke away at me, demanding they be told.

"Tell me, Dr. Hadfield, what is right about women being treated with less respect than men? Or why women should earn less for the same work? Why a woman cannot own land, or a house, or see her children if she chooses to divorce? Tell me how it is fair that a woman walks away penniless from an abusive husband or children live in fear of their fathers."

"A feminist, I see." Hadfield chuckles deliberately in his attempt to undermine and demean me.

I should feel angry, but he's so certain of his views that his ignorance is laughably pathetic.

"Do you have daughters?"

"Yes." He grins proudly. "I have four," he replies as if it bears no consequence.

"Then I pity them for having a father who is quite unwilling and unprepared to stand up for them."

I climb back into the bed, deciding that I do not need his medical opinion or any other, and besides, I have already deemed myself fit.

His face scrunches up irritably. "And I pity you when you return to your cell—which will be tomorrow, by the way—to live out what is left of your miserable life there."

Dr. Hadfield lifts his stethoscope from around his neck and inserts it into the pocket of his jacket and leaves the room. Beyond him, I see Mo smirk.

**

Later that night, Mo clocks off and is replaced with a different guard, who I am able to convince that doctor's orders are that I move around to exercise my knee.

I walk around the room, pausing at the windows, bending and stretching and thoroughly putting on a show while I check the resolve of the bars that I have no hope of getting through.

Beyond this room, there is a small, windowless bathroom to the right, and Dr. Hadfield's office to the left, which is kept locked. The floor is concrete and the ceiling solid with no vents or hatches or anything that might suggest a way out. Aside from using my soup spoon to dig myself out in full view of the guard, it's hopeless and escape from this room is impossible.

Still, I pepper my resolve in the knowledge that I have the solicitor to meet with, and maybe Danny will come eventually. I refuse to believe that he knows about my whereabouts and doesn't care. There must be other reasons he has not come.

I put Ruth to the back of my mind, convincing myself that she was a figment of my imagination, but not long later that night she comes to me—not in a dream, like I imagined she might—holding a bowl of something and telling the guard she is here to feed me supper, even though I am now perfectly capable of feeding myself.

"Go along with it," Ruth whispers then casts her eyes at the guard.

I reply in a hushed voice, "She's seen me walking about the place, she'll never believe I need feeding."

"That's Mildred. The warden only trusts her to guard this lot because they're bedridden and stand no chance of escape." Ruth winks then spoons a mouthful of oats laden with sugar into my mouth.

I can't bring myself to smile at the delicious sugary oats or laugh at her joke. I'm caught between wonder at her face and convincing myself this is not real. I must be imagining that she looks almost identical to the woman from Nanna's photographs.

"We have a lot to talk about," Ruth whispers as though she can read my thoughts directly from my expression.

"I recognised you, when I first saw you," I say. It's vague, but it's true, and as good a place to start as any.

"I'd heard your given name mentioned before I met you. It made me wonder how many Roseanna's there could be in this world... in this time... Thousands perhaps."

She stops feeding me and her comment is so enlightening that I almost forget to swallow. Her hair is red, but not bright like mine, faded like red hair tends to over time. The pale complexion and sallow skin that hangs from her delicate bone structure is suggestive of light malnourishment, yet it's easy to imagine how she once may have looked. Even easier to envisage, thanks to the photographs Nanna kept of my mother. Photographs I couldn't bear to look at and locked away only to bring them out whenever I felt sad or lonely. Now, it is as though a ghost of the photographs stares back at me.

"I can't imagine there are many Roseanna Chapman's in 1920s London," I say once I have been able to find my voice.

Her eyes shimmer as she smiles at the sound of my name. Her voice breaks during her reply so that it is barely audible. "No. Not many at all."

"You're my mother?" I shakily whisper.

She nods and spoons more oats into my mouth and I swallow quickly.

"You're an inmate of Holloway prison?"

She nods again then sighs. "Nigh on twenty years."

I start to question if I did, in fact, time travel. For if she is here, and I am here, could my existence in the twenty-first-century have ever been real?

"It happened. We were there and now we are both here."

It's my turn to nod. "How?"

Ruth opens her mouth to speak but my second question overtakes her answer to my first. "Why?"

She looks behind her at Mildred, who is walking the line of beds and checking the patients with a grave expression. It's a peculiar sight. As if Mildred is a child playing a game of dress up, pretending she is a nurse.

"If I answered your questions and someone heard me, we'd both likely end up on the asylum wing." Her smile is watery. She spoons another mouthful of oats into my mouth.

"You left me."

It's all the reminder I need to cast aside any doubt of where I have been. I existed, and she left me and every part of my life since has been tied to this moment.

She shakes her head. "I would never leave you. Not the way you think I did. My child. My beautiful child." She attempts to put her hand on mine but I move it away.

"Then how? I've spent my whole life lost. I need to understand what happened." My voice comes out louder and higher pitched than I intended.

Mildred must hear me because her face swings in our direction. "Shh. Patients are sleeping and they need their rest."

We both nod and Mildred goes back to inspecting their charts like she knows what all the words and numbers mean.

"I took you back to get your vaccinations—"

"I was born here?"

Ruth nods. "Do you remember anything?"

I shake my head.

Her voice becomes nostalgic though she is talking about events that theoretically haven't happened yet. "We went forward. You had your vaccinations and after, as a treat since you were so brave, we visited the cinema…. There was a movie theatre and we watched a replaying of *The*

Wizard of Oz and ate a huge bucket of popcorn. You tried nachos for the very first time and said you didn't like them." She smiles fondly.

I remember the film—I liked it. And I *don't* like nachos—Katie thinks I'm mad but they're just too crunchy.

"We were in modern London for six months. We stayed at Nanna's house and had a lovely time, but eventually it was time to go home. You had a new doll but you dropped it. You ran back for it but it was too late—our connection was broken. I waited on the other side for you. I waited until the moon was replaced by the sun. You never came." Her eyes are glistening, and as she paints the picture before me, it is like I am there.

"I never told you about the stones—too worried you'd blurt it out to a stranger. I supposed, after you picked up your doll and looked back, it appeared like I had vanished. It's haunted me ever since that you would believe I left you."

Mildred comes closer. "Taking a long time over that food. How is the patient?"

"Struggling with deglutition. Do I have permission to go slow to minimise the choke response?"

Mildred nods seriously. "Yes, that is very important. Choking can be deadly. As you were."

"You were taking me with you?" I check.

"Yes. I did everything to get back to you. I swear." Her eyes, the exact same colour as mine, become misty, her beautiful face drawn with enduring pain. "But the very next day I was thrown in here and this is where I've been ever since."

I slide my hand over hers.

"What do we do now?"

Chapter 23

Roseanna

Live and Learn

The next day Ned escorts me back to my cell. "Thought you could get me the boot, did ya?"

I walk beside him, carefully assessing the risk his mood might present.

The feigned confidence of his tone and nervousness beneath his smug facade is plain on his face. Ned fears "getting the boot" more than he regrets his actions.

I keep my tone conversational but ensure the threat is clearly weaved within my comment. "I hear the *Herald* want someone convicted for my assault. They're willing to pay for the finest legal representation to bring the perpetrator to justice. After all, I defended the darling Diamond Duchess from a disgusting rapist… if anything happens to either of us, the public will make sure you swing from a rope."

Of course, I'm lying, but Ned doesn't know that.

I hear him swallow.

"They ain't going to want to do that. 'Tis in the past. Now, get into your work clothes or there'll be no breakfast for ye." He shifts uncomfortably in the same corridor where I cowered beneath his relentless beating.

I take a step into my cell before turning to him. "If you ever lay a hand on another woman in this prison, it is not the *Herald* you will need to fear." I pierce him with my most angry and violent of stares and he nods. "Shut the door, man. Give me some privacy," I demand, suddenly fearing I have pushed my luck, but to my surprise, Ned closes the door.

I rush to the window and stare at the rooftops. No one is there, but I check the surroundings just in case. I don't know why I thought he might be there—Mo said he hadn't come. Danny probably still doesn't even know I am here, but it doesn't stop me needing him, even if he's on the other side of a wall.

Dropping my shoulders in disappointment I turn back to my cell and notice on the desk are two envelopes, a fine fountain pen, and a stack of writing paper. Placed on top is a note from Beatrice:

Words can never be enough to thank you, but I hope they can help you reach your love.

B

**

Sometime later, as I enter the workroom, I am met with the slow, rhythmic, steady bringing together of hands. Mo orders the women to stop clapping, and after a while they do, then they smile and pat my behind as I pass. All except Bet, who has the greenish-yellow coloured tinge of a bruise beneath her eye.

"Good to have you back," Beatrice says from the corner of her mouth as I seat myself beside her.

From beneath the pile of fabric on the bench in front, she slides me a newspaper. A copy of *The Daily Herald* it details the incident that has intrinsically marked us both.

Diamond Duchess Assault

Two nights ago, under the "supposed" care of His Majesty's guards, the dear Duchess of Suffolk, incarcerated for crimes yet to be established, was attacked in her cell.

The attack, which was allegedly committed by a male guard with long-standing employment at the prison, was fought off on this occasion by the bravery and selflessness of a fellow inmate: Roseanna Chapman, who sustained a life-threatening beating.

Westminster is now calling for an investigation of these claims and said there would be no comment until such time.

The "Making Prison Pay" report, penned by parliament, is due to be published next month when it is likely the public will be questioning: Are prison conditions for women too harsh?

I thank Beatrice, then slide the newspaper back beneath the material and start to sew. "The conditions in this prison are disgusting. The guards should not get away with it... it's a complete breach of trust and utterly barbaric." I chance a glimpse at Bea who seems much stronger than the last time I saw her.

"I'm working on it," she whispers. "I've written to some very important people about these matters, and if something isn't done about it... well, I will not rest until something is done about it."

"It's other things as well. I told Dr. Hadfield as much—not that he would listen, the bloody idiot! Sanitation must improve if he is to stave off an epidemic in here. Maternity care." My voice hushes to a whisper in case Verity overhears us. "There isn't any. There is only the hope that one of the inmates knows a thing or two about saving infants' and expectant mothers' lives. It's not good enough, no matter the mother's crimes!" I huff and then move the conversation to what has also been a constant weight on my mind. "Danny hasn't come."

Beatrice's front teeth hold her bottom lip.

"He's not going to, is he?"

"Perhaps he didn't see the article?"

"Maybe…" I snap the cotton and thread the needle. "It's possible it escaped his attention."

I remember the times we sat in his office at the Alderman Manor, me reading the newspapers to him and dissecting the information while he would tell me I had too many opinions in my head, even though I could tell he didn't mean it.

"He'll come once he knows. Write him a letter. I'll make sure he gets it."

"You're right. He loves me. I know he does…"

And I do. I know it.

This place. This prison. It messes with the mind and convinces you what you know is wrong.

Holloway Prison: Captor of Hope.

#Notanymore!

Chapter 24

Roseanna

It Ain't Over Till It's Over

In the queue at supper, Verity lets out a squeak of excitement when I am handed a big chunk of bread and something that strongly resembles meat and potatoes. She's so thrilled at the gesture of acceptance that I tear away half the bread and spoon some of the heartier elements of the dish into hers so that we can better share the moment.

Then I seat myself in the available space opposite Bet.

Her cronies stop talking and stiffen in their seats while the atmosphere turns volatile.

Bet clutches her spoon as though one might a dagger. "You've got some front coming over here and sitting with me."

"We need to talk."

"Ain't nothing I want to say to you unless it's over your dead body."

"I understand why you want me dead." I nod slowly. "I wanted someone dead too once, but nowhere near as much as I wished that a boy lived…." I tear off a chunk of bread and put it beside Bet's bowl.

She looks at me suspiciously.

"Benjamin Alderman was fifteen and tall and gangly for his years. He wouldn't eat meat if he'd met the animal it came from and he never cussed, not even when he was in pain and his life was ebbing away." I picture Benjamin in my arms during his final moments, staring up at me with a strength and dignity that was beyond his years, and remember how he stole my heart. "Benjamin had a family. A good one. A little brother, Henry, who races around like his pants are on fire and a younger sister with the same blonde hair who talks and talks about every detail of her life with a sense of wonder that makes your heart feel like it might burst with love.

"He didn't invite pain into his young life, yet he was recruited by it nonetheless. A senseless, pointless death that rippled through the lives of others until it almost drowned them. Eventually you have to ask yourself, where does it stop? When is there enough death?"

I shrug and dip my bread into the gravy just so I have something to do with my hands.

"I didn't wake that morning planning to shoot your son, just like I don't think he left his house that day with the intention of murdering a child. Sometimes, events escalate beyond our control and we become mere vessels for our values."

I let go of the bread and it sinks inside the bowl. Then I stand.

"Death cannot be honoured by more death."

Bet's gaze moves from mine to glance around her table of supporters who have been quietly listening—the same as the rest of the room, but I don't dare turn my attention from her—not when she could turn on me in an instant. When Bet turns back to me, her expression is unreadable.

"I came over here to call a truce with you. Life thrives best through living it, and Benjamin wouldn't want further bloodshed."

And I refuse to die in honour of a man such as Eli Harris.

Despite the deep lines in Bet's face, it's difficult to tell if her expression has softened, and so I walk away and hear her mutter to her friends, "Stupid cow."

Chapter 25

Roseanna

Come Rain or Shine

The next day, after I have passed a long and detailed letter to Beatrice for Danny, I am instructed by Mo to take the women's dirty sheets to the laundry. At first, it feels like a punishment. The load is bigger than I am. The metal crate for carrying it in has rusted wheels that have a mind of their own and threaten to snap as I manoeuvre it down the steps to the basement laundry.

Once I am there, I hand it over to the woman at the entrance of the laundry and then turn to hurry back to the workroom when I am pulled inside a storeroom housing large canisters of detergent.

I immediately swing around and raise my fists.

The woman before me grins wildly at me.

"Mum?" I realise it's the first time I've said the word aloud in a very long time and tears prick my eyes.

Unable to hold back, Ruth casts me in a cradling hug that caresses deep into my bones. Then she breaks away and tells me, "We don't have long. The sheets only come once a week, but Mo'll make sure it's you that brings them each week."

"Mo?"

"She's all right, is Mo. She's been seeing that I get updates as often as she can. Told me about Bet Harris giving you grief."

"That's over now, I think."

"Damn well better be." Ruth looks ready to fight.

"Motherly retaliation?"

"I'll kill her if she ever lands a finger on you again."

A watery smile lifts the corner of my mouth. "I thought you left me."

"Never. Your dad and I, we worshipped every hair on your head."

My heart almost stops.

"Dad?"

She smiles and nods.

"I knew I had a father, obviously. But it was useless asking Nanna anything. Her replies were always so extreme in vagueness and prone to sounding fantastical."

Ruth doesn't seem surprised. "She's been forgetful for as long as I can remember, but then she lived half in one world and half in another. And when my father died, well, she lost more than just her husband." Her eyes gloss over as though remembering her mother in the time that came before me and she pulls a brave smile to her lips. "Does Glenda still take care of her?"

"You know Glenda?"

"Of course." Her face becomes confused. "Do you know anything of where you come from?"

I shake my head. "I gave up trying to make sense of any of the things Nanna said when I was in my teens." I remember feeling so utterly helpless to get her the care she needed. "Her memory got really bad. I took her to the doctor with Glenda and he did a memory test. He said her long- and short-term memory were impaired by dementia and there wasn't anything we could do to delay the progression. Of course, he asked if there was anything we needed, but Glenda said we could cope fine and for the most part, we did." Selfishness spins my stomach. "I was worried they'd put me in foster care if anyone knew how bad she was, and so we just muddled along."

Ruth lowers her gaze morosely. "That's exactly what Mum would've wanted. She hated interference and is a stubborn old goat sometimes."

I laugh gently, remembering how her intransigence ways would cause us to butt heads even though she was often right. "She certainly is." I grip Ruth's arm a little tighter. "She's in the future. I didn't know I'd be transported here. It happened suddenly and well—"

"I know. It happened to me, too, and to your grandmother."

"You've got to tell me everything. I need to know."

"I will but not today. You're in danger of being missed if you take much longer and Ned is on shift in the sewing room. You need to get back."

"I'm on trial for murder. They've mentioned the death penalty." Just saying the words aloud sends a shiver down my spine.

"It won't come to that. We'll get you out of here and on your way back to Nanna."

"And you too. We both have to escape somehow." Ruth nods as though persuading herself. Part of me wishes I could hand my fate to her to deal with, but she has been in Holloway twenty years without managing to escape.

"When will I see you again?"

"Soon. I promise." She throws her arms around me in an embrace and then pushes me out the door. "Go back the way you came and try to stay safe until I can find a way to bring us back together." I thank her then turn to walk away. "Roseanna," I look back, "I love you. I've always loved you."

My eyes moisten at the unfairness of Ruth spending twenty years in this hellhole and realise there is so much I don't know about her. Had she been unfairly incarcerated, too, and what about my father? Is she missing the man she loves? I've been in Holloway five months and it has almost broken me numerous times. My mother seems content here, though I suppose with the passing of time and the application of strength, one becomes used to this life. I throw her a watery smile. "I think deep down I've always known you loved me."

I continue walking and pass a guard who hurries me along and the corridors take me on a journey further than just the workroom.

Growing up, I couldn't make sense of my mother leaving me. Nanna was so loving towards me that it was impossible to imagine she'd behave any differently towards her own daughter. And if my mother grew up with that kind of love, then surely, she would love her own daughter the only way she knew how—with all of her heart and soul.

I remind myself that it was a tragic turn of events that lead to our parting. Yet, that tragedy led me to Danny—and I would never undo that.

Chapter 26

Roseanna

Curiosity Killed the Cat

Bet doesn't declare whether she accepts my offer, but the threats stop as suddenly as they began and I am left to wonder whether the peace is intentional, or if it is to get me to drop my guard when Bet will surely strike.

Either way, I keep my wits about me.

Ned orders Titty to take the laundry on Friday, and though I ask to go with her, since she is in her last trimester and because I am desperate to get some answers from my mother, I am told no.

So I go through the motions, held captive by the passing of time and wonder about my mother and if Danny has read my letter yet. Now I have a news article and the letter I wrote to try to reach him, and still, I am no closer to holding him in my arms. I start to wonder if perhaps he was just a figment of my imagination. He always felt too good to be true. What I wouldn't give for a mobile phone.

Dammit, I'd send smoke signals if I knew how. In the absence of any opportunity to see my mother, I ask vague questions about her. "Ruth's been here years. She's the best carer in the infirmary. Knows as much as the doctor himself, more I'd say." Mags lowers her voice. "She was first brought in as a lunatic. Spent years in the asylum, but eventually Dr. Hadfield said she wasn't crazy no more and moved her to the main wing. She proved herself enough to get a job in the infirmary, and they say if you get a job in there your set."

"Why did they think she was mad?" I ask casually, though my interest doesn't go unnoticed by Verity and Beatrice.

"I heard she was bought in spouting all sorts of nonsense with crazy in her eyes and the devil inside her head. Reckoned she was the lover of a highborn and that they were going to marry!"

Mags and Titty laugh loudly at the revelation, but Beatrice's face is deadly serious as she watches me absorb the information.

"Course this was good ole' Duke Eddie—God rest his soul—that she was talking about. He was known to be a right randy bugger, *if you know what I mean*, so maybe she bedded him in one of the brothels, but marry? HA!"

"No. I don't know what you mean." My comment is delivered more tersely than I intend, so I qualify, "Please explain."

"You must have heard?"

I shake my head.

"Well, he was reluctant to marry, so the people just assumed he was getting his end away anyway…"

"And did this Duke, Eddie, come for her when he found out she was here?"

Titty and Mags begin chuckling loud and deep belly laughs. Even Beatrice, who only sometimes involves herself in idle gossip, has a smile on her face.

"A Duke of England, come to Holloway prison, the asylum wing—no less, on the word of a lunatic?" Beatrice questions.

A sickened chuckle leaves my throat. "Of course, not. Just kidding." But I spend the rest of supper deaf and locked inside my own head at Mags's revelations.

Am I the illegitimate child of a duke?

**

Exactly one week before my trial, Mo collects me from the workroom and deposits me in the same office that I met in with Detective Scott, only this time it is to see the solicitor and I'm delighted that it is not the same man from my plea hearing.

"Sit down. We have a lot to get through and not very much time."

The man is wearing an expensive suit. He's older and has a serious look about him. He calls me Ms Chapman and asks me to call him Sir Dunn.

I gawk at his title and then wonder how I have such expensive legal representation—and then I imagine Danny's face and remember the lengths he will go to for the people that he loves.

"I have no money to pay. How much is this consultation even costing? He can't afford it. Danny has to pay for the business and the children and their schools—"

"Ms Chapman, there is no need to worry. The Duchess has—"

"Beatrice?"

He nods and even though it is the kindest thing a friend has ever done for me, I can't help feel wretched in the knowledge that Danny still hasn't come.

And so, I sit and the solicitor, Sir Dunn, goes through everything in his stack of files. After over an hour, and although he is dubious about my story regarding shooting Eli in the street after happening upon him, Sir Dunn becomes complicit in the story and suggests this is the best defence.

"How I see it is that the eyewitness can be easily discredited. Frank Alderman is a well-known bootless buzzard. Given the right judge, I think we can quite easily change the narrative to suggest that you had no choice but to fire the gun. You're a fair woman, aristocracy no less—"

"Wait, what?"

The side of his lip curls up at my confusion and he checks his pocket watch before sliding a birth certificate across the table to me. "That is your certificate of birth?"

I read the sheet of parchment twice, then confirm that it states my name, the location of my birth City of London Maternity Hospital, and date of my birth—May 9, *1898?*—and also my mother's name. Along the line where my father's name should be, there is the name Edward Chapman.

"Are you quite all right, Ms Chapman? You look like you've seen a ghost."

I splutter a non-sensical reply. All my available headspace is rocked to its very core, but I manage to catch Sir Dunn saying something about my good standing, he thinks I will get off—

I am led back to my cell in a daze.

I was born in a hospital in London in 1898.

And I am the daughter of a Duke of England?

Chapter 27

Roseanna

Every Dog has His Day

The next day as I sit beside Beatrice in the workroom. I thank her for arranging the legal assistance for me, but she frivolously dismisses my gratitude under the guise of a debt now paid. And even though she is acting as though it was nothing, I can't help notice the kindness in her eyes and beneath it her glee at helping me, even though she tries very hard not to revel in the joy of a good deed.

Still, I intend to make use of the representation and it renews my hope that I will someday, hopefully, and finally leave Holloway—though the thought that I may have to leave my mother here dampens my new sense of pending freedom.

Days creep by as I wait for something to happen in this endless snake of an existence, and I only notice it is the ninth of May as Mo mentions it in passing on her return to work.

Captive Songbird

It is a Sunday, so we're dressed in our "Sunday Best" which is a gown similar to our brown work-gowns only black in colour and with a white tie at the neck and white sack-like bonnets atop our heads. But I'm so glad I don't have to sew mailbags on my twenty-fifth birthday that I don't complain about the scratchy material and the lack of a lie-in.

Beatrice, Titty, Mags and I file across to the chapel in the sunlit grounds and suddenly, I feel strangely blessed. I have good friends by my side and my mother, who was for so many years absent—whereabouts unknown—is alive. What I thought I knew was wrong but I'm not dwelling, I'm looking forward and feel prepared to face my future with a new sense of possibility.

With empty stomachs, we all discuss the foods that are special to us that we eat on our respective birthdays from the pew of the chapel, and Titty, who is in her last trimester, is drooling by the time Beatrice has finished describing the feast that is held for her at Cambridge Hall.

The priest stands in the pulpit and demands quiet amongst the crowd, when Mo taps my shoulder and hisses that I go with her at once.

I follow dutifully, ignoring the gazes of the congregation who are burning curious stares upon my head—wondering what I have done to feel Mo's wrath.

Outside of the doors, I'm met with blinding sunshine, and so it takes a few moments to notice my mother before me. She pulls me to the side of the building where there is a row of bushes, and we crouch as Mo informs us we have ten minutes and that is all or we'll see the back of her baton.

"I've been waiting to see you. I thought I'd get to see you during laundry time but the damn guards kept sending other inmates," I blurt out and my mother urges me to sit beside her with our backs against the chapel. With the sun beaming down on our faces and my hand in hers it feels almost heavenly, were it not for the reality of our situations.

"We have no control in here. I've been waiting to see you, I've missed you," she says. "Not just since I saw you last, but for what feels like forever. I've missed you." She pushes aside a piece of my hair and it shines under the glare of the sun. "Bright as the day you were born." She holds the lock in her free hand and marvels at it. Her own hair, faded by years, is a similar shade to my own. At almost fifty and having been subjected to a hard life, her face is captivating and suddenly I feel like I am remembering her smile though I have never been able to recall such a memory prior to now.

"I have so many questions, I'm afraid I won't get all the answers I need. Like, where was I born? I seem to have a birth certificate in the nineteenth *and* twentieth centuries."

She releases my hair and lays the hand that was holding it over mine until my hand is clutched in both of hers. "You were delivered on this day in 1898 in the City of London Maternity Hospital with your father right by my side—which was almost unheard of in those times. Still unpopular now," she chuckles. "How times change… But I suppose your grandmother arranged the other birth certificate."

"And my father, where is he? Who is he?"

Ruth's smile falters and her eyes glisten. "He passed away. Right before your seventh birthday. They were my most difficult of days in here, not being with you and not being with Eddie." She looks up to the sky and then her hand squeezes mine. "I'm so sorry. This must be incredibly difficult for you."

"I… I don't know how I feel or what to believe. Is my father… was he a duke?"

She nods and the delicate point of her chin remains downcast. "I met your father shortly after I transported to this time. We met by chance and he took care of me and we fell in love." She's smiling so fondly that the vision makes it difficult to swallow. "But that is a tale for another time. Your father's family wouldn't accept me—it was a condition of the times that he marry well. He was ordered to marry a highborn woman—several were already picked out. So, we were keeping our love quiet. You were born and not exactly planned, but we knew it wouldn't be long until his own father passed and once your father's inheritance was granted no one could argue who he married. He visited with us as much as he could and you knew him. He'd walk in and you would run to him and shout, 'Daddy, Daddy!' In the most highly pitched of voices and he'd pick you up and spin you around, calling you his little red princess." Her voice drops to a barely-there sob and her arm loops around me tightly like I imagine she would if I were a child. "There were outbreaks of Spanish Flu everywhere. Then I found a lump in my breast. During that time, there was no way to know if it was cancer, so your father demanded I take you back, get treatment if I needed it and then return. We were both concerned that you could become ill from a preventable disease and we wanted more than anything for you to be safe, so you and I returned to the future. The lump was benign and we spent time with Mum. I managed to get your childhood vaccinations and as suddenly as we arrived it was time to go, but at the doorway, we were separated. I couldn't come find you until the next solstice. It was impossible."

I hug her back, grateful that she didn't have to endure cancer treatment and that she still seems to have good health.

"Your father and I were going to marry, but I was thrown in here before I could get to him and no one would listen to me. The warden at the time wouldn't help me. Many members of the royal family wanted me out the way—there were alliances they wanted to form through his marriage and I was a threat to their plans."

"So, my father's family arranged for you to be jailed?"

"Not exactly. I don't think they planned it, but if they knew of my incarceration it was probably convenient for them, and they didn't help me. A police officer found me right before midnight on June 21st. I was inconsolable waiting and hoping you would follow me through the doorway, and he took me to the station. I kept repeating your name as though I could summon you out of thin air. I thought that if time travel were possible, then surely my love for you could conjure you somehow. And then… they asked me what I had done with my daughter….” Her eyes are filled with moisture now and I clutch her back as desperately as she holds me.

“They thought you killed me?”

My mother nods and the dam of my lower lids breaks under the weight of my pain for her and tears streak down my cheeks.

“I’m so sorry,” I blub.

She holds my head and kisses my temple. “It is not your fault. It is not anyone’s fault. Your father would have moved heaven and earth to find us, but he thought we were locked in a future he would never see. I know he died waiting for us to return home to him.” She squeezes me harder. “He loved you so much. Our lives were on the fringe of perfect….”

“And everything was ripped away. I’m so sorry,” I say, mostly comforting her since her story is one of utter heartbreak and also because I have still not processed that I knew him. I knew my father, he loved me, and now I know he is dead.

“I am sorry. I should never have allowed your hand to slip from mine when I touched the arch."

“How is it even possible that we can travel through time from just some stupid stones?”

“I wish I knew. There are standing stones from the Emerald Isle imported all over the country, Roseanna. You can pass through so long as it is a solstice. Same for me and same for your grandmother. Though, the headaches, the toll it takes on your mind, it must not be done too often or, well, your grandmother… when I was a child her mind was as sharp as pins and now… I researched the women in our family as much as I have been able to. No women in our tree have ever had a son, and all of us lost our loves.”

Our grip on each other relaxes and we stare up at the few clouds that pass in the light breeze. "So, we're cursed. I'll never get back to Danny and now you will never have the chance to reunite with my father."

"You met someone special as soon as you arrived here too?"

I nod and then I tell her everything because after the weight of the news my mother has shared, something good—even if it is likely doomed—feels needed, and I want her to know how I met the man I love.

Mum's cheeks rise and she glows pridefully. "I need to get you out of here. My father died before we could have a life together and so did yours. I've carried on every day in this place in the hope that I could somehow, one day, make a change and yet, here you are and I have done nothing to prevent history repeating."

Her face is torn and I clutch her hands tightly in mine.

"Is there any chance that you are pregnant?"

"It's been five months since I saw Danny. I had the depo injection before I was cast back. I'm still not having regular periods." It's been almost a year, but I remember at my last appointment the nurse told me in some cases it can take up to two years to become fertile again should I decide I'd like to get pregnant. "I have a solicitor trying to help me get out of here. The duchess, Beatrice, she fronted all the costs. My lawyer thinks it should be easy. I'll talk to him. I am here and obviously not dead, we can get you released, surely?"

My mum looks doubtful. "Where will we say you've been all these years?"

I shrug. "We'll think of something."

"No. You can't risk it. You have no alibi as to where you've been."

Mum blinks away tears and then suddenly, Mo's face pops up over the hedgerow, "You've had your ten minutes. Move it, both of ye."

We both stand and a flash of fear rushes through me that Mo might have heard our conversation. "She'll have been getting her end away with one of the guards at the gate the whole time, don't worry." Mum winks and I can't help grin—somewhat shocked that hard-ass Mo, is inclined to any kind of intimate liaisons at all.

"The saucy old mare." I elbow Mum and we both laugh at the shared joke, and I can't help think how much Danny and his family, even Ida, would like my mother… but once again, I'm left with the deepened sense of longing and unfairness that I can have one of the people I love, but not all of them at once.

And it sucks.

Chapter 28

Roseanna

Going Down in Flames

As my trial creeps closer, the mood in the prison—mostly from the guards—worsens and the inmates get used to walking on eggshells particularly after the last of Valentine's serialised articles for *The Daily Herald,* and the long-awaited report on prison conditions is published by the state.

Suddenly, as if drawn like rubber-necked drivers during a collision, the long driveway to the prison fills up with members of the public holding placards reading misspelt messages to: "leave the women alone" or to "stop hurtin' 'em!"

It raises energies inside the prison, and during an endless night, Titty, who is almost at full-term and now constantly hungry and irritable, takes it upon herself to fill the time we spend locked in our cells to rally the women's sense of justice. She yells, as once again a man stands on the rooftop across the wall, that "Women need feeding proper," and the inmates echo her

163

sentiment by following whatever she yells. "The beatings and rapes must stop!" she yells again, and the women go crazy for her commanding the narrative.

I join in, too, and the ruckus is only brought to quiet when physical threats are made by Ned through Titty's door.

Titty stops yelling and I expel my held breath when I hear Ned's boots retreat down the corridor. Suddenly, and in the hope of getting out in a few days, I feel very proud at what the women in here have achieved. We were warned not to speak out, and yet with Beatrice and her contact's help, we managed it and it seems people are actually listening.

The next morning, as our doors are unlocked for washing, Beatrice slides a copy of *The Daily Herald* beneath my door. It states on the front page that the warden of Holloway, in consultation with his clinical director, has pledged to improve sanitation inside his prison and review physical punishments and maternity care. Beatrice has drawn a loop around the sentence in her neatly drawn pen with a comment beside it that reads: *Who gave them that idea?*

And I wonder if beyond my release, there will be positive changes for the women of Holloway prison.

**

A few nights later, and with the mood still volatile, we're lined up for supper—which is late, thanks to some of the workers struggling to get through the blockade in time to start their shifts. As such, and in an environment where clocks could be timed from the yawls of women's stomachs, there is a provocativeness in the atmosphere that taints the air like a foul stench.

Captive Songbird

When we're finished slurping our disappointing bowls of lentils boiled in water, Ian Copley appears and stands before us, with his usual smugness at our feebleness, only today, the women look ready to lynch him.

"Now, now, calm down or you'll not eat for a week. I have news…"

The women hold themselves in their seats, angered that there was no meat or potatoes in their dish. "The good news is that conditions here have been stamped by parliament for improvement, and in a very small way, you have your dear friend Roseanna Chapman to thank." The women look at me with hope lighting their eyes as Ian continues, "Roseanna has been talking to the doctor and our visiting journalist about the conditions. They're too dirty, she says. You're all putrefied and verminous worse than pigs, she says. And so, with her concern that you are all slovenly cretins, she has inspired a revolution in the way you will continue to be housed. From today forth, you will all clean harder. Starting before and after your work shifts, the areas of the prison will be divided up and you will each take a section and clean it until it sparkles like the divine message from God himself. Any person seen slacking or not administering exemplary cleanliness, will receive twenty lashings of the rod." Ian's expression turns sour and devious. "Now, can we all stand and applaud Ms Chapman for her due care and attention for conditions in this prison."

Exhausted, the women stand and turn to me with outrage. Then as ordered, they begin smashing their hands together—as if my face were between them—in resented, sarcastic praise.

Ian Copley looks on, gloriously happy with the women's response. "Ned will hand out your orders. If you all work diligently, you will be finished in time for midnight."

He smiles at me one last time and then walks from the room while Ned barks out sections of the prison to clusters of inmates and they all turn to me, underfed and utterly exhausted and scowl.

And though I mouth apologies, even my own friends turn their backs on me as they leave to complete their duties.

**

I put my anger into the work at hand. Scrubbing floors reminds me of Ida and I picture her telling me I am not doing it right. None of the other women talk to me while we clean and even though I offer to clean Titty's half of the communal bathroom, she stands firm that she will not accept my help.

And so, we clean quietly and diligently until Ned comes to check our work, makes us do it again—even though he wouldn't know cleanliness if it drowned him in a bath of bleach—and then we are escorted to our cells where we collapse into our beds.

The following morning at four a.m., we are hauled out of our cells and ordered to clean the same areas again.

"This is pointless. No one has used these areas since we cleaned them last night!" Titty protests.

"You've your friend to thank." Ned puts his grimy thumb so close to me that I can smell the unwashed stench of tobacco. "Don't go thinking you can chat back at me. I preferred it when I got a longer shut eye in me quarters on a night shift." He screws his face up at me.

"I'm not doing it." Titty leans back and her hands knead the small of her back.

I step in front of Ned's view of her. "Let me do her share, please. This is after all, my fault. She's fit to pop with that baby inside her and should be resting."

Ned shoves me out of the way. "I should be bleedin' resting. But the warden has a dozen people to show around later and this place has got to sparkle." He rushes right up to Verity and his paw lands on her shoulder, forcing her down onto her knees. "Ye'll clean that floor like I said."

"I won't!" she replies and sits in a childlike pose. From this angle, and with how emaciated she has become, it's difficult to even see that she is with child.

"Ye damn well will!" Ned's boot lurches out and connects with Titty's abdomen. It happens so suddenly that I am powerless to intervene, but I immediately rush to her, cowering over her in case he attacks again.

Verity lets out a howling shriek and the colour drains right from her face. She falls to her side, her face against the cold hard floor, as she cradles her bump. Tears spring to my eyes and I stroke Titty's hair from her face as she convulses on the floor.

Then she goes deathly quiet.

"Titty," I sob. "Are you okay?"

I hold my hand to her stomach, waiting to feel a nudge or something to confirm her baby is okay. One solitary tear falls from Verity's face and her eyes flutter closed.

I stare back at Ned who is shaking his head disbelievingly.

"Whatever is going on in here," Mo says, walking in the bathroom. "I could hear the screaming right from the kitchen!"

I stand, looping my arms beneath Verity's and pulling her up. "HE. Attacked. Verity. For no damn reason! You have to help me get her to the infirmary. NOW!"

Mo brushes roughly past Ned and takes one side of Verity's weight by levering her arm beneath Verity's, and with her tiny body dangling between us, we carry her through the corridors.

"Get Ruth and bring her to the infirmary, you stupid fool!" Mo calls back to Ned who is taking a drink from his flask.

I try not to focus on the bright red blood that seeps through Verity's underwear as we advance towards the infirmary. The placenta has likely detached from the uterus and meanwhile, the baby might not be getting ample oxygen. I hold my available hand against her stomach and feel it is hard as a rock without the telltale wave of contractions.

The pain keeps Verity conscious and she howls and complains of stabbing pains as we rush as best we can towards the infirmary.

Verity vomits but after we keep going.

"I'm scared, Roseanna. I'm going to die, aren't I?"

I try to keep a positivity in my voice, though inside all my worst fears are surfacing. "No. You're going to be fine. Your baby is just coming early now, that's all."

"It hurts, Roseanna."

"I know. But that's good. The pain will help you push the baby out when the time comes. Me and Mo, we've got you."

"If I die, Roseanna, you've got to take the baby. You'll love it, I know you will. Sammy's useless, he won't know what to do and my mum, she's already got all my sisters to look after. She can't afford another mouth to feed."

"Verity, listen to me. You are raising your baby. No one but you. You hear me?"

Inside the infirmary, Mo and I lay Verity on the one available bed, and without any privacy curtains or anything to protect Verity's modesty, I proceed to remove Verity's pantaloons. Cotton that should be white burns red with danger. Mo's expression is one of horror and I yell at her to find me some scissors and a scalpel.

Mo flounders.

"I think there's been a placental abruption," I lower my voice but use my tone to urge Mo to act, "which can be catastrophic to mother and child." When she still doesn't lurch into action, I yell, "Mo, move!"

Blood continues to spill from Verity but it is now mixed with amniotic fluid; then finally I feel her stomach contract.

"I'm going to perform an exam. Verity, I need to put my hand inside you."

She's clutching the sheets and her face is agonised. "Just do what you got to. Get him out!" I wash my hands quickly and thoroughly. I can't see any surgical gloves, so I do without and insert my fingers inside of her and feel for her cervix. There is no need to feel for how dilated she is, I can feel the top of the baby's head.

"Verity. The baby is almost ready to be born. I'm going to need you to use all your strength to push down through your hips."

"I really need to poop!" she growls.

"It's not poop. He's coming. Now get ready to push, and in between when I tell you, you're going to pant and stop pushing."

I feel for the contraction, and as it crests I call for her to push. All around us, the women have sat up in their beds as though watching a movie.

"Now. Titty, *push…*"

She growls and pushes and I feel the baby advance slightly. A metal tray with implements on it jangles as Mo puts it on the bed beside me.

"Go to Verity and clutch her hands," I instruct Mo and am pleased to see that she does. She holds onto both her hands and provides reassurance and encouragement.

"Now, Titty, push again," I tell her. Her face is red, sweaty and she's panting, but as the contraction rolls in, she pushes her baby closer. "That's amazing, Titty. You're doing great! He's almost crowning now. Just give me small puffs and tiny pushes so your body can stretch."

Verity's voice is broken with pain. "It's all right for you to say. Me hoo-ha feels like it's bleedin' caught fire!"

"That's it. Now stop. Breathe. You're doing so great, he's almost here… Now push your hardest."

And then, suddenly his head is free and I insert my finger and clear his airway. The next contraction rolls in fast and I order Verity to push, and suddenly his floppy little body advances forwards and I grip his arms and pull him into my arms.

"Verity, he's… he's perfect."

I wait for his first lungful of air and the proceeding scream but only harrowing silence follows.

Then the door opens and in walks Ned.

Chapter 29

Roseanna

Deafening Silence

"Why isn't he crying?" Verity's voice is barely a croak.

My mother, who is behind Ned, rushes to me, taking the baby and turning him over and patting his back.

A red mist has descended over me and I narrow my eyes on the monster capable of kicking the life from an infant.

I have a hold on his shoulders and am pushing him down to the ground before I have even noticed I've moved. Ned's shock at my attack makes him easy to accost and my fists rain down on his face. His blood mixes with Verity's blood that still coats my hands and the sight makes me even more furious. His hands try to bat me away, but I am quicker and more precise as his face slickens and blood covers his eyes.

I keep beating and clawing him, I don't know how many times but the sobs and pleas that come from him only make me want to make him suffer more.

And then something miraculous happens.

A baby cries.

Howling into the vacant, dark and damp space, it fills the air with warmth and comfort like an apple pie straight from the oven.

I stop hitting and Ned's hands clutch his face.

"I should put you in the hole," Mo says, arms folded and standing at the jamb to the infirmary doorway.

I stand on shaky legs and back away from Ned. Suddenly, all fortitude has evaporated from my body and I crumple to holding my knees. Then I look beyond Mo and see Verity feeding her baby and I don't care what the punishment is.

I hold my hands out as though she welds handcuffs. "I'll go wherever you want me to."

"Not you. Him!" Mo sneers down towards Ned. "Get up. Fool." When he doesn't move, she leans down and grabs him by his hair, dragging him up to a standing position. "You'll not get away with it this time!"

Mo drags Ned down the corridor with such ease that Ned looks pathetic and weak. Free of guards, the infirmary is just a room full of happy, thankful women, grateful more than anything that mother and baby survived.

Chapter 30

Roseanna

Always Darkest Before Dawn

Verity's colour has returned as she nurses her infant. Mum watches me taking Verity's vitals and seems confused. I whisper that I am a paramedic and she smiles. "I always knew you'd be in the caring profession. Even as a girl, you'd nurse your dolls like their lives depended on it."

We're left with only Mildred watching us for the rest of the day, while Mum and I care for Verity. Beatrice arrives with fresh tea and an entire loaf of bread toasted into slices and thick with butter, and we all eat until our bellies are full.

Eventually a full moon hangs high in the sky. Mum and I take turns to cradle Oswald and fuss over him while Verity rests. And when Mildred embarks on her usual routine of pretend nursing the elderly, we talk.

"You slept eight hours a night from the moment you left the womb." My mum grins and nuzzles Ozzy's face, inhaling and revelling in his fresh baby scent.

"I don't tend to get much sleep these days."

Her smile falters. "No. I don't either." She tucks the blanket more tightly over Verity using just one hand. "The beds. I miss the beds from the twenty-first century the most. What I wouldn't give for a pocket-sprung, memory-foam mattress." She giggles.

I chuckle lightly. "And mobile phones," I whisper. "God, I wish I could just call a person directly at any given moment, night or day."

Mum looks at me questioningly and I realise, she won't have been around in the future for the invention of mobile phones. She walks around the bed to where I am seated next to a sleeping Verity and places her hand on my shoulder while she shushes Ozzie.

"I have a plan. It's not much at the moment, but if your trial doesn't go our way, then we'll need to act quickly. There's no way I'll have my daughter die in this place."

"Mum, it's too risky. Mags said anyone caught trying to escape is swiftly executed—though they record it as the fever."

"Then it's die or die trying, my love. There's no other way to get you back home and safe in the future."

"I can't return through the arch, not before I've seen Danny. But you can."

"You want me to go home and look after my mum, your nanna, while you stay here with your love?" She raises an eyebrow and then brings Ozzie up to her nose and sniffs his hair. "I think that's a grand plan." She taps my shoulder and then changes the position of the baby in her arms.

"Perhaps once you're there, I could come back and visit, at least, I'd like to," I muse. There's something comforting about planning the future, even though it will likely never happen.

"No. You'll fall in love and lead a happy life, breaking the cycle of the women in this family's bad luck with time travel," Mum replies. "And I will always thank my lucky stars that I got to be even a small part of your life."

Verity shifts in her bed and we change the subject of our conversation to everything Momma has missed while I have been growing up, leaving out such details as advanced technology and mysterious standing stones in case anyone hears.

**

On the morning of my trial, Beatrice stands in the doorway of my cell with a flock of navy-coloured material looped over her arm and a pair of expensive-looking heels hanging from her index finger.

"You'll want to look your best," she huffs and enters my room uninvited.

Beatrice glances down at the pale blue dress I was wearing when I arrived in Holloway prison, which is strewn on my bed and still has the stains from my struggle with Copley; she shakes her head. "Thought so… you need my help."

Beatrice combs and makes me over until I look and feel like a normal woman again. I find myself drawn to my copy of the Old Testament and find the words that the previous reader etched into the parchment.

"You will die here."

I take my earrings from it and close the book, throwing it onto the planks like I did on my first night here and insert my earrings one at a time.

Beatrice watches me. "They don't match your outfit."

"I don't care." I grin at her and she shrugs ill humouredly.

When Mo comes for me, her mouth momentarily falls open with shock at my appearance. Beatrice holds both my hands as she stands before me. "I hope I never, ever cast eyes on you again."

"Likewise," I reply stoically but can't keep the grin from turning the edges of my mouth up. Neither can Beatrice, and before I follow Mo's orders to leave, she pulls me into an embrace.

"I'm sure he'll be there this time."

I nod, hoping I see Danny, too, but also ready to do this part alone if I have to.

**

The courthouse is the same as before, and I am crammed into a holding cell with multiple women all looking resigned to terrible outcomes.

I glance down at my watch, stroking its face and I marvel that Mo gave it back to me before I was hauled into the truck. "You did good," she told me and actually looked like she meant it. "Ned got the sack. He ain't gonna hurt the women here no more." She grinned conspiratorially before adding, "And his face looks like he had a fight with a bull and came off worse."

If I never return to Holloway, knowing that Ned can't enforce his regime of sickness on the women is a comforting thought, and I find myself agreeing with Mum that "Mo ain't too bad."

Next to the holding cell I am contained in, there is only a barred barrier from the men, and some of them call out insulting comments as though they have never seen a woman before and their encouragement might just implore one of the women to, "Get ye tits out!"

"Roseanna Chapman. Roseanna Chapman!" a voice booms and I look up. "Your turn."

I follow the sound mechanically and am marched up steps until the lit courtroom blinds me. I'm seated behind a barred partition and notice it is the same judge who heard my original plea. He seems to remember me, shaking his head as though I am a waste of his precious time.

The jury sit on benches adjacent to the judge. Twelve white men of varying ages, they get to wager my innocence and decide my fate. Opposite, the gallery is filled with onlookers who seem conditioned to expect a ruling of guilty and call for justice like contestants in some kind of warped reality TV show.

There is also no sign of Danny or any other Alderman member and a sick churning rolls deep inside my belly. I had hoped Danny would be here. Even said a prayer that if he had not seen any evidence of my incarceration, that he would somehow know to come here, on this day, at this very time and meet my eyes one last time.

My vision blurs, but through it I see Sir Dunn and throw him a watery smile. He opens the case with my charges and I admit to myself how terrible it sounds.

What proceeds next is a vortex of legal jargon and argument.

Detective Scott is interviewed and gives his opinion of how and from what distance the pistol was fired. His assumptions are grossly accurate probably due to no small amount of experience in firing guns himself. He explains that the fingerprints on the pistol match mine and then goes onto explain where the body was found and in what condition it was in. And then, when probed, he admits that his own officer failed in his duty to follow procedure. By the time Detective Scott leaves the stand, Sir Dunn is winking at me like he did good.

Then Frank Alderman takes the stand and I brace myself.

He's wearing a suit and is somewhat groomed in appearance. I wonder where he is living and what poor soul is at his mercy.

Frank doesn't make eye contact with me, despite me glaring at him to get his attention. He confirms his name and states that I am of no relation to him. The Crown Prosecutor then asks Frank to walk the jury through the night in question and he does so with a solemn face and an air of drama.

"Was just out walking… knew Eli from old… good sort, wouldn't hurt a fly… his mam was heartbroken… then that woman," he points at me and every member of the jury looks my way, "she opened fire on the poor bugger for no reason. No reason at all!"

I shoot to my feet and point right back at him. "You lying bastard! You know he was going to kill—"

"Miss Chapman. Silence!" the judge orders and the jurymen look to their neighbours and whisper.

Sir Dunn throws me an irritated glare.

"Mr Alderman. Can I ask what exactly your relationship is to the accused?"

Frank shrugs.

"Is she not, in fact, engaged to your son?"

Frank shrugs again. "One split-ass he uses is much like another."

My stomach spins with bile.

Danny loves me.

"Do you disagree with your son's choice?

Frank screws up his face.

"Is that why you are here falsely accusing an innocent woman of good standing?"

Frank laughs. "She's a whore and a killer. That's why I object to her."

"No further questions, Your Honour."

I continue to glare at Frank who looks entirely unremorseful, even winking at me as he passes my box.

A gentleman from the sewage works is then called up to answer questions. He tells of happening upon a body being dumped in the sewage works and remaining out of sight. Then he watched the police arriving shortly after as though they knew exactly where to find it. Crown Prosecution asks if he can pick out the person dumping the body and the man says it was dark. They rephrase the question and ask if the person *could have* been a woman and the man reply's that yes, perhaps it might have been. The people in the gallery gasp and once again, the jury mutter to one another.

"Objection! Speculation."

"Sustained. Clive, keep it factual," the judge orders, speaking to Clive like they are old golf buddies. But the damage is already done. I can tell from the faces of the jury they already believe it is a done deal and panic creeps through my veins.

By the time I am called to the stand, it is past lunchtime, but I couldn't eat even if a banquet were laid out before me.

I find myself analysing the faces of the jury, who seem to all be middle-aged and disgruntled about something or other. While the man on the end, a dark-haired chap in his fifties checks his pocket watch, I wonder if my freedom might be inconveniencing him from his lunch.

The prosecution asks me questions about how my prints came to be on the gun and focus on my motive for killing Eli. They suggest I am a scorned ex-lover of his, which I laugh disgustedly at.

I tell them that shooting him was self-defence and they call me a liar.

In his line of questioning, Sir Dunn minimises my knowledge of Eli and asks if I was rough handled. I think back to the night I first arrived in 1921 and testify that yes, indeed I was beaten by the man and feared for my life. Sir Dunn suggests that the gun was Eli's and I was defending my honour. He paints Eli in the truest of lights and I agree that yes, lives were at stake.

"No further questions, Your Honour."

Sir Dunn delivers his closing statements first. He details my unfair handling by the police and the dubious relationship with the prosecution's star witness. He describes a "victim" who was out on the prowl for defenceless women and alleges my upstanding nature as a teacher of the Alderman children. He tells the jury I was merely defending myself and if it were their daughters, the jury would want them to behave exactly as I did, and I'm left feeling hopeful that his statement will swing the lead in my direction.

It is then the turn of the prosecution.

"Men of the jury, I put forward today a case of a woman of unsound mind, creeping around past dark, looking for men to exact her bloody-minded foibles on. A dancer of men, she is no more a teacher than I. Instead, she is a singer in one of the roughest taverns in all of London—a place of crime and debauchery. Her own mother is listed as a resident of the asylum and such affiliations run in families as we know. An eyewitness saw her shoot the pistol for no good reason. Her fingerprints were on the pistol. Another eyewitness saw somebody, who could have been her, disposing of the body and trying to cover their tracks. The question you must ask yourselves is: are your sons safe on the streets with the likes of her, posing as just an innocent damsel in distress?"

With doubt put firmly in the minds of the jury, Sir Dunn approaches me. "I did my best, but you really didn't help yourself. Refined women don't stand up and call gentlemen doing their civic duty in court 'bloody bastards!'" He shakes his head. "Beatrice told me you knew how to play the part, and if I lose this case it'll be a black mark on my otherwise impeccable record. I took your case to pay a debt and I have done my best, but Lord knows you have not made it easy."

"Wait. What do I do now?"

"You go back to the cells downstairs, cross your fingers and pray to the Gods because after that debacle, only they can help you now."

Sir Dunn storms away and I am returned to the holding cell to await the decision of the jury.

Chapter 31

Roseanna

Hang in There?

I'm strangely relieved to see that my name, which I carved when I came here to make my pleas, is still etched in the wooden bench I now sit. In the years that come, perhaps it will wind up in a museum and someone will google my name. I wonder what they will find.

Will it be:

Roseanna Chapman bravery award winning paramedic.

Or

Roseanna Chapman, crazy woman, hung at twenty-five for murder.

I'm violently sick on the dirt floor beside the bench, retching and retching though barely anything is dispersed thanks to my missing breakfast, and now lunch. No one even bats an eyelid or asks if I am okay.

I move along the bench away from the small puddle and watch as a foot-long rat scuttles towards it and stops for a while.

The men beside my cell, like a male mirror image are now bored with being crass, sit and stand, their faces deeply lined by their woes. Among them is a small boy with his back to me, keeping himself small to avoid detection. I watch him at first to pass time. He has a mop of dark hair and when I catch glimpses of his face, I surmise that he cannot be much older than Henry.

He picks up a stone from the floor and throws it towards the rat.

Then my heart quickens. I recognise him. "Billy?" I whisper in a croaky voice.

His eyes meet mine and his mouth pops open. He takes a step back while I take one forward.

"It's okay, Billy. You're not in trouble, I swear it. Come closer, please." My voice is a beg. I'm strangely pleased to see the boy that so many months ago led me into a trap that almost got me kidnapped by Eli's men.

He takes a tentative step towards the bars that separate our quarters, and I do the same until we are held apart by mere inches and thick, iron bars.

"Why are you here? Surely you're not old enough for court."

Billy's bottom lip protrudes and he shrugs. "Turned twelve last month, din' I. The whistles been waiting to get me for ages. Then they bleedin' got me on pocketing from a lady, but since it's me first time I'll get let out by supper unless the judge hates the look of me face."

I wonder how anyone could hate his face. He's a cute-looking child, that was why I was so easily reeled in by him.

As though reading my thoughts, he looks at me adequately abashed, since after all, "pocketing" is exactly what he did to me nearly a year ago when he stole my watch.

"Who were you stealing for this time?"

He looks genuinely sorrowful as he replies, "Got to feed me sister, don't I?"

It's quiet for a while and then he says, "'Ere, I'm glad you got away from Eli. I didn't want to get you down to Simon and Eddie but they made me. Did you really shoot Eli?"

He's looking at me in wonder as I nod.

"Shitbag had it coming. I'm glad you're all right."

He grabs the bars and I find my hand wandering to find his. "I'm glad you'll be out for supper. Do you think it's time you found a less risky occupation?"

He kicks the toe of his sock that protrudes from his shoe against the bar. "Ain't no job they'll give me that'll keep the roof over me and Elsie's heads…"

It gets me thinking. "Billy. There's something I need you to do for me. It's really important and my life may depend on it…" He asks me what and I tell him as quickly as I can and then I discretely pass him one of my earrings as payment before I am called back before the jury.

**

I am asked to stand as the judge enters and then again while the verdict is read.

"How does the jury find Roseanna Chapman on the count of murder in the first degree?" the judge asks the jury member that is closest to him.

The man holds a sheet of paper and refers to it before declaring the verdict: "Guilty."

Guilty?

GUILTY!

The sounds in the courtroom blend into one muffled crescendo of noise, my legs give way and I fall onto the chair.

"Silence!" the judge orders and I stare helplessly at him as he speaks to me directly.

"Roseanna Chapman. You have been found guilty by a jury of twelve honest men of the cold-blooded murder of Eli Harris—a man in his prime and an honest citizen of London. As such you will be hanged for murder in the first degree not sooner than three Sundays from now to allow adequate chance for prayer and repentance."

He stands and all the courtroom stand, too, except for me; my legs won't respond.

"May God have mercy on your soul."

I watch him walk away as though it is a TV show and I am waiting for the commercial break before making Nanna and myself a cup of tea.

This can't be happening.

I'm going to be hanged for murder.

Chapter 32

Danny

Clouds on the Horizon

The passing of time between March and May dragged by, painfully slowly, and I found myself in a deep depression, wondering if my Red will be home to me in June or if it might be years yet, or worse, never at all. So, I vowed I would not dwell and put all my energy and focus into running the business.

Ida quietens her nonsense about the family not having room for her and even though she interviews plenty of maids, there are none she approves of, so instead she spends her time cleaning and complaining she has no help about the place—though really I suspect she misses Roseanna.

Every day after finishing work at the factory, I visit the King's Head and meet with Jimmy. On this particular day, I have big news for him.

"Boss." Jimmy nods his head as he carries a wooden box of liquor through the pub. "Got you that delivery of gin you asked for." The bottles chink together as he drops the crate on the mahogany surface of the bar and takes one out to examine. "Can't see this muck selling round these parts. *Gin*. It's a woman's drink."

I chortle. "And women are now visiting the pubs and clubs just as much as men. They're working and have money in their pockets, same as men. You keep a drink in for the women, and they'll show their gratitude by buying it all up."

Jimmy replaces the bottle and lights a cigarette; I decline as he offers me one. "S'pose they are coming in more often. When I was a kid, you wouldn't find a pub in the whole of England that wasn't a whorehouse that'd want the woman in."

"Since the war the women have been running this town. It's time us men started accepting that. Times are changing, Jimmy, and for the better too."

"They do give us something better to look at than Harold and his snuff pot." Jimmy puts the bottle on the shelf and quietly seems to think on this matter. "I'm happy to take a woman's money same as a bloke's. 'Ere, I've also found a singer, not as good as Roseanna but she can carry a note."

"That's good news, Jimmy, well done. The place could use a little livening up." I look around. It's only 7 p.m., so the majority of the drinkers aren't here yet, but it's busy enough. I know from checking the accounts that the place is running well and doing so without illegal activity.

"Do what I can." Jimmy flicks the ash from his cigarette on the floor. He acts like he couldn't care less but I can tell he's in his element running the pub. "You said you wanted the place running proper, so that's what I bin doing."

Jimmy pours one of the regulars an ale and I wait until the man leaves to continue.

"You've been on my back about when the next job is coming in and when I'm going to go out and do another gun deal, and I have told you many times that our illegal dealings have stopped now."

"Boss, I haven't been doing any dirty dealings behind your back. I've been waiting to see if given time you'd change your mind but I'm beginning to see you ain't never gonna go back to that. Your life, well, it's going good and I am happy to see that. I want things to be good for you, boss. But I want them to be good for me too." His lip curls up, torn between being happy for me and pining for the purpose and illegality of the former life that I know he thinks he is destined to live.

Then I look across the bar at Agnes. "I thought you and Agnes might become a thing."

He glances at Agnes as if thinking about it for the first time though I know he has taken a liking to her.

"I ain't getting involved with no working lady even if she does make my balls ache."

I shake my head. "Jimmy, you've been with plenty of working girls. What's the problem?"

"Yeah, I've been with them but I ain't never had one as me woman. Official, like." He glugs at his pint of ale and then slams in down on the counter, then uses the sleeve of his jacket to wipe the froth from his mouth. "It ain't right. She could be out there, making a crust," his eyes widen as he attempts to emphasise his point, "you know, with other men."

I suppose I get his point. The very thought of Roseanna being with anybody else makes me capable of murder. Yet, what Jimmy is missing is that he can't pay for sex and then disapprove of the women who provide it.

"Have you talked to Agnes about changing her lifestyle?"

"Ain't no point. She'll just tell me to fuck off," Jimmy says between pouring me a brandy and sliding the glass across the bar to me.

I chuckle deeply. "And I suppose she'd have a point, you do after all employ her to do exactly that."

Jimmy shrugs. "Ain't me what employs her, it's you."

"Which leads me to…" I take the papers from my bag and slide them across the bar to Jimmy. He picks them up and his nose crinkles like I handed him some magical device from the future that he doesn't know how to operate.

"You know I ain't a reader, what does all this say?"

"It says you, Jimmy Watts, are the new owner and proprietor of the King's Head." An expression of confusion sinks onto Jimmy's face, so I explain. "I had the licence and everything put in your name." Jimmy's brow furrows as though he is angered. Many years of mistreatment has him dubious about accepting kindness, even though he knows me well enough to know that this is a genuine offer.

"You did that for me?"

"Jimmy, you are like a brother to me. As good as any brother I've ever known. You've been patient while I've been sorting out the factory and such. You've been loyal, and I respect you. This is my gift to you. You have proved you are an excellent landlord and this way you have your own business to start you off. Your very own opportunity at a good and decent life." I click my glass against his and stand to make an announcement.

"Everybody spread the word, the new owner of the King's Head is Jimmy Watts." The patrons of the pub erupt into cheers and I watch as Jimmy becomes bashful, batting his hand at them as though their praise is unwarranted, though I can see beneath it that he is enjoying it.

"Does that mean there's a free drink?" a man calls out.

"Fuck off!" Jimmy says quite jovially. "I've got me a business to run. I don't make money by giving away free ale."

A chuckle erupts in my chest and I feel good. It's just like Jimmy to worry more about profits than celebrating. "And who knows, maybe you'll need someone to help you run the place." I casually look at Agnes and then check Jimmy's expression, noticing that he is pondering the idea. I pick up my briefcase and prepare to bid good night, assuring him that just because he now owns the bar, doesn't mean I won't be in quite often—only this time as a customer. Just as I am turning to leave, a young lad, younger than Henry, dressed in rags, wanders straight up to the bar and straight into me.

He's a mere two feet away when it becomes evident he is quite desperate to see me.

"Sir, I've been looking for you everywhere. You weren't at your house. There's some old woman there that told me if I didn't piss off, she'd belt me."

I smirk at this news, guessing exactly who the "old woman" is and betting good money that Ida would belt him if she heard him call her as much.

"Thank God I found you. I had to find you. See, it's an emergency." The boy is breathless and stuttering.

"Whatever is the matter?" I ask him.

"Whatever is the matter? It's the lady. The beautiful lady with the bright red hair. Her name is Roseanna Chapman, that's what she said it was. And she said I must come and find you."

White-hot fear runs through me and I immediately check the boy's face for any sign that he is lying or trying to trick me.

He seems genuine.

I muse aloud, mostly to confirm facts to myself. "Roseanna is away. She is caring for her sick grandmother."

"No she ain't, sir. She's stuck in Holloway prison for murder and she's gonna be hanged."

My knees almost buckle.

I shake my head firmly. "You must be wrong, boy. She's not in prison."

"She bloody well is." He thrusts his fist into one of his pockets and then holds his hand out to show me. "Look, she gave me this to show you, in case you thought I was making it up." In the centre of his grimy palm is one of the green and gold clip-on earrings that Roseanna was wearing when she arrived that godforsaken night.

I snatch it from his hand, bringing it closer so I can examine every part of it.

"Mister, she said I could keep that earring for passing the message to you."

I marvel at the shining piece of metal remembering the very first time I saw Roseanna in her green dress with her glorious red locks that looked too bright to be real. She looked like a vision, a temptress sent to destroy me. Except she didn't destroy me; she saved me and now I am on the cusp of thriving.

And now she could be hanged for murder.

My stare pins back on the boy and I realise with utter maddening certainty that the boy is telling the truth.

"Holloway," I repeat. "Murder?"

Then I picture Eli Harris lying dead in this very bar, and I know exactly who she is accused of murdering.

"She had sentencing this afternoon. She was found guilty on all counts. Roseanna will be hung three weeks from Sunday."

"Sentencing? Why wasn't I told?" I bellow but the boy just shrugs.

"Beats me, but I hope they don't hang her 'cause I think she's all right. You will get her out, won't you?"

"Come on, let's go!" I reply, wrapping my hand around the gun that's neatly tucked inside my jacket, wondering why I ever thought I might no longer have need for it.

Chapter 33

Roseanna

The Best of Both Worlds

I'm scrubbing the bathroom floor when Verity comes in, since even death row inmates are expected to clean floors in the hope it sanitises their souls.

"Mo said you've to go to the infirmary, apparently your wounds need checking."

"Wounds?" All my injuries from Ned's attack, though still angry and red, are fused and I have no sign of infection.

Verity's cheeks rise up in a smile.

"Get going with you, your mother will be waiting," she hisses beneath her watery grin.

I return her smile and then, without warning, Verity rushes me, pulling me into a bone-crushing hug. "You're a good sort, Roseanna Chapman, the best, in fact!" She snuffles lightly into my shoulder and I pat her back. "I suppose this'll probably be the last chance I'll see you. They'll move you to the execution wing tonight." Her hands crash against her mouth as though she has said something awful.

"It's okay. It's what it's called," I reassure her. "I'll be moving to the execution wing tonight. I already knew that was going to happen. The guards told me when we got back from the court house. I'm prepared."

I'm not prepared. But I'm trying to hold myself together so I don't make this harder for everyone else, and myself. Losing myself in tears right now is not going to do me any good.

"You won't be my neighbour no more. Me mam's coming for Ozzy tomorrow and I'll be sent back to the cells until it's time for them to let me out. I won't see you no more." Her eyes are filling and I can tell Verity is about to gush so I pull her close.

"I'll miss you too, Titty," I say and try to blink away my fear. Since I was sentenced to death by hanging earlier today, I have tried to get through the day refusing to think about what my death may look like and who I will leave behind. I thought knowing people might miss me would be a comfort, but actually it just makes me feel even more wretched.

Beatrice and Mags also know I'm being executed in three weeks, though I haven't managed to see my mother to tell her. On the way down the corridor, we pass Mo, and I see Beatrice and Mags.

"Thank you for everything," Beatrice says from the doorway of her cell.

"You're welcome," I reply. "I hope you get out of here soon and give your husband, ex-husband, hell!"

"Oh, I intend to," she replies and her mouth widens into a smile that doesn't reach her eyes. "It was good meeting you. I didn't think I'd make friends in here." She glances around at the drab of women who have come out into the hallway, shaking her head as though she still can't believe that she has made friends with so many criminals, and then she adds, "Guess we're all the same, aren't we? No matter where we come from or where we've started, just pounds of flesh trying to keep our hearts beating."

"Jaysus, Beatrice. Why you go and say something like that, ay? She ain't gonna have a beating heart come next month," Mags replies, and then, realising she has dropped the bombshell in front of every woman in our wing, her hand flies to her mouth. "I'm sorry, Roseanna. I didn't think. I just, none of us want you to go. We like ya', and death, it's not right. It's not fair—"

"I know, Mags. It's okay, don't be sad."

"But I just… it ain't right and it ain't proper. Me, an old lady, still here and someone like you in their prime getting the rope for saving one of their own…" She lets out a sob and I pull her into me and try to offer some comfort, but the words remain hitched in my throat. I will die soon and Danny doesn't even know where I am.

When I pull away from Mags, she forces a glass bottle that I hold up to my face to examine. "Hide it under your smock." She bulges her eyes urgingly at me and I hold the canister quickly before the guard can see it. "It's moonshine. My finest batch. I wanted you to have it. Me and your mum go way back. She's looked after me and me bad back more times than I care to count. Lovely woman."

"Thank you, Mags. I'll see that she gets it."

"It's for you both." She rubs my arm. "Share it. A final drink between a mother and daughter that should'a never been parted."

I nod my head and follow Verity and Mo down the halls on our way to the infirmary. Mags doesn't know that my mother and I are time travellers, and I wonder what my mother told her as to why we were parted.

When we reach the infirmary, Verity takes baby Ozzy from my mother and climbs back into bed and then Mo looks at her pocket watch and says, "I'm off on me rounds. Be back soon." Her eyes wander down my body and for a moment I swear they settle on where I have the concealed bottle beneath the waistband of my apron. Then she leaves the room and my mother rushes me.

Since news spread that I will be hung for murder, I've been treated with a certain kindness even from some of the guards. And as my mother pulls me down into one of the wooden seats that skirt the room, I decide that Mo isn't so bad. She's given me back Nanna's watch and somehow managed to find me time with my mother, again, and on my last night on earth, too.

When an old lady coughs, my mother leaves me to tend to her, wiping her brow and then picking up the bowl beside her and feeding her soup. I find myself glad that if I'm going to die, that I got the chance to meet my mother and to know that she never intended to leave me.

While Mo is gone, I pour two cups of the moonshine and take it over to Mum while she works. Her hand cups mine for a moment longer than it takes to receive the cup and our eyes meet. Unspoken pain and loss crosses between us and a shared understanding of the hopelessness of my situation.

The moment is broken by the old lady coughing and then Verity, noticing we are drinking, asks for a cup and I pour her one and hand it to her.

We drink from the same metal cups that we use in the dinner room and the hit of alcohol hits my throat like petrol on flames.

Verity lets out a splutter as the liquor hits the back of her throat.

"You know, you could try and escape. We'd all help you," Verity says, pacing the small window beside her bed while nursing Ozzy.

I smile lightly and take another sip of the moonshine. "It's not like the thought hasn't occurred to me. I've thought of little else, but I was told by the warden himself that anyone trying to escape is shot on sight. With no weapon, keys or the brute force of an army, it's impossible."

My mother glances over at me, her eyes dimmed by pain.

"I've been thinking of nothing else since I heard of your sentence. I've been here all these years and know the place inside out. No one has ever escaped."

When my mother has finished nursing a desperately ill patient who should be in a proper hospital, she moves onto the next but she continues to check on me often and, in an odd way, the mere act of knowing she cares helps me to feel at peace with leaving this earth, though I wish I could see Danny one last time to explain.

"If you write him, I'll make sure he gets it. I'll deliver it myself the second I am released," Verity says, somehow knowing that I am thinking of Danny.

"I passed another letter to Beatrice already. She said it was sent today, so he'll get it in a couple of weeks… It could be too late by then but if he reads it, at least he'll know how I felt about him."

Titty's eyes swell and so I change the subject and she tells me about motherhood. "It's not at all like what I thought it'd be. When he gets on my nipple, it hurts like hell, but in a good way and I like it. Makes me feel closer to him, you know?"

I shake my head and blink to keep the water filling my eyes. I'll never know what it is to be a mother. In the twenty-first century, I was on birth control. I had no way of knowing if I could get pregnant in this time, but it didn't happen and I suppose that may have been because the chemicals were still protecting me from an unplanned pregnancy.

I hold Ozzy while Verity uses the bathroom and wonder what a child that was both me and Danny might have looked like. In this parallel universe, I only ever seem to get one love at a time. As a young child, I had my mother, but not my Nanna. Then Nanna, but not Danny, and later Danny but no mother or Nanna.

I've often wondered if I am somehow cursed. If I can only have one person I love at one time, and if that is the case, I choose Danny. But in here, I have no choices, no control, and my fate seems sealed. I slug back more of the moonshine and the burn of the alcohol numbs the static sensation of fear in my gut so I slug more.

When more patients require help than my mum alone can provide, I stop drinking and support one of the patients to the toilet and then settle her back in bed and then help another person dress for bed. We finish the last of the moonshine and then as though worn out from the day's activity, the patients, including Verity, one by one, drift off to sleep, and then my mother comes to me and holds my hand.

"We will not let them hang you. It's not possible. We will do everything we can to get you out of here. Maybe we can…"

My mother's face, deeply lined by pain and fear hurts my eyes to look at. When I speak, there's a potent strength to my voice that I don't recognise.

"It's no good. You'd be shot if you even tried to help me escape. Mo is outside that door somewhere and there're guards. We'd never get past them."

"But you could appeal, surely?" Mum says.

"Beatrice already asked her lawyer friend. They say the evidence, it's irrefutable. And they're right, it is. I did murder Eli, and they have proof—fingerprints and an eyewitness."

"Nothing is ever irrefutable."

"This is. I'm never getting out of here, not alive anyway."

"Don't talk like that, Roseanna. We will find a way. I'll think of something. It's so cruel for me to find you, or for you to find me at least, only for it to end like this. I can't believe it. I can't believe we would go through all this just to have things blow apart so callously."

My mother hugs me and her warmth seeps into my body.

"Do you know," my mother says, "I've seen terrible things. I have lived through terrible times but there's always been one thing in my life that has given me hope and joy and that thing is you. We must find a way to help you escape."

I shush my mother's lips with my fingers.

"You've been planning your own escape for almost twenty years, where has it gotten you? You're still here. I've written to Danny and he hasn't responded. He either doesn't know I'm here or perhaps he does. I can't get away from the feeling like he knows I'm not in the future. A part of me wonders if he's figured out I'm not worth the trouble, but the other half of me knows that our love was a force to be reckoned with. But not even the greatest of loves can survive death."

"In all my years I've never seen such a kerfuffle," Mags says, bristling into the room. "There's a watcher on every corner." She drops the rest of the stale bread from dinner onto the counter.

Mo walks in abruptly behind her, looking seemingly stressed.

"What's going on, Mo? Why we got so many guards here?" Mags asks.

Mo glances at me curiously then looks away and shrugs. "Beats me. Go on, Mags, back to your cell."

Mags makes no effort to move. "Word in the kitchen is that Ian Copley drafted guards from all of the other prisons in London."

I examine Mo's face but she remains guarded.

"But why would he do that? It's not like there's even enough money for soap around here let alone extra rats... I mean, guards..." Mags's face turns awkward and I try not to smile at her sass which will only wind up getting both of us into trouble.

"That's not any of your concern, Mags. Now, come along back to your cell, or do I need to show you the bat?"

Mags shakes her head and quickly takes Mo's threat as her cue to leave. While my mother drops my hand and once again begins tending her patients—though before she starts, she throws Mo an expression of sheer gratitude for the time we have shared together, and I look at Mo with fresh eyes. Here on the countdown before my death, I find myself appreciating things I had never paid much attention to before.

Mo notices me staring and narrows her eyes with a look that's stern enough that I know there is no point asking her to help me escape. Such a question would probably ensure my last nights on earth are painful ones.

My mother glances at us both and attracts Mo's attention by asking her a direct question, "The extra guards from other prisons are probably something to do with the Duchess, is that right, Mo?" Mum looks away as she busies herself by turning down the sheets on one of the empty beds. She's acting casual but something in the way she bristles about her activity suggests she is highly strung, verging on desperate as our time together begins to run short. "Hear the Duchess'll be going to trial tomorrow. Created a stir, has it?"

"Stir in a tea cup," Mo huffs, "and that's all I'll say on the matter."

Mum doesn't press, and a little while later Mo announces she's going for a toilet break and warns us after that she must take me back to my cell.

While Mo is gone, my mother and I immediately gravitate towards one another. Between the light snores of the patients, the mood in the room becomes sombre.

"I suppose this might be our final goodbye," she says and I nod.

"At least we get to say goodbye this time," I reply, pushing a watery smile onto my face. "And now, we know the truth."

"Yes, truth is best," she says. "I wish I could get you out of here." She dabs her eyes with the sleeve of her dress.

"You must not blame yourself. Things are out of our control and none of this was your fault. I told Danny in my letter yesterday that you're in here. I asked that he try and get you out, and if you do, please will you return to Nanna. Tell her that I...."

She embraces me and it gives me the strength to continue. "Tell her I'm okay. That I met a boy... she'll like that."

Mum pulls away to see my face and smiles. "Always was a sucker for romance, was Connie." Her smile is affectionate.

"I'm glad I had the chance to meet you, Mum. To tell you that I love you, and I'm sorry for blaming you for your absence all these years. I didn't understand what we were up against was the very hopelessness of time itself."

Mum nods. If anyone understands, it is her.

"And I'm sorry I ever let go of your hand." She squeezes my hand tightly as though to check it is there.

"Do you think there's a life after this one?" I ask.

"I hope so. It's something I have thought of often. If there's one thing this place provides above all else, it is time to think." She strokes her thumb across my face, wiping away a stray tear of mine as if I am a child and also as though studying and committing every part of me to her memory. Then she continues, "You haven't even been born yet. If you die, after everything we've been through," she shakes her head as though she doesn't quite believe it has come to this, "if I can somehow change the path of history and get you a message never to come back to this time, I'll do it. I'll do everything I can to prevent you living this trauma—"

"No!" I tell her, rising to my feet and pacing. "If I never came to this time, I would never have met Danny. Somehow, despite all the pain, the time I have had with him has been everything. This life has been enough. I found love and family and friends." I stop pacing and turn to her. "Is there anything else I'd like to have accomplished? Of course. It hasn't been a perfect life, but I wouldn't change meeting him."

My mother's lips turn up in a sad smile. "It was like that with your father. All these years in here, I'd do it again. My time with him was everything. My only regret is not having a life with you."

"Time can be wicked, evil, even, but love is worth it."

"It is," she whispers as she stands and moves to be next to me.

Suddenly there is a ruckus from outside the window. The usual yelling of the women as they pass contraband to one another, some are having a song or a laugh, it reminds me. "On my first night here there was a woman singing a song I remembered. Or, maybe I just wished I remembered the song. It was so lovely and it sounded familiar."

My mum starts humming a tune and I instantly recognise it.

"I used to sing it to you as a child. So did your father, though he couldn't make a tune to save his life." She smiles fondly.

All of a sudden, a vision of parquet flooring and me and a man scooting across it in our socks comes to me. "I think I remember him." Once I have one memory, another quickly follows: my father holding my hand and sweeping my hair behind my ear, him singing to me.

"I remember him."

"Tell me what you remember," my mother says through shining eyes and I realise my memories are just as valuable to her as they are to me. We share a history that extends beyond this miserable place to a time of happiness and love.

Cloudy memories of a man with a big smile and a bulbous nose seep into my conscious. "He was happy to see me and when he picked me up and swung me around, I felt loved all the way through to my bones." I'm smiling and Mum is too. It's a simple moment of sharing a history, sharing one man, but between us, the moment is extraordinary and instantaneous bonding between mother and daughter.

The women outside become even louder.

"I wonder if the extra presence of the guards is putting them on edge," Mum says, moving to the window.

Lights from the spotlight at the guard tower flash past us. Curiosity wins out and I move to Mum's side and look out the window at the 1920's London skyline.

The moon is at its highest point, like an overhead light illuminating the rooftops. The women quieten long enough that I hear yelling.

More than yelling.

A ruckus.

Followed by gunfire.

Chapter 34

Roseanna

What's Going On?

I stand on a chair to look down through the open window at the commotion below.

In the blackness of night, the spotlight of the lookout tower shoots from left to right at the ground so quickly it's like the strobe at a nightclub, illuminating random heads in the throng of the crowd outside the gates.

There's a chanting, something to do with the Duchess that I can't quite make out. A quiet disappointment settles in my gut, churning as though to goad me for even thinking that the crowd might be here to rally my pending execution.

"You think they want to break the Duchess out?" Mum asks right as the main gates into the prison grounds break open and a flood of people spill through them. Shots are fired by the guards but there are hundreds of civilians, some carrying placards of varying demands to free the Duchess, and some waving their arms around to goad the officers attempting to round them up.

It's carnage. People run towards the entry beneath us, while others dart off around the grounds that we sometimes get to walk. Another set can be seen darting towards the small chapel that's set across the green. Setting off in all directions like unruly fireworks, the guards chase in all directions, shooting into the air and yelling to stop where they are or gun fire will be opened upon them.

They don't stop. The condensed crowd disperses across the ground, lit up by the overhead spotlight like particles of glitter in the wind.

The women in the prison bellow from their cell windows, cheering the intruders on, gloriously buoyant in their tones like a symphony at the sudden break from mundane, when the sound is broken up by a deeper, more chilling sound.

Dogs.

At the perimeter wall, dozens of guards with vicious looking, barking and gnarling dogs march towards the still dispersing crowd.

The members of the public don't stand a chance against these gnarling beasts and gunfire but such is the guards desire to bring the situation back under control, that the beasts are released from their restraints and they immediately make chase after the intruders.

I don't realise I'm holding my breath until I attempt to speak. "I don't know what they plan to do, but surely they can't have thought this through. They'll never get through the doors to the main prison. It's suicide."

I cover my mouth as a person is dragged to the ground by the jaws of a violently trained mut and wince as I imagine the pain of flesh ripped between its jaws.

At that moment, Mo enters. "Get down from that window at once, Chapman!" she orders and Mum holds out her hand to steady me while I clamber off the concrete sill of the window. "Say ye goodbyes."

Mo grabs me by my arms and pulls. I instinctively reach out to grasp my mother but Mo pulls me away, out of her reach and as I look back, I see tears streaming down my mother's face.

Mum calls after me, but Mo locks the door to the infirmary with her and the patients inside.

"What's going on?" I try to keep up as Mo pulls me down the corridor but instead of going up the stairs back to my cell, we descend the steps.

"You're a death row inmate now, Chapman. You'll have a cell in the bowels."

"But… my things are in my cell, I need to get them." The one earring I have left of Nanna's is in the pocket of my dress but inside the bible in my cell is the selfie picture Danny drew of the two of us.

"Tough. There'll be no buts. Got enough to do tonight with the protesters without wasting time with heirs and graces on you. I should never have gave in and let your mother snatch a moment with you. Coulda got me a sacking like Ned. Now I've got a nightshift ahead of me where I won't get so much as a wink of sleep and all because someone wanted to punish a duchess."

Her grip on my arm relaxes slightly as she becomes out of breath from the exertion of rushing to another part of the prison. We pass guards dashing down the corridors in what seems to be a mass exodus.

"Where are they going?"

"Outside! It's like a flaming circus out there. People everywhere and they seem determined to get inside to the Duchess. Warden Copley is on his way back in, but heaven knows how he'll get through the blockades."

"Blockades?"

We step aside to allow more guards to pass and for Mo to catch her breath and unlock a door to a wing I have never entered before.

"Blockades. There're cars, hundreds of bleeding cars blocking the road into the prison. I've never seen so many bleedin' cars." She pulls the door open and her hand grips my arm to lead me down the almost pitch-black corridor. "Still, you'll be all right down here. Quietest place in the block apart from the leaking pipes."

A rodent scuttles past my ankle and I leap to the side, pushing into Mo. A fleeting thought of if I were to escape, this might be my only chance, but as though reading my mind, she glares at me. "Don't you even think about it." Her hand reaches for her baton and I hold my palms out.

"I would never."

Mo unlocks the windowless cell at the end of the row and angles her head to the open door. "In you go."

Apprehension holds me still, so Mo uses the flat of her hand to shove me inside and then the door closes behind me and the lock mechanism slides into place.

Chapter 35

Roseanna

Great Escape

I strain my ears to hear but there is nothing of any consequence. If the protesters did manage to get inside, it is certainly beyond the reach of my ears.

The cell is smaller than my other and completely empty of any furniture even a bed. There is no light. No bell to request assistance and no sound except the light rush of water and the echo of the sewer rats.

My stomach grumbles and I realise that I have missed supper. Still, I suppose with most of the guards outside trying to control the crowd, there'll be no supper for anybody tonight.

"Hello," I call out, wondering if there are any other inmates in the bowels of the building with me, but am only met with silence.

I dig the toe of my boot into the soil floor and wonder how long it may take to dig my way out and if it is even possible when I hear the echoed sound of a door closing.

I press my ear to the door and listen intently.

"Roseanna!" It's barely more than a hiss. "Roseanna!" The hiss becomes inpatient.

"In here." I wrap my knuckles on the door and then do it again as the gentle sound of footsteps come closer.

The lock churns and then the door squeals as it is pushed open.

"Danny?!"

He is almost unrecognisable wearing a prison guard uniform though his dark hair is the same shiny swept-to-the-side style that I am used to.

His hand remains fixed to the door, gripping it as though that is all that is holding him standing.

"You're really here," he says, barely louder than a breath.

The months of missing him and turmoil over how he would feel when I never returned comes crashing down on me all at once and I launch myself at him, swinging my arms around him and squeezing until I can feel every part of him against every part of me. The chest of his jacket smells like tobacco and stale sweat, not like him at all so I lean up into his neck and inhale.

Danny's gaze settles on mine and a subtle frown is quickly replaced with a look of sheer adoration. "I've got to get you out of here, Red. Someplace safe."

"I've missed you." Tears are welling in my eyes with months of built-up emotions boiling to the surface, and my small sentiment is nothing compared to the pain I have endured being apart from him, but in case we don't make it out safely, I need to tell him. "I love you."

"My God, Red, living without you has been more than I can bear. We have to go. Is this all your clothes. Is there anything else in here with your scent?"

He brushes my tears away gently, then checks over my shoulder, gazing around the empty cell, probably wondering if I have any normal clothes to wear.

"I just moved cells today. This is the execution wing. I had a dress on for my trial but I gave that back to the Duchess. The one I was wearing when I got here was ruined, I don't know where it is. All I have is this." I gesture to the burlap-like material dress and fleetingly think how terrible I must look.

"Good." Danny's answer surprises me.

"Why?"

His hand clenches tighter around mine. "They'll use anything they have with your scent on it to excite the dogs."

Bile slickens my throat and I remember the man I saw taken down by the jaws of one. He places a chaste kiss against my lips and swivelling, he takes one long stride to pull me away.

"Wait. My mother. We have to get my mum. She's here. She's been here all this time."

He pauses and then turns back to me. "Where is she?"

"She's on the third floor. G wing, in the infirmary. She's the only semi-nurse they have."

His jaw stiffens and he shakes his head. "We don't have time." He strokes my hair, holding a piece of it between his fingers, then trails his thumb along the line of my jaw.

He pulls me by my arm again but my legs stiffen. "I can't leave her here. This place, it's hell." My voice is a desperate beg.

"Red, Ian Copley's made a call for reinforcements. The police are on their way and once they get here, every one of the guards stationed outside of the prison will be back inside, counting the inmates and punishing anyone who isn't where they are supposed to be." His expression is torn and for a moment I wonder if I should try harder to persuade him but then he says, "Do you know what the penalty is for inmates who try to escape?"

"I have to—"

"Do you know what the penalty is for people helping them escape?"

A chill travels up my spine.

"Jimmy, Ida, Clifford… they're outside rallying the crowd, distracting the guards, you and I need to get as far away as possible. I swear to you, we'll get your mother out but not now. Not today, okay?"

I barely have chance to nod before Danny is pushing the door to my cell and locking it behind us—to delay anyone checking on me from realising I am gone?

He pulls a torn piece of paper from his pocket and we dash through the dark corridors, left then right, right then left. I am disorientated and wonder how on earth we will get out of here safely.

He slows as we get to a corner and hear voices; then pulling his gun from the holder, he tucks me between his back and the wall and we listen. "D and E wings are accounted for. You want me to go check on the execution wing?"

I'm holding my breath while I wait for the guard to consider it. If he turns this way, they'll see us for sure.

"No. Go to G wing. None of them have eaten since midday and Mo said they're ringing the damn bell. Any of them making noise, threaten them with isolation."

"Yes, boss," the man replies.

Once they've gone, Danny checks the corridor is clear and then pulls me along until we reach a door that he unlocks from a key on the hoop on his belt. I have so many questions they're swirling at speed inside my head but the constant fear that we could be found at any moment prevents them from spilling from my mouth.

Through the door, we transcend more steps. If we were already in the "bowels of the building," by now we must be approaching the core of its hell. The deeper down we go, the darker and more uneven the ground beneath our feet becomes. Danny's grip on my hand tightens and his other arm reaches behind me and he grips my elbow as we dash, side by side to an unknown destination.

Down here, there are even more rats and frequent puddles beneath our feet as though the area is prone to flooding. Huge, like cats the rodents scuttle along the edges of the corridor, their eyes lit up red as the meagre, haphazardly placed lights on the walls glint upon them.

At the end of the corridor, we reach a round steel grate in the ground, with bars that are blackened by grime. Beneath it lies blackness.

Danny rechecks the paper he carries, a hand-drawn map.

He lets go of me and yanks at the crossed bars, carefully checking for weakness but it doesn't budge. It seems to be connected to the floor with no obvious means of opening it. The side section is rusted and one of the bars is shorn off at its middle.

Danny glances back impatiently at the door that we entered the corridor through. Then bends towards the grate, leveraging his foot on the wall and bending his knees while he tries to pull the lower bars away from the horizontal fixings using sheer brute force.

I check for anything that might work like a crowbar to release or bend the metal grate enough that we can get through, but the corridor is empty except the dirt and puddles beneath our feet. My feet squelch inside my shoes as I walk and the stench of sewage is so overpowering that I stop breathing through my nose.

I follow Danny's lead and crouch beside him to his left, put my foot on the wall and together we pull against the long bar that's next to the broken one. We pull for long enough that my hands smart and I'm gasping for air, but it budges… an inch. Beyond the door I can hear dogs, whistles and indelible screams.

Danny's expression is pure determination and will. He grips the rod of the bar and rips it from its lowest point using two hands and it moves again. The metal creases in its middle and bends enough that it sticks out from the grate in a right angle.

"After you." He gestures and with his other hand uses his cigarette lighter to cast a glow inside the grate that's just bright enough that I can see the metal ladder headed down.

"Always a gentleman," I joke, lowering myself through the small gap and taking Danny's hand until my feet meet the first step.

"Keep going, I'm right behind you."

I do as he says, moving as quickly as I can so that I free enough space above me for Danny to get on the ladder and lower himself down also.

The ladder is slick with damp and mould and I lose my footing several times. We appear to be in some kind of sewage system tunnel. I'm reminded of a long-discarded memory of a school trip from my childhood to the London water supplier, Thames Water. I remember learning how the water was abstracted, cleaned and sent into use, and also thinking how disgusting it all sounded. And I remember the maps of the London sewage system that was built during the late nineteenth century. The sewage system was built following disastrous epidemics of cholera from raw sewage being poured into the River Thames. They span hundreds of miles.

"You okay?" he whispers down to me and I tell him I'm fine even though the smell is bringing up last week's lunch.

I don't get as far as the bottom step when my feet meet frigid liquid.

"Danny, there's water."

"Hold onto the ladder. Don't let go. We're going to have to wade through it."

I was afraid he'd say that.

Chapter 36

Danny

The Same but Different

She looks thinner. Fragile. Maybe a stone, but more likely two lighter. Her body appears shrunken, it dips in and arcs at unnatural angles, weakened and vulnerable. Still beautiful. Still perfect to me, but neglected, damaged and in need of love and care so that she can become strong like before.

Red, my Red, used to have soft flesh and milky skin that curved in a manner to set my flesh on fire. Now her bones stick out at sharp right angles beneath her pale, almost translucent skin that's marred by scars and bruising. The urge to nurture and protect her is so overwhelming that I am already sitting beside her, waiting for her to wake so I can feed her the bread, meats and cheese that I know she used to enjoy, remembering the way her eyes used to flutter shut when she was eating with gusto after a long day cleaning the house with Ida.

Captive Songbird

I have bandages and pain relief at the ready. Ida prepared a case of anything we might need in the safe house and then she left to go join the riot outside the prison. At first I had told her no, but she wouldn't hear of remaining at home and left the children with Harriet while she went to jostle the people that were already there to hold a protest for the Duchess. And it worked out well. I can even imagine my grandmother, inciting the protesters to "Put their money where their mouths are and to get on and do something!" Such is Ida's grit, I imagine they were more afraid of she than the guards.

I memorised each and every freckle and blemish on Red's body. Every scar too. The scar on her hand from having her fingers crushed in a drawer by Lorenzo. The faint flicker of the scar on her temple from being smacked against a wall by Eli. The perfectly round scar on the upper flesh of her left arm that Red tells me came from a vaccination that protects against measles, mumps and rubella—a vaccination that hasn't even been invented yet, not in this time at least.

Now there are new marks and scars, and they're all over her body like the map of the sewer system we climbed out of just yesterday.

Ida organised the supplies but the safehouse was arranged by Jimmy—a place he used to use when he needed space. The little house is located on the Welsh border, neighboured by no one and surrounded by fields. It's hard to imagine my city-boy brother here—but we should be safe until we decide what to do next.

We arrived at the crack of dawn and the first thing I did was bathe her as she dipped in and out of sleep. The adrenaline from her escape long since evaporated, she's been in a slumber for sixteen hours now and I'm getting worried there's something wrong.

She sleeps fitfully like she used to when she first came into my life and was plagued by the dreams that tormented her. The memory of her body and her smile are what carried me through in the dark days we were separated. She hasn't smiled yet, but I'll make it my mission to make sure she does.

I want to care for her but I'm reluctant to wake her, so instead I go to the fireplace and light the fire. It may be June, but the house has been empty a long while and the sun is not yet high enough in the sky to cast its glow through the window. When the fire is raging, I toss in the rags she was wearing when I found her—she has no need to be reminded of that godforsaken place. Still damp, the material crackles lightly then disappears in a puff of smoke that is sucked up the chimney. I only wish her memories of Holloway will be just as easy to erase.

Whatever awful events she went through in jail, I know someone did this to her and they will pay. It will be my mission.

Red mutters in her sleep and tangles in the sheets on the bed, her delicate hand reaching across the sheet, searching for solace, so I move quickly to the chair beside the bed and take her hand in mine. I use my other hand to stroke her hair while muttering to her that she is safe. She is loved. She is cared for.

"Sleep, my love. I am watching over you."

**

Her eyes burst open before she is fully awake and I can tell she is startled.

"Roseanna, it's me, Danny." I try to make my voice reassuring but it sounds cold and lifeless in my unpreparedness for her sudden waking. "I am here."

She swallows loudly and I offer her a glass of water that I had ready and sitting on the nightstand. "Thirsty?"

She nods, lifts herself to a seated position and takes the glass from me, drinking it down until it is gone, never taking her eyes off mine. "Shall I get you more?"

"No. Stay with me." Her hand slides across the mattress searchingly and I take it in my two hands.

"I'm not going anywhere."

She glances around the small room, taking in the fire and the solitary single bed she rests upon. "Where are we?"

"A little house in the belly of a valley. There're no phones for miles or people we're likely to happen across."

"You broke me out of jail?" She looks confused.

"The moment I discovered where you were, I came for you. I'm just sorry I didn't come sooner."

Her hand reaches out and she grips my chin. Our eyes focus on only one another. I wait for her to yell. To tell me that I should have come sooner. I wait for any sign of righteous anger but none comes. Her expression is sheer adoration.

"Thank you." The words leave her lips in a sob and so I inch closer, beside her on the bed and wrap my arm around her.

"I thought you were…"

"In the future? I never made it that far."

"I want you to tell me everything, but first you need to tell me how you feel. Are you in any pain? Do I need to get you a doctor? I will, Red. Just say the word and I'll drive you to the nearest doctor and demand he fix you."

She smiles sweetly. "I'm fine. Or, I will be. My mother, Danny, we need to get her out."

I kiss her temple and inhale her sweet hair. "I will, but first you need your strength. Are you strong enough to walk?"

"Yes," she replies.

"I'll give you a tour?"

She nods and I hold her hand and help her up off the bed. Her legs are unsteady at first, like a hatchling taking its first steps. Her thighs are now mostly skin and bone as if the muscle just fell right off. I try not to convey the anger I feel at her treatment on my expression, but she must read it because she gently massages away my frown with her index finger and kisses my cheek.

I force a smile that's as comforting as I can. "So, it's not much. Two rooms upstairs and two down. The tub that I bathed you in last night is just made of tin, kept in the garden and brought in when its needed." I lead her downstairs to the kitchen and sit her on a stool at the table and turn to fill a pan to boil water for tea.

"I remember," she murmurs, her cheeks flushing. "You waded in sewage to save me." She shakes her head in disbelief.

I stop the tap, put down the pan and turn to her, crouching, placing my hands on the bones of her knees and look up into the most honest green eyes I have ever seen. "Sewage." I shrug. "Red, I would walk through the flames of hell itself to get to you. When I discovered where you were and what the jury decided, terror filled me." I stroke the soft skin of her neck and marvel at the feel beneath my fingertips. "The very idea that anyone would tie a noose around a neck so fair…" My jaw tightens and I try to breathe through my anger since she has already been through enough without me frightening her. "I'd kill every man in England before I let that happen."

"Just one man. One man who caused all of this pain."

My fingers twitch for my gun.

"Who?"

Compassion fills her eyes.

"Your father. It was Frank. He testified that he saw me murder Eli Harris in cold blood."

Chapter 37

Roseanna

Naked Truths

"My father?"

He's guarding his expression in that way he does when he thinks it'll frighten me.

"It's okay if you're angry. I'm angry too."

Danny nods. "I'll kill him."

I shake my head. "No, you won't. He's done his worst. His absolute worst and I'm still here. After that night at the King's Head, he went straight to the police and told them that he saw me kill Eli. He testified in court that I killed a man in cold blood and they believed him. But I did kill Eli, even though I truly believe that's the only thing that would have stopped him from killing again. From killing you. The question is, what are we going to do now? I'm a wanted woman. You've disappeared from society. The authorities must have realised I am gone by now and they'll be looking for us both. I'm so sorry you've been dragged into this—"

"Sorry. You're sorry? Red, it's my lifestyle that put you in there in the first place. I had to get you out. I wish I'd known you were in prison sooner; I'd have raised hell to get your name cleared. This is all my fault. My fault."

My hand grips his in my urgency to make him realise. "No. You cannot blame yourself. These events, all of them, have been out of our control. And, even though you weren't in there with me, you were in there with me. In here." I raise his hand to my heart. "I thought of you every day and thinking of you kept me alive."

His hand flattens against my beating chest. He's still crouched before me and we're eye to eye, only truth exists between us.

"I breathed you every day. Everything I did was with you in mind. I was preparing a life for us. Damn it, Red, I worked so hard to give you something to return to. A life you could be proud to live…" He shakes his head. "Now, I can only offer you the life of a convict on the run." He laughs cynically. "A life I would not wish on my enemy let alone the person I love most in this world." He briefly squeezes his eyes shut. "Roseanna, do you think… Would it be better for you if we took you to the arch. Solstice is just a few weeks away. I won't leave your side, not until you're safe back in the future."

I move my other hand and rest it on the hardness of his chest. The feel of his heart beating beneath my palm is a steady rhythm that's as comforting as the air in my lungs, for without it I would surely die.

"My life is with you. If you plan to send me into the future without you, then you'd just as well put a bullet between my eyes, here and now, because I have no life without you, being apart from you has shown me that."

Danny pulls me into him and sighs against my neck, then he says, "I thought you'd say that." He gazes up at me and strokes the side of my face with his index finger. "I can't bear to give you up, not now that I've got you back, but I'd understand. I'd understand if you wanted your old life back. You've been through enough. Too much."

Fear prickles beneath my skin. Terror that he might want to send me away in some kind of misguided manner meant to protect me.

I grip his jaw with both my hands so he can't look away. So that no part of him can be unsure that I want to be right here with him no matter what our future holds.

"I'll go through whatever it takes to start my life with you. I've learned that love is precious and it overrides any pain. What we have, it's like nothing I've ever felt before. I don't understand why we were thrown together, if not to find love from within all this craziness. It makes no sense. Nothing makes sense, only that I love you and you love me." I suddenly need to hear him say the words so I check, "You do love me, don't you?"

He analyses every part of my face and laughs bitterly. "Love. Such a stupid little word. One syllable and too short to convey the breadth of its meaning. The word could contain every letter of the alphabet and could pull every breath from my body to speak it and it still wouldn't cover the depth of my feelings for you. I've been walking about the place without you, listening to people speaking of love, but their use of it sounds shallow and paltry when I compare its use to how I feel about you. Love doesn't come close, but there are no other words capable of conveying how much you mean to me. I would die for you. I would kill for you. I would do whatever it takes just to see you smile. But I fear you will never smile again and that thought alone terrifies me."

I pull a very wide and deliberate smile onto my lips.

"I love you too. You need not worry about how often I smile, just know that all my smiles are because of you." I trail my index finger along the sharp edge of his cheek bone. If it were just me and Danny, in this tiny little house in the middle of nowhere for the rest of our lives, I would never stop smiling.

He strokes my thigh and looks up through his thick, dark lashes and gently smiles at me. "I didn't think I'd ever see you again." His hands reach around my waist and meet at my back. He nuzzles his face into my middle and I fold my body over his. I'd often wondered if the time away from each other would change his feelings towards me in anyway, but now I know for certain that he has found our separation as tormenting as I have.

We stay locked together until the quiet is broken by a growl from my empty stomach, and he lifts his head and smiles at me. "We'll figure everything out, and you *will* rehash all the ugly details about Frank—do not think I've forgotten—but not until you're strong." He stands and returns to boil the water and then he goes to the pantry and pulls out some bread, knocking on it with his fist. "It might be a little stale," his smile wavers, "I'm sorry."

I stand and take the loaf from him, tearing a chunk and taking a huge bite because I can't help myself. My mouth salivates the second my jaws wrap around it. "This tastes better than anything the finest chefs in England could prepare." I chuckle and take another bite.

He leads me by the hand to the small sitting room. I stare out the window at the rolling hills beyond. It's a perfect day. The sun is shining and the sky is a glorious shade of turquoise.

Danny stands behind me and wraps his arms around me. "Difficult to believe life has been so cruel lately with a view like that extending beyond us," I murmur.

"Then let's not think of that. Let's live together in this house as though God himself intended it."

I turn in his arms and face him. His beautiful face lit up by the sun's rays shining through the window. He's so utterly flawless it hurts my eyes and makes a lump form in my throat.

"Sounds heavenly."

"Nothing's stopping us. I've left Clifford in charge of the factory. No one will find us here and I've enough money to carry us through. Maybe I could find employment locally. Farm work, perhaps?"

I find myself grinning. "Tending pigs. Now there's something I'd pay to see."

He grins too. "You're smiling. That's something I'd give everything I own to see continue."

His lips inch closer to mine, slowly as though asking permission. But he doesn't need permission and so I meet him halfway.

The press of his lips against mine creates an electrical charge through every nerve until a fire spreads through my veins, warming my skin and causing heat to pool deep in my belly. My arms reach up and around his neck, pulling him closer, drawing him into me until it feels as though we are one. Together. Finally. My mouth opens and I push my breasts against him. Every part of me aches to feel him and I am relieved when his tongue brushes against mine. It feels like I am winning. Like I am healing. But then he stiffens, closing his mouth and lifting his lips until they are on the tip of my head and not at all where I need them. Tightly tucked in his arms, he doesn't let me go.

"Not yet. You need to eat."

I look at him and smirk. "I have a hunger for more than food."

His finger lightly taps the tip of my nose. "When you're healed." I shake my head but his expression is resolute. "I won't take advantage of you after the ordeal you have been through. Even if I really want to."

He sits me on the small loveseat in front of the sofa, pulling my legs up onto it, and then tucking a heavy fur over me.

"Don't move. I'm making you food."

"But—" He leaves the room and I rest my head on the back cushion. I hear him quietly pottering in the kitchen and rest my eyes for just awhile until he returns.

Awhile later, I wake and Danny brings me an enormous plate of freshly cooked eggs, toast and bacon. My mouth is watering before I have even tasted the first bite. He insists on feeding me and I let him because my body is exhausted and it seems to make him happy, caring for me in this way. He asks me often if the food is okay and seems overly concerned whether he is taking good enough care of me.

It continues like this throughout the day until my stomach is continually refilled and, rather than feel energised, I feel sluggish and tired. Later, he fills the tin bath, and since it is not big enough for two, he insists I bathe. Whenever I try to discuss what we do next, he quietens me with offers of more food and promises that we will figure everything out. That for now, I concentrate on rest and recuperating.

So, I do exactly that. My mother has been an inmate of Holloway prison for almost twenty years. We can't risk trying to break her out yet, not when there are likely swarms of police looking for us, so I put my fears in a box for now and allow myself to enjoy my freedom and time with Danny.

I remove the cotton nightdress that Danny dressed me in last night and hold his hand to steady myself while I step into the tub. The way his eyes scan my body in a concerned glance doesn't escape my attention. "I suppose I won't need to go on a diet for a while," I joke in an attempt to alleviate his concerns over my appearance.

"You never needed to diet anyway. Perfection in its entirety. Before and now."

"The food wasn't so bad, once I got used to it, but it was used as a form of punishment. Meals taken away if we didn't toe the line… that kind of thing." I clamp my mouth shut, if I want him to make love to me tonight, reminding him about any mistreatment is probably not going to help my cause.

He soaps up a sponge and takes hold of my ankle, gloriously massaging my foot.

"Tell me how you found your mother. That must have been quite a surprise."

"Surprised, yes. Dumbfounded more like. All these years…" I explain that I met her in the infirmary. "It was like she immediately knew who I was. And I felt I knew her. As soon as I saw her, I felt something. Does that sound dumb?"

He stops concentrating on my foot at looks at me intently. "Nothing you say sounds dumb."

I explain what I know about my origins and then he interrupts as though the thought just occurred to him. "What were you doing in the infirmary." He lifts my foot higher, examining my leg, then he trails his finger down my arm where a long scar is healing.

I stammer.

"You don't have to talk about it if you're not ready, but I've seen your scars. The ones on your body, at least. I know you were beaten."

I take a breath, lean back in the tub to wet my hair and then sit up and look at him, deciding that his imaginings of my incarceration are probably worse. So, I tell him. I tell him everything.

He's silent the entire time he pulls me from the bath and wraps me in a towel. He leads me to the bedroom and helps me dress in another cotton nightgown.

"Did Ida buy this?" I ask, thumbing the material that reaches past my knees.

He nods and a barely-there smile tips up his lips. "A boy came to tell me where you were—"

"Billy," I interrupt.

Danny nods.

"After I'd made enquiries, I realised breaking you out was the only way. It's almost unheard of for a person sentenced to execution to get a pardon. I couldn't risk using legal methods in case it didn't work, so Jimmy and I planned everything and Ida helped. The men from the factory took as many Alderman motorcars as they could and blocked the road." He smirks seeming to rather enjoy this part of the plan. "That way if the police or army were called in, it'd delay them, and it did. See, the protesters were already there for the Duchess so we added to their numbers with our own men. By all accounts, it wasn't difficult to rile the crowds and get them to storm the building which gave us the distraction we needed. And, Ida packed my car with all we'd need to keep us alive here until the fuss dies down."

"It was a great plan." I stroke his hand, still thrilled that he is before me. "I hope I get the chance to thank Ida and Jimmy one day."

"You will. We'll find a way to see them again eventually. But mostly, I don't fully understand how you ended up getting arrested for Eli's murder?"

"It was Copley who arrested me. He told me he started the fire at the factory—"

"Copley?!"

Danny's expression pinches with an angry glare that he quickly neutralises. He pulls back the covers on the bed. "No one who has hurt you will survive. I'll make sure they can never hurt anyone again. Into bed. You need to rest."

Feeling exhausted, I do as he says, scooching all the way to the wall so that he can climb in beside me. He seems to hesitate, then strips down to his underwear and climbs in, pulling the covers over us.

"How was it for you, while I was… away?" I ask.

He lies on his back looking up at the ceiling.

"Torture. Though I don't like to think of it that way when you were actually undergoing torture."

I roll onto my side and trail my finger across his collarbone, drawing it down between his pectoral muscles. The hardness of his muscles beneath my fingers sends heat directly to my core. I had visited the sheer perfection of his body in my dreams over and over again during his absence, but having him here, almost naked beside me is too much to resist. I've been aching for this moment for too long.

He catches my finger before it reaches his navel, bringing my finger up to his lips and kissing the tip.

"I won't take you until you're recovered."

"I'm recovered."

In the light cast by the moon, I see him smirk.

"I won't take advantage of your fragile mental state."

I kiss his temple.

"My mental state is just dandy."

I edge closer to his lips, kissing him gently at first but he barely responds.

"I know what you're doing, and you need rest."

"One of the benefits of being from the future is all the access we have to modern, scientific information." I kiss his neck, slowly trailing my tongue across his Adam's apple.

"Really," he replies.

"Yes, really. Did you know, endorphins can be healing when set off under the correct circumstances?"

"Endorphins?"

"Yes, like tiny explosions set off all over the body, they are released when a woman orgasms."

I feel him twitch beneath the covers.

"They have been known to heal, cure pain, ease depression…"

He turns to face me. "You're half starved, sleep deprived, beaten and goodness knows whatever else. You need—"

"I need you. I need to remember how good you feel and why I've been fighting to get back to you. And I really need those endorphins… with or without your help."

"You'd…" His eyes flick downwards to where I am lifting my nightdress up over my breasts.

"A girl's gotta do what a girl's got to do."

I trail my hand across my breasts and use my other to reach down and stroke down between my legs but before I reach my goal, he has a hold of my wrists and is anchoring them above my head.

"If anyone is healing you with endorphins, it will be me."

A smile creeps onto my lips.

"If you insist."

He rolls on top of me, bracing his weight on his elbows so that not one part of him presses against me.

"Keep your hands up here or I'll stop."

"Yes, Mr Alderman," I reply already becoming breathless in anticipation.

Danny places a teasing kiss on my lips and my toes curl. His kisses trail down my neck and I gasp in pleasure when he reaches the buds of my breasts; arching my back and pushing into him, his tongue on my breasts alone threatens to send me over the edge.

The sensation is overwhelming after months of not being touched, not feeling a loving touch. "Please, Danny I need…"

He lowers himself down the bed, spreading my legs and trailing his finger through my wetness. He growls in appreciation and the sound is like bass on full vibrating against my clit. When his tongue dips out, I buck against him.

"My sweet girl, you taste so good."

He's gentle at first, so achingly slow that my fists grip the pillow beneath my head as the sensation builds. It feels so good that I want to grip onto him in case I float away, but I tuck away the temptation to tangle my fingers in his hair in case he stops. Danny seems so concerned that I will overdo it that I don't dare risk this moment by doing anything other than allow him to bring me into this higher state.

My breathing hitches. The swirling sensation building to more than I can manage to hold within, I call out his name, and all notions of remaining still evaporate with the setting off of fireworks deep inside me. I buck and mewl as I come apart with his mouth on my most sensitive place. My hands fist his hair and I pull him towards me, kissing him deeply and feeling his hardness against my thigh.

"I need you. I need you inside me, now."

"I don't want to hurt you."

"You won't hurt me. I need you. I need to feel you. Be a part of you. Danny, please—"

No further persuasion is needed. He slips inside me, filling me until we are one. A perfect union of bodies, it feels as though we were never separated as he moves slowly until he is gloriously deep. Kissing me on both cheeks, he tells me, "You're so beautiful. We fit perfectly. Mine. My Red."

My body is warmed as if by the sun, his nakedness against mine is sheer heaven. I run my fingers through his now mussed hair and trail kisses across his cheek. I cannot get enough of him. Meeting his moves with my own, I lock my ankles around his back and call out his name, showing him I am relishing in the delicious friction that builds, that I need the pleasure he gives me.

My fingernails dig into his shoulders as the sensation builds. I'm hanging on the edge and can feel we are both close. Too long apart, too explosive to come together for long, we both need this moment. Together. Finally.

His eyes are locked on mine, lit with desire. He and the look of desperation in his eyes intensifies with every thrust. I cling to him, hanging on for the payoff that we both know will soon be upon us.

"I love you."

His thrusts deepen and build pace.

"You're mine."

"Forever," I reply, panting.

I can feel all of him against me in exactly the right places. I grip him tighter as we ride the force of the release together. Falling into me, he buries his face into the nook between my throat and shoulder as the orgasm that has been building explodes, shattering me into tiny pieces that are held together only by his touch.

We lie together, both of us panting and utterly spent. I run my fingers over the muscles of his sweat-covered back while he pants into my neck.

"I missed that the most. Not the act, though the act is always spectacular, but the closeness, you know?" I muse.

He kisses my jaw. "Always spectacular, but yes, I know what you mean. This closeness, it's incomparable to anything."

He rolls onto his back, beside me.

"Welcome home, Red."

Home.

Daniel Alderman *is* my home.

Chapter 38

Danny

Taking Care of What's Mine

We spend all of the next week together. I can't get enough of her. Fear pulsates beneath my skin if she is out of my sight for more than a second.

"It's beautiful here," she says.

It's a glorious summer day and the temperature is hot but it's nothing compared to how beautiful my Red looks, larking about bare feet in the small stream we found at the bottom of the land our current house sits upon. There's barely even a breeze, and the sun warms my shirtless chest. Nearby, birdsong and the splashing of Red's feet is the only sound for miles. It takes quite a bit of getting used to after a lifetime of London bustle, but I find myself quietly enjoying the pace, until I remember why we are here and murderous notions fire into my gut.

All in good time, Danny.

They will pay.

All of them.

Red told me about some guard at the prison called Ned, he's already as good as dead. He'll be easy to find and I'll make him pay. Red won't need to know about that, she's seen enough death and destruction, but he will be taken care of. Copley and my father, I will make sure they can never make Red vulnerable again.

Another issue is that Red says she wrote me letters while she was inside Holloway but I didn't get them. She couldn't be sure if they were posted to the factory or the manor since one of the other lags sent them out, but I intend to find out who intercepted them. If I had received those letters, she wouldn't have stayed in prison anywhere near as long as she did.

I lay on a blanket we brought down here from the house. Watching her, as I find myself doing a lot lately. Always watching. Watching for signs that the Post Traumatic Stress she described to me has returned. Watching for signs that she misses her nanna, her mother. Always watching and waiting for something to go wrong. So precarious is our current predicament, it feels likely to be snatched away at any moment.

"Stop worrying," she says as she plops down beside me and takes the sandwich I am holding right out of my hand to take a bite. I don't try and snatch it back. In the past week, I have watched as the colour has returned to her cheeks. The flesh on her bones. Still, she moves around quietly pondering, and that's what scares me the most. The pain she is in on the inside.

"I'm not worrying," I lie. "Tell me, how are you feeling?"

"I'm fine." She shrugs but I know from the way she curls her lip as she speaks she is hiding something. Raising my brow at her is all the encouragement she needs to enlighten me. "I feel guilty."

"How so?"

"Me, here, enjoying all this." She sweeps her hand all around at the view of the picturesque landscape. "Enjoying you." Her finger lightly trails up my chest. "It's so unfair that I am here and Mum is…"

I wince. Every day Red has been eager to plan. To put into motion some kind of action to free her mother, and even though I try to put her off, I know I won't get away with it for long and I feel like a bastard for trying to distract her. I won't risk her safety so I try once again to placate her.

"When the dust has settled—"

"I've thought of a way."

Her green eyes, lighter than the shade of the grass in the bright sunlight, she pins me with a serious look that shows determination.

"I won't risk you. We'll hide out a few months longer, and then we'll talk about it."

"Months!"

The high pitch of her tone warns me that I'll have to try hard to persuade her to wait.

"It has to be planned precisely. If your mother is caught escaping, you know what the penalty will be." I feel like an ass using her mother's safety to keep my love safe, but the fact of the matter remains the same. Her mother would be executed if she was caught trying to escape, not to mention that if Red goes within fifty miles of Holloway she'll be locked back up immediately, and having escaped once already, they'll shoot her on sight.

"I have an idea that won't put me within so much of a hundred miles of the prison. One that doesn't require any risk at all."

I sit up. She has my full attention.

"I learned something while I was in jail. Something that didn't mean all that much at the time, but now that I think of it, it will prove everything my mother needs to be released."

Red had already told me how her mother was locked up. Roseanna dropped her mother's hand and her mother travelled back through time without her daughter. On the other side of the gateway, her mother waited for her kin, but at only five years old and with no clue what was going on, Roseanna never walked through. Her mother was locked up with signs of lunacy, calling for her child. The police officer who found her assumed when they could find no sign of her daughter, that Ruth had gone mad and killed Roseanna.

"I have a birth certificate. It was used by my solicitor and mentioned in court. They know who I am and they knew my mother was locked up for lunacy. It will just take someone to present this information. My mother can't do it from inside jail. No one would help her. But even though I have absconded, they can't argue the fact that I am alive. It proves she didn't kill me, and so it's new evidence. They have to take it seriously, don't they?" Her voice is desperate, her expression hopeful.

"We'll walk into the town. I'll call my solicitor and have him make the necessary arrangements to have the case looked at."

"There's someone I think might help."

"Who?"

"Detective Scott."

"No."

"Danny he's always been kind to me, even though he knows I killed Eli. He seems… fair."

I've known Scott since he arrested my father and "fair" is an accurate description.

"I want to write to him. Tell him about my mother. I think if he knew someone was unfairly incarcerated then he might act. It's a theory, anyway. It might not work but I have to try."

My immediate urge is to keep her away from anything that could put her in harm's way—even writing letters that might trace back to her—but the sadness in her eyes is too much for me to bear to even attempt to shield her.

"There's some paper at the house. You write the letter and we'll drive twenty miles north to post it."

She smiles so widely that my heart aches as it expands.

"I'm also going to tell Scott that Burt admitted to me that he was responsible for the arson at the factory. I was too overwhelmed when I saw him last. I didn't get to mention it, but he should know. If he can find any evidence that Burt did it then he should be held accountable."

I link my fingers through Red's, appreciating the softness of her skin and how good her hand feels in mine. "Whatever you want to do, beautiful. I'll help you." I don't sully the moment by telling her that Jimmy is already waiting on the word to end Copley in case I can't get back to London to do it myself.

He'll wait, but only for now.

Chapter 39

Roseanna

News

It's been nearly two weeks now, and when food stocks run low, we head into the small village for supplies. As we're coming back up the long path to the house, we spot a man looking through the window.

Danny pulls me to the side to hide behind a tree and immediately reaches for his gun. "Stay here."

He wanders to the house with purpose and intention. The man, who is dressed in a dark suit that looks too warm for the climate, is startled when he notices Danny behind him.

"Who are you and what are you doing here?" Danny's voice is a million miles from the loving, endearing tone I am used to.

"I.... didn't think anyone lived in this old house. The chap who used to stay here hasn't been back in years. We had a letter delivered at the post office for here. I was just bringing it by."

Danny snatches the letter. "You can go now."

The man raises his palms in a gesture that suggests he means no harm, then he turns his back to Danny and begins walking up the path. Danny doesn't take his eyes off the man and I stay out of sight until he has gone. Then I rush to Danny.

"What is it?" I ask, but quickly I change my question because it's obviously a letter. "Who's it from?"

He pulls me inside the house, checking through the windows. Suddenly I feel nervous. He rips the letter open and scans it.

"What does it say?"

"It's from Alice. It says your mother has been freed. Jimmy collected her from jail. Apparently released on the same day as the Duchess and Alice got to meet her. Blah, blah blah..." He continues to scan the letter while I imagine Alice's wonderous face taken in by Beatrice's movie star good looks.

"She's free? Mum's really free?"

He hands me the letter.

"Yes, you did it, Red. You freed her. They couldn't argue with birth certificate and court papers. Can hardly jail you and then claim you're not who they said you were. They had all the evidence they needed."

I clench my eyes closed to prevent the tears from spilling. Danny wraps me in his arms. "It's okay. She's safe. She's with Jimmy. He'll look after her."

I nod through my tears. "She'll go through the arch on the solstice to look after Nanna. It's what we planned." I'm smiling despite my sadness. "I'll never see her again. But at least I will know Nanna is looked after and safe and my mother's finally free! I can't believe she's actually free."

The tears I have been trying to hold back spill free from my eyes and I'm so happy I let them fall.

"Ida says that Burt Copley has been suspended from the police force. They found a petrol canister at the factory after the fire and kept it as evidence. And after a 'tip off'"—I grin wildly as I wonder if the tip off was the letter I send to Detective Scott to alert him to Burt's confession—"they matched the fingerprints to the canister, and along with the burn marks on his arms and known vendetta against the Alderman's, they are pressing charges. In Alice's words, 'it's going to court and everything.'" I feel Danny watching me as I read aloud and pause to take in the sentimental expression on his face as I mention Alice.

"You did it, Red. You got your own back against Burt Copley. Not the justice he will face from me, no, that will be much darker, excruciating, in fact, after everything he has put you through, but still a good dose of karma."

"Burt Copley won't survive jail. You won't have to worry about exacting your own revenge, I'm sure of that." And I am. Having lived through the terrors of a 1920's prison, I am sure that a man, no a weasel, like Burt Copley will be in sheer hell.

I glance back down at the letter, not wishing to spend even another second thinking of Burt Copley. "Alice says that she met my mother. She likes her very much and that my mother has a plan to get our names cleared. Mine and yours, Danny, my mother believes she can clear our names. She says to wait for another letter." I wonder what this could mean. What her plan could be but don't dare hope it could actually happen. "My mother won't put herself at risk, will she?"

Danny's arms lock around my waist. "I don't see that she can. You mentioned that you discovered that your father was a man of means, a duke? I wonder if perhaps your mother has connections related to your father that can help?"

I suppose that could be true. Duke's tend to know royalty and the wealthy, maybe there is some sort of family related reason but I don't dare hope.

I read to the end of the letter, mostly just Alice updating us on how they all are and baby Ellen cutting her first tooth, and then I get to a part that sounds mysterious.

"There's something in the envelope that I thought you'd want." I look at Danny questioningly. "What does Alice mean by that?"

He shrugs. "You know Alice, her thoughts run ahead quicker than any of us mere mortals can follow. You rest. I'll prepare dinner," and with that, I let Alice's mention of something else being in the envelope go and position myself in the loveseat and wait for my man to cook while I bask in the knowledge that my mother is free.

**

We dine on bacon chops, potatoes and vegetables. Danny even manages to find a bottle of wine to have with dinner, and we sit in amicable silence savouring the food.

"You've been quiet today."

"Just missing everyone, I suppose." I spent the entire afternoon reading the contents of Alice's letter over and over. Clifford is running the business and it's doing well. Danny told me that Clifford plans to marry Harriet, for namesake only, and I wish once again that I was there to be able to talk to him about this. I wonder if he has anyone to discuss his sexuality with and hope he doesn't make a mistake he'll come to regret. Likewise, I wonder how Harriet will feel about a marriage not built on love. She and Clifford are both still grieving Benny; we all are, and I can't see that a marriage for the purposes of reputation alone will make anyone happy, least of all Clifford and Harriet.

"The letter says baby Ellen is thriving. I wish I'd met her. Henry now plays on a football team and Ida has been out of the house more and more. It makes me wonder if she has met a man."

Danny smirks. "Be a fine man that can put up with Ida's caustic tongue. I think more likely that she has found something she disapproves of in the city, and she's decided to make her mark." He ponders quietly for a time and then adds, "I miss them too." His voice is neutral, much like his expression, but it makes me realise no matter how much I am missing them all it must be worse for him. They are his family, after all.

"Do you think—"

"No."

"But what if we—"

"No. I won't risk it."

"But Mum, she'll be gone soon. I might never see her again."

"Alice's letter might not state it outright, but there'll be police keeping an eye on the Alderman Manor. It can't be risked. I'm sorry. I wish we could chance it, but if they got their hands on you..." I watch as his hand curls into a fist. "We can never go back."

I nod. He's right. It's not like I didn't know before now that I don't get to have everyone I love all in one place. Whether it's thanks to a curse or not, just having Danny, it's enough. He's everything, I remind myself.

"Okay," I reply and then I move the conversation to other matters.

"So, should we look for jobs here?"

"How do you feel about America?"

"America?"

"A friend of mine has a ranch in Texas. He left right after the war but we kept in touch. I have some money tucked away. Enough to get us started. A fresh start."

I watch his expression for any glimmer that he is joking but he is deadly serious.

"You'd give up your life here for me?"

"Red, you gave up your life for me. It seems only fair I return the favour. Besides, I can ride a horse."

I guffaw at the thought of Danny astride a horse. Always so proper in his suit with his hair perfectly combed. "I can't imagine you in a cowboy hat."

"Hey, I'll have you know I'd make a very dashing cowboy."

He walks around the table and pulls me up into his arms. A pulse of electricity shoots through my arms straight to my heart at his touch. Danny kisses my lips and my eyes flutter closed. "You are very dashing." I find myself sighing.

"Dashing enough to marry?"

My eyes open with a pop. His expression is utterly serious, if verging on a little nervous. In his fingers, he's holding a ring. It's white gold and three diamonds are set vertically in a way that elongates my finger as he slides it on.

My eyes are unmoving from the ring. The three main diamonds are surrounded by smaller, yet no less dazzling, stones to form an art deco style frame. It is quite simply the most beautiful piece of jewellery I have ever seen.

"I can get you something different, if you prefer. Something more modern, perhaps?"

I tear my eyes away from the ring and stare into Danny's eyes which, in the dim light, look almost white like the diamonds themselves.

"When did you get this?"

He bashfully smirks. "I had a lot of time to myself while I thought you were in the future. I visited many jewellers but nothing seemed quite right... So I drew..."

"You designed this?"

He shrugs as though embarrassed.

"A unique ring for a unique woman. I had it made and kept it in the bedside drawer at the manor. I suppose Alice must have found it because that was what she put in the envelope that she 'thought I might want.'"

"She posted it to you?"

"Yes. I think Alice would very much like to see us marry."

"I don't suppose she will, though. Not unless my mother can find a way to get us pardoned. We'll never be able to return otherwise. I imagine there are penalties should anyone know where we are and if they are harbouring us." I begin to feel sad so I change the direction of the conversation. "Can I see the drawing you did of the ring?"

"If you wish." He hesitates and then pulls a sheet of folded paper from the pocket of his trousers. I examine it on all sides. He's drawn the ring from each elevation, but around it he's drawn me. My face multiplied several times only with different expressions. In one, I look as though I might cry. He's sketched the light perfectly reflecting the ring in my eyes. In another, I am biting my lip as I am now, in an attempt not to cry. And in another, the one I feel myself reflecting, I am smiling. I turn the paper over and see that he has drawn the ring on my finger. I stroke my ring finger with my thumb and turn my hand until it perfectly resembles the drawing, including the small scar I have on my index finger from catching my finger in the chain of my bike when I was a child.

"It's flawless," I murmur. "You captured everything."

"Three diamonds. One for the past, one for the present, one for the future." He shifts awkwardly on his feet and I realise I still haven't given the poor man my answer. "Red, I am not a perfect man. You deserve a better man, one whose temper is even and his manners mild. I am not worthy of your love, yet I feel its warmth even when you are not with me. Times change and, in some respects, so do people but I know the way I feel about you will never change. You are mine and I am yours, not even time can change that.

I will always love you. Will you share a future with me? I can't promise it will be straightforward, but I can assure you that I will love you every moment of every day until the end of time."

I place my hands on his firm, broad shoulders and tear my eyes from my beautiful ring to look into his crystal blue eyes.

"Yes. Of course, I'll marry you. You've had my heart since the day we met. Any future with you, even if it is just one day, it's all I need. It's everything."

His arms tighten around my waist and his chin angles down until his lips press against mine, sealing the deal we have made to one another. He breaks our kiss, leaning back and examining my expression.

His lips tip up at the corners. "Roseanna Alderman, my wife."

"You know, in the future women often keep their own names, or add their husband's on at the end." I'm teasing but he doesn't seem to notice, pondering my suggestion as though taking it seriously.

"I'd understand if you didn't want to take my name."

"I like Roseanna Alderman very much. It has a ring to it. Mr and Mrs Alderman, no one and nothing can stop us."

He sweeps me up into his arms, carrying me as though I weigh nothing at all up the stairs, all the way to the tiny bed that we now share.

Danny moves slowly, savouring every touch, every kiss and stroke. It's tender, loving and feels as much as if we are consummating our promise to marry, and as much a union as any vows could secure, for we are one. Now and always.

Chapter 40

Danny

Time to Go Home

Something I learned being away from Red, nothing, and I mean nothing is better than being with her.

And so, the fear of losing her and being without her is more real than ever.

She snuffles lightly on the bed, still fast asleep, her hair splayed across the pillow even more vivid against the white cotton of the sheets. It makes me wish I had access to more art materials. Wax and paints, I could paint her in all her dramatic beauty, but still, even my best attempts could never do her justice. There is not a face in the whole world, of this one or any other, that fascinates me as Red's does. It's probably why I have never drawn another.

Her hand reaches across the mattress for me and her diamond ring glints in the sun cast through the window. It's almost midday but I won't wake her, not when I've been keeping her up as late as I have. She needs her energy, for today will be a big day.

I move to her, still in a state of undress following our lovemaking, her skin is a peach glow against the backdrop of the bed.

I comb her hair back to prevent it tickling her cheek and she slowly opens her eyes. "There you are," she says, her voice unsteady with sleep.

"I never go far."

She glances behind me to where I have moved the seat and placed my paper. "Drawing me again?" She looks embarrassed.

"I've never had access to a model before. I cannot afford to waste a second if I am to fill a gallery. Ten galleries. I shall fill them across the world, all with your face."

"The visitors will be quite bored if it is only me, even if you do make every drawing look unique."

"The visitors will revel in your beauty, how can they not?" I draw my thumb across the swell of her now flushed cheek.

"You make me blush."

"You make me want you."

"Again?" She raises her delicate brow. "I'm still sore but I think I could suffer it." She has a cute look on her face, a glint in her eye as her vision travels down past my navel. Her hands reach out but I edge away. "I'm not sore, not at all. You should come here so I can show you just how good I feel."

I snigger at her wanting and am eager to give into her, but first I have news to share.

"Haven't you had enough of me yet?"

"Never," she answers instantly and I grin. I could stay here with this woman forever, just she and I and never tire of her, but I have news that will make her incredibly happy and I am eager to see her resulting smile.

"That may be so, but I thought perhaps you might like to change things up. Have a change of scenery."

"I suppose we ought to keep moving around so that we are not caught. How long do we have to pack?" She glances out the window to the perfect June day as though the house may indeed be surrounded.

I've kept a patrol, but the area we are in is so remote there has been no need. Not even the national newspapers tend to be delivered this remotely. It's one of the reasons Jimmy kept the place as a bolthole, almost completely away from civilisation.

"As long as you like, but you may want to get a move on…" I lean over—unable to resist planting a chaste kiss on her lips—and pick up the letter I collected from the postman earlier, while Red was still sleeping. "We have an invitation."

She sits up, pushing her auburn hair behind her shoulders, revealing her perfect, milky breasts, distracting me.

"An invitation," she reminds me.

"Read it for yourself." I hand her the letter.

"From Alice. They… we've been pardoned! The Prime Minister?"

I've already read the letter several times and even drove to the village to use their phone. I spoke to Jimmy directly while Red was sleeping and he confirmed the truth of it.

"It seems your aunt, your father's sister, is married to the soon to be Prime Minister of England. Jesus, Red. You could've told me you were practically royalty; I'd have cleaned my act up long ago." I wink at her. "So, your mother has friends in high places, it seems. She, Beatrice and Valentine went to your aunt and her husband and he agreed to arrange a pardon. After all, the daughter of a duke couldn't possibly have killed a person or escaped from London's most notorious women's prison. And they also don't want any negative link to the PM published in *The Daily Herald,* especially with an election looming. Afraid that voters will question the appropriateness of links to crime and gangs…" I find myself smirking. "I would never have thought my criminal links would pay off in a manner that could save you."

"Danny, it's…" Her eyes fill and I catch a tear before it wets her lips.

"It means we can go back to the manor. You can see your mother before she leaves in two days. You can even…" I swallow and the sound is loud. I don't want to say what I am about to, but I must if I am to be sure she is certain. That her decisions are not based on the limitations of our predicament. "If you decide to leave with your mother, then I understand. I cannot offer you everything that the future can. You may be better off—"

"Don't you dare even say it, Daniel Alderman! I am not going anywhere. I miss Nanna terribly. So much it tears me up inside but living without you is an impossibility. I have tested it and I know there are no alternatives. I stay here, with you. For better or worse, that's what you asked me for and that's what we agreed. Us. Forever. That's what we promised to each other, you can't—"

"I'm not. God, I want you to stay. But not because it is your only option."

Her lip juts out as though she is affronted. "Well, I have choices. Plenty of them. And I've chosen."

I lean towards her, dipping my head, until my lips crash against hers. This moment, knowing she can leave, but that she chooses not to, it is everything to me. My own mother left, yet Red, she chooses me even though it is the most difficult option.

"I love you," I mutter against her skin, kissing a trail down her neck.

"I love you too. More than life."

We spend the rest of the morning making love and then we prepare for home.

To our home.

To our family.

And with it the promise of forever.

Chapter 41

Roseanna

Home Sweet Home

Alice is the first to reach the car when we pull up outside—flinging herself at me like a missile, I'm almost knocked off my feet.

"Roseanna, I've been waiting all day and it's almost dinner time, and I was worried you'd never get here and... it's so good to see you." Alice wraps her arms around me, locking her hands at my flanks and pressing her body into mine so tightly that it's almost difficult to breathe.

"I missed you too," I reply, peering at her cherubic face and noticing she looks different somehow, older? I hadn't expected much change, but I suppose by the way she is examining my face, Alice has noticed changes too.

"You lost weight."

I nod. "Just a little."

"That's okay, Ida will have you fed up in no time."

"She has me fed up every bleedin' day, washin' dishes," Henry remarks from behind her and I can't help chuckle.

"Come on, Henry, if you didn't do dishes then how would we keep you out of all that mischief you like to make?" I joke and hold out my free arm so that there is room for him to snuggle in for a hug with me and Alice. The feel of holding the two children that I have spent so much time thinking of is almost too much and my throat swells with a heart-shaped lump. "I've missed you both so much. How are you liking school?" There's so much I want to ask them but I hold back in the hope that there will be plenty of time to talk and because, beyond them, I see the rest of the family have followed the children outside, and now here they stand, on the steps of the Alderman Manor. Ida, wiping her hands on her apron as she often does when she is in the midst of preparing supper, Clifford with his arm around Harriet who is clutching a baby that I assume is Ellen, and on the other side of them is my mother.

Danny comes around the car and ushers the children inside with the promise of time with me later and then he takes my hand and leads me up the steps.

"You got out," I say to my mother, disbelieving that it is so despite Alice's letter confirming the fact.

"And you are free too." She glances over my shoulder, presumably at the arch. "Whatever will we do with all this freedom."

"Well, I don't know about anyone else, but I could quite do with a sherry," Ida provides. Then leaning into me, she says, "I'm glad you didn't rot in that place. Though by the look of you, you weren't far off."

I try not to snigger and reply, "Thank you, Ida."

**

The next day is a haze of strange contentment as I adjust to life back beneath the Alderman roof.

Ida is surprised but welcoming to my mother as a house guest and doesn't ask the probing questions about my mother's sudden appearance that I've brace myself for. Our story is that the authorities wrongly incarcerated my mother and never checked my whereabouts, which was in fact with my grandmother (only we don't mention the timeslip). It passes well enough and at dinner, with all of the family as well as Jimmy in attendance, Danny clinks his fork against his wine glass and stands to make an announcement.

"I'm not a man of many words so I'll make this brief so's Henry can get on and eat this fine beef that Ida has prepared for us all." He smirks down at Henry who nods approvingly. "I'd like to welcome a new member to the family. Ruth Chapman, thank you for giving my love, Roseanna, life and freedom. It is a debt that cannot ever be repaid. Your daughter has come to mean very much to me and I intend to take great care of her from here onwards by making her my wife, if you'll allow it?"

Danny looks to my mother for her approval. It's an old-fashioned gesture but one that I find endearing and sweet.

"Married?" Mum raises her eyebrow questioningly and I lift my ring finger to show her the evidence, smiling widely as I do so.

"Danny asked me at the safe house. I said yes, of course." Since we have been home, we have tucked all thoughts of Texas away and decided to remain in England with the Aldermans.

"Then I suppose, since my daughter said yes, you do not need my permission at all."

"Still, I would be grateful for your blessing," Danny replies.

"Then it is yours."

He proposes a toast and I notice Alice practically hopping in her seat. "Will I be a bridesmaid. I mean, you don't have to say yes but—"

"Of course, Alice. You and Harriet, Ellen won't be walking by then but she will be a bridesmaid too—"

"When will you do it? If Ellen won't yet be walking, it must be soon," Ida says.

Turning to Ida, Danny replies, "Twenty-first of June. I've spoken to the church and the bishop himself will marry us, here, on Alderman land."

A smile licks at Ida's lips though she does her best to hide it. "That's tomorrow. Have you taken leave of your senses, boy?"

Danny grins at Ida. "I have never been more serious or saner."

Ida nods as though she is decided. "Then there'll be much to sort and it won't leave me long to make the spread. I suppose you've already spoken to Marjory Gibbs about a bridal dress?"

Danny nods again. "Marjorie says she saw this coming and already has the perfect dress. She's coming over tomorrow morning to check the fit but Marjorie has a good eye for such things, so I imagine it'll be perfect. The service will be at three, isn't that right, Red?"

"Sure is." I still can't believe we're attempting to pull off a wedding in such a short amount of time but with my mother leaving soon, I couldn't bear to say no when Danny suggested marrying on the day of the solstice. A part of me also hopes that the curse, if that's what started my time travelling adventure is, will have come full circle. According to Norma, it began at a wedding on a solstice by a scorned woman pulling lovers apart. I only hope that can be the end to it and nothing, not even time and fate themselves, can intervene.

"Well, at least that's something. We'll all need new threads and Clifford, you'll need to speak to Trevor, make sure we've all we need in to cater for a crowd."

At the mention of Trevor, Clifford shifts awkwardly in his seat.

"It's the day I leave, but I'd be proud to stay for the ceremony," my mother says drawing my attention away from Clifford. "Thank you for holding the ceremony while I am still here."

"I'd like you to walk me down the aisle, if you'd do me the honour?" I ask mum.

She snatches her napkin from the table and dabs her eyes. "I'd be very proud to walk you down the aisle."

Ida frowns at the leap from tradition. Deep inside, I am sure Ida has much to say about the appropriateness of a person who is not the bride's father or grandfather walking her down the aisle.

"That's settled, then." Danny's smile is beaming as he looks down at me, then he proposes a toast, "To the soon to be Mrs Alderman. May time always be on her side."

Chapter 42

Roseanna

Wedding Plans

The next day I have not a moment to myself for all the plans that must be made for the wedding. Even though I already declared that I would happily marry Danny in a sack, Marjorie arrives to fit me for a dress becoming of a 1920's bride, since I know not much of the era's customs or fashions.

Harriet is excited to be tasked with styling my hair and also arranging my bouquet, and so Mum and I help Ida by baking tarts and cleaning the house.

Later that morning, while my mother and I are picking strawberries from the garden to decorate the wedding cake she has baked for us, she explains how she and Beatrice visited my father's sister. My aunt, who married well and was surprised to learn of my mother's incarceration, was even more surprised to learn that I, too, had ended up inside Holloway prison. She agreed to help and secure mine and Danny's pardon but mostly because she was concerned about the stir it would create for her husband and the pending election.

"I don't suppose I'll be looking Aunt Jenny up anytime soon," I joke. "At least she helped, and Danny and I can live our lives here as we intended."

Over my mother's shoulder, I glance at the arch and ask her, "Do you think Nanna will remember you?"

She pauses and leans back on her heels, stretching her back. "From all you say, her memory is quite impaired now, though I like to think there'll be sparks of recognition."

"Perhaps she'll know you. You remembered me as soon as you saw me, after all."

"Perhaps." My mum smiles whimsically. "You sure I can't persuade you to return? You could be my guide. A lot has changed since 2002, I'm sure."

I lean over the fruit bed and place my hand on hers. "My home is here. Danny and I are to be married…"

My wedding is bittersweet since it marks the date my mother will leave me, but this time I know the reasons and I also have the knowledge that I was loved by her.

"I understand. Wild horses wouldn't have driven me from your father. Daniel's a good man. I look forward to looking you both up when I return to the future." She smiles warmly while I think on this.

"I wonder what the history books will record of us. In the time I came from, this house wasn't in the Alderman family. It makes me wonder what becomes of us all." I ponder this for a while. "There are so many possibilities, I suppose I shouldn't dwell."

"No. One can't predict the future and you can't live your life with what ifs and maybes. Besides, I have a strong feeling that only good things lie ahead."

I find myself hoping her premonition is correct, but we are jarred from the conversation by a truck pulling up outside the house.

With the strawberries collected, we stand and walk to the house to see Jimmy and Agnes disembark. In the back of the truck there is furniture from the Kings Head to use for the wedding, and also plenty of alcohol.

We chat and Jimmy comments that he will lose a day's takings by shutting the pub, but he does so without complaining which takes me by surprise.

More surprised still am I by the way his eyes linger on Agnes as she orders some of Danny's men to arrange seating in the garden. Then Jimmy announces that he is going to find Danny, and I am commandeered by Harriet who wishes to trim my hair before she ties it with ribbons.

Once Harriet has shorn around five inches of my hair off and I am now sporting a "more modern" style, I look for Danny, finally finding him in his office, with Jimmy and several of his men. The door is a few inches ajar and I hear him before I see him.

Pausing behind the door, I hear him say, "He hasn't just vanished. Where is he?"

"I don't know, boss. There're rumours that he got work on the railway. Someone else said he was going down to Southampton and getting on a boat set for Canada. He ain't in London, though. I've looked bleedin' everywhere."

I hover at the doorway, listening as the men speak.

"Jimmy, put word out there's a reward. Five hundred pounds to anyone who brings him to me. I want it impossible for him to so much as come within one hundred miles of London without me knowing about it, okay?"

"Got it, boss," Jimmy replies.

"Now, what about that other person I mentioned?"

Other person?

"Already dealt with boss. He was exactly where we thought he'd be," Jimmy replies.

"Good. And Burt Copley?"

"About that…"

"What about him?" Danny sounds furious, and even though I can't see his face, I can imagine the hard line of his jaw and icy glaze to his eyes.

"Were'nt my fault so don't give me your hard eyes. Police let him out. Snitches said his brother paid his bail since he thought the lags wouldn't give an ex copper an easy ride in jail. He's at home. Probably waiting on a visit from yourself." There's a joyful sound to Jimmy's voice that suggests he's enjoying the notion of Burt Copley at home fearing for his safety.

"You know idle hands make for the devil's work. I'll not do all the work for the nuptials myself. There's still sheets to press and flowers to arrange, not to mention I've a two pound of tongue that wants slicing." I allow Ida to usher me into the kitchen but vow to find Danny later before he does anything that might land him in trouble.

Chapter 43

Roseanna

Coward by Name Coward by Nature

"Where did Danny go?" I ask Henry after helping Ida in the kitchen.

"Beats me. No one tells me nuffin'. All I get told is 'go to school Henry', 'Wash behind your ears, Henry.'"

He does an impression of Ida that brings an instant smile to my face but it falls when I notice Henry isn't smiling, he looks sad. Lost.

"Is everything okay?"

He shrugs.

"Looking forward to the wedding?"

"Will there be cake?"

I grin. "Absolutely loads of it."

He rubs his stomach. "Then yep, I'm looking forward to it all right. Even if Ida says I got to wear a jacket and tie, even though it'll be boiling." He pulls a putrid face and I squeeze his shoulder.

"You'll look dapper as can be and years from now, when folk look at the photographs, they'll say, 'Who's that handsome young man?'" I wink at him.

"You think so?"

"I know so," I reassure.

"Henry. You'll go and wash behind your ears before you put your smart clothes on. Off you go," Ida says from behind me.

Once Henry has left I ask Ida, "Where's Danny gone?"

She turns to face me, slowly, then leans to clutch the counter behind her to take the weight off her hip. "He wouldn't say, but I think we both have a good idea where he'd be off to…"

She raises her brow at me.

Then it dawns on me.

"Burt Copley will be on his way to jail as soon as the trial is over."

"He might, eventually. But while he's in his home, he's not repenting for his sins, is he?"

"Danny hasn't gone to—"

Ida's nodding before I've even finished speaking.

"I need to go."

"There's a car around back. You can take that. You'll want to drive towards the King's. Copley lives above the Cobblers on Tanner Street, but don't be gone long, the wedding starts in two hours and you've still to dress yeself."

I scramble to the hallway and take a set of car keys from the drawer and dash to the car, hoping I can get there before Danny does something he'll regret.

**

There's an alley at the side of the cobblers with a door that leads to a staircase to the flat above. The door is open and I walk straight in, up the stairs, only pausing when I hear voices.

Danny's voice.

"You could have destroyed her!" There's a crash—something hard, wooden perhaps, splitting as it hits the wall. "Your need for vengeance was so great that you decided to take it out on my woman?!" There's another crash and I hasten my pace.

"Danny, please, I—"

"You what?! She was almost hung for murder!"

I dash in the room in time to see Danny's fist fly into Burt Copley's face. Burt's nose crushes as it splits down the middle and blood gushes out from it.

I notice a repugnant towel resting on the small, wooden table in the middle of the room and hand it to him.

Burt looks surprised to see me, Danny even more so.

"I came because there is no use in you hurting him," I say to Danny. "No good will come from you being imprisoned for murder. And Detective Scott will know immediately that it was you."

"Red, go. I can't let him get away with it."

"You go. I won't let you do it."

Burt nurses his nose with the dirty towel, his eyes darting between us both.

"I can't let him get away with it. You… You nearly died!"

"You're right, but I didn't. I'm here and killing Burt won't make you feel better."

Danny grabs a hold of Burt's neck and headbutts him, then punches him in the gut until Burt is doubled over and wheezing.

"See!"

"What?" Danny asks.

"Do you feel better?"

I can tell right away just by looking in his eyes that he doesn't feel better for hurting Burt. "One thing I have learned since I have been in this time and also while in jail is that revenge doesn't make us feel better. I often wondered if I would feel better about Benny's death if Eli were dead… and then he died and I still don't feel any better about him not being here, and neither do any of you."

"So you think people should go unpunished, is that what you're saying? Because, Red, I let Frank go and look what happened to you as a result of that. And if Eli were still alive, he'd be coming back to hurt us again. It's the only way to make sure these sewer rats don't come for us again and again. It's the only way to get any peace."

I walk to him and put my hand on his arm. He has it raised like he wants to hit Burt again, so I move my hand down his arm and cup his fist, angling myself until I am standing in front of him with Burt behind me.

"He can't hurt us from jail. We just have to wait for him to get there."

Behind me, Burt takes a step towards the door. "Sit the fuck down, Burt," Danny orders, and then rubs his thumb along my jaw. "Go wait in the car. I'll handle this and then I'll drive you home."

I shake my head. "I'm not going anywhere. If you're going to kill him, you'll have to do it in front of me."

I take a step away so I can see both men and I wait.

"You don't understand this life, Red. Men like him, they don't stop. Bitterness eats them away until they will destroy everything you have. He wants to, he still wants to hurt what's mine."

"Your father took everything mine had and then he shot himself in the head," Burt states bitterly.

Danny's nostrils flare and he turns his attention to Burt. I'm tempted to slap Burt myself and tell him to shut the hell up.

"Really, Burt. And what was your role in your father's death, huh?"

"I din't do nowt. Was your dad who took all his money. Man had nothing left. No pride. No money. No house. He did all he could and wiped himself from the earth in all his shame."

"And did you try and stop him, Burt?"

Burt's face screws up bitterly, but when he speaks it is as though he's talking to himself, not Danny or me.

"Want no point trying to save my old man. A man is nothing without respect and he lost it all. Like me. Scott fired me from the police force. Took my fingerprints like a common criminal. Found out I torched the factory and now I got no job." He holds his head in his hands and inhales deeply before continuing. "Sarah left me. She said no point staying if there's not a wage coming in, and who can blame her?"

"You torched my business and put my woman in jail and kept it from me to punish me for the sins of my father."

As though waking from his reverie, Burt looks up at Danny. His nose drips blood down onto the table in front of him though he doesn't seem to care.

"Yeah, I did. For what good it did me. You could fall in shit and come out smelling of roses. Me, I got no job, no wife, even the roof over me head is rented and I can't afford rent with no job." He shakes his head dejectedly.

I can't help thinking its karma but I don't say as much. Burt Copley may be a bitter little man who has put me through hell, but even I can't seem to kick him while he's down.

"And what did you do to your father when he was in a similar position?" Danny asks him.

The question confuses me.

Burt looks down at the gun in its holder at his chest. He takes it out and puts it down on the table in front of him, spinning it slowly as though playing spin the bottle with it. It spins around twice and slows to a stop to face him. He does it again and the same thing happens.

Burt's reply is again said to no one in particular. It's like he is thoroughly alone in his mind, destroyed by his own doing. His voice is cold, unfeeling. "My father was ruined. No point in him going on and he wanted to end it all, so l left him with the gun and told him to get it over with if that's what he wanted."

Burt spins the gun that rests on the table again while my mind reels at his revelation.

"He left his father with a gun, knowing he would use it to end his life?" I ask and Danny nods.

I feel like I might be sick. Flashes of Nanna, my mother and all of the Aldermans play like a slideshow in my mind. Burt would've been a young man back then, but old enough to know that pride is no substitute for love and family.

"I'm gonna to be a jobless laughing stock. The force'll never hire me again. Sarah won't come back to me. Ian will disown me."

"And all with good reason," Danny replies coldly and then he takes a step to me and takes a hold of my hand, never taking his eyes off Burt and the gun.

"Come on, Red. No need for revenge today. Burt'll either end up dead at his own hand or rotting in jail where he'll be treated accordingly as a hard done by bent copper with a grudge against anyone trying to get on in life."

He pulls me to the door where I pause and turn to look back at Copley, remembering all the misery he has caused. He's spinning the gun as though trying to decide what to do.

"Come on," Danny urges. "He'll not have means to hurt you again."

My feet won't move. I hate Burt Copley with a fire that makes me want to shoot him myself, but the more rational part of me feels sorry for him, even though I shouldn't. In a way, it seems poetic that we should leave him with the gun like he did his own father. Yet my conscience won't allow me to walk out of here without saying something to make him reconsider.

"Burt, anyone can be a better person if they want to be, but it lies within. You can let go of the bitterness or you can choose to let it pull you under, but only you can decide."

Burt seems to nod his head, though I can't tell if he hears me.

I let Danny pull me away.

Moments later, when we're outside on the cobbled streets beneath the glow on the sun, the boom of a gun cracks through the air.

Chapter 44

Roseanna

Wedding Bells

"It's looking wonderful downstairs. Your Danny's team have decorated the entire place with white roses and ribbon streamers. Enough roses to fill the entire Chelsea flower show, I'd say," my mother says, dabbing at her eyes. "Think it's set off my hay fever."

I peer at her through the mirror in front of me while Harriet wraps my hair in ribbons. Now that it's bobbed, she's created Marcel Waves using a curling iron that she heated on the stove, and the look is perfectly in keeping with the decade and also looks rather flattering.

"Ida sent you up a sherry for your nerves." Mum hands me a glass and I take a long sip. "I took one too. After all, it's not every day that a mother gets to have a drink with her daughter on her wedding day."

We clink glasses. "I'm so glad you're here for the wedding."

"Me too. But you talk like I won't return. I hope to, someday."

The thought is sobering as that day will be when my grandmother has passed onto heaven.

"I wish she were here."

Sensing I am becoming sad, Harriet taps the brush she is using to tease my hair against my head. "No tears. You'll smudge your lashes."

"A toast, to Nanna," my mother says, and all three of us lift our glasses and toast the incredible lady who raised me.

"I hear it'll be you next," my mother says to Harriet.

She looks down, fiddling with the bridal corset that Marjorie brought for me to wear beneath the wedding dress she has hung from the top of the wardrobe.

"Oh. You heard."

"You said yes?" I ask.

Harriet nods awkwardly. "It'll be a long engagement. Clifford's not yet eighteen and we thought it proper to wait until he has means. It's not very romantic, but we want to do things proper, you know."

"With the business doing so well, Danny mentioned that you will receive Benny's share of the profits. You'll be a woman with your own means soon," I reply, hoping to help her see that finances are not a reason to marry.

"It doesn't feel right me accepting that money. I'm not an Alderman, after all, and I wanted Benny, not for his money but for him, you know."

"That money is yours and Ellen's. Benny would've wanted you to have it. Take it. What will you do once you're married?" I ask.

"Same as you. Stay in the house, cook, clean, make a home." She shrugs. Her lack of enthusiasm makes her seem almost detached from her decision.

"Harriet, I don't intend to stay in the house and make a home. I've already told Danny that I want to pursue my dream of becoming a doctor."

"And he's letting you?" Harriet's mouth pops open. Her hand lands on my shoulder as she studies my face in the mirror before us, as though to check I am being serious.

I find myself chuckling. "He'll not stop me. But, yes, he's also supporting me."

"Hmph. And you two, so in love," she muses. "I'm happy for you both. You deserve good, great things."

I move my hand to my shoulder and rest it on top of hers. "You and Clifford deserve the very best life has to offer too."

"Yes, but I'm a mother with no husband. I'm not the same as you." Her voice is soft, friendly, but her tone makes it clear she really believes what she has just said.

I turn in my seat so I can look at her directly. "You are a strong, independent woman who has survived more than any woman should, including losing the love of her life. You can be anything you damn well want to be and no one is going to tell you otherwise, you hear me?"

She nods placatingly.

"Harriet, I am serious. You have access to money. A sound place to live and the support of the Aldermans should you need it. What would you be teaching your daughter if you settled for anything less than what would make you happy?"

She raises her head and seems to ponder what I have said.

Then Alice storms into the room, spinning on her socks and twirling around in her dress. "How do I look?"

"Beautiful."

"Stunning."

"Gorgeous."

We all comment and then Alice replies, "They're almost ready for you, and I've a bag full of rose petals to throw."

"Best get you in your dress, then," Mum says to me. I stand, giving Harriet one last squeeze to her hand to thank her for my wedding makeover, but she seems miles away in thought.

Chapter 45

Danny

Patience is a Virtue

The heat is beating down on me like the door has just opened on the furnace from the factory. Behind me, in two sets of rows of chairs, are our wedding guests. Though it is customary to have the bride's family and friends on one side and groom's on the other, we have mixed them together. Everyone here, from Marjorie and Harold, Jimmy and Agnes, even Beatrice and Verity, who my beautiful Red met in jail, have become friends and family to us both.

Interestingly, as I spoke to Beatrice and Verity, to thank them for protecting my Red, I remembered the letters that Roseanna said she sent me from jail so I checked with Beatrice and she confirmed that she passed them out of the jail through her solicitor and that he had written the factory address on the envelope since a business address is generally the most readily available one to find for a person.

As I scan the crowd, wondering who might have intercepted such important news from my love, I find a possible culprit and zone in.

"June, you decided to come to mine and Roseanna's wedding." A notice went up on the board at the factory announcing the wedding and also that the men had the day off. The wedding was so rushed we didn't give out any invitations. It makes me wonder if people believe our wedding is of the shotgun variety, not that I would in any way mind if Red were with child. In fact, it would be the icing on the cake.

I don't smile or give June any indication that I am pleased to see her here.

"Daniel, yes. I thought it was an open invitation. The notice on the wall. I wanted to come support you both." She smiles broadly. Her yellow hair looks brittle in the sunlight and hangs limply at her shoulders despite having the appearance of being styled.

I decide to go straight in for the kill. I'll know if June lies to me and Red will be walking down the aisle soon. I don't have time to waste with soft questions and coaxing meanderings.

"And were you supporting us both when you withheld the letters Roseanna sent?"

Her mouth pops open and her breath hitches on the intake. Her skin colours just enough to give me a sign. "Don't you dare lie to me. I've shot people for less."

"Daniel, I'm sorry. I…"

"Why?"

She nibbles her lip and pathetically looks as though she might cry.

"The envelope had her name and Holloway's address printed on the back. I thought if you wanted to hear from her then you'd have visited."

"Visited? How, when I didn't know where she was?" My fists are balled. If she was a man she'd be dead by now.

There's a guilty expression to her face that is doing nothing to quell my anger.

"Her name was mentioned in *The Daily Herald*. I figured there can't be too many Roseanna Chapman's."

"And again you didn't think to mention this to me." My blood is boiling through my veins. I haven't picked up a newspaper since Red last read one to me. I couldn't bear to read one without her at my side. Now, I'm almost as angry at myself as I am at June.

Almost, but not quite.

"She's not right for you Danny. You have to see that. She's no more than a common—"

"Shut. Your. Rancid. Mouth," I growl. Then I inhale deeply through my nostrils and then out through my mouth, just like Red does when she's trying to stay calm amongst the midst of something unpleasant. "You're going to take your shitty excuses and lying, deceitful ways and leave this wedding so that you can't tarnish it. Roseanna Chapman is an honest to God, loyal, beautiful woman, and you had the power to help her and you did nothing. Nothing! You are not an employee of Alderman Inc. anymore. You're fired and I never want to see your face again, understood?"

Tears are streaming down her face so I usher her away. "Go on off, you fuck." I feel no pity for her and just want her gone.

Once I'm satisfied that June has left and take a few cleansing breaths, I go stand beside Clifford, my best man, at the front of the alter.

"Nervous, brother?" Clifford asks.

I see the arch beyond him. "Always, brother, but not for what I am about to do. No, marrying Red is the easiest thing of all. Being the man she needs and giving her the future she deserves, that is my greatest concern." His expression carries the weight of a man with his own worries. "Still, you'll be standing up here soon, contemplating your own marriage."

I leave my words to rest, and he seems to be chewing them over for a while until he replies, "Harriet deserves a man who can give her everything too."

"She does," I reply. "Benny would've wanted the best for her."

He slicks his hair back and I notice beads of perspiration on his temple. Then he looks back into the crowd and I see his eyes meet with Trevor's. A shared glance that holds the weight of a secret shared.

"Do you think I should call the wedding off?" Clifford asks.

"Only you know what's in your heart. If that is Harriet, then proceed with full steam, but if it is not, spare Harriet and yourself a marriage that lacks love."

He has a resolute gaze in his eyes. "I think I love another."

I rest my hand on Clifford's shoulders and fix my eyes on him. "Then love this other person. The swell of your heart when it is filled with joy should not be compromised out of duty of fondness. It is to be enjoyed, revelled upon. Clifford, I support your choices and am here for you whatever you decide."

Clifford claps me on the back. "I know you do. I'll speak to Harriet. She'll understand, won't she?"

"She will, brother."

Ida appears suddenly and taps my shoulder. "It's time! Quit your whisperings and look lively!" She juts her chin and bulges her eyes at us, but as she turns herself to return to her seat I notice she is smiling in the direction of the small aisle that I had my men arrange.

And then I stop breathing entirely and everyone ceases to exist while I take in the vision before me.

My Red.

A vision in an ivory dress. All slim lines, a dropped waist and a shorter hemline, the dress is a sight to behold and shows off her slender calves and delicate ankles. The bodice is ornate with the sun glimmering from stones expertly sewn by the hand of the woman who, along with Ida, as good as raised me.

Red's face is covered by a cloche veil, and in her hands is an enormous bouquet of white roses streaming with ribbons that billow down to her knees.

Never before have I seen a more captivating bride, and as the pianist plays, she makes her way towards me and I find myself eager to meet her halfway, lift the veil and kiss her plump lips.

I hold myself still, reminding myself to breathe. My cheeks ache from smiling, but still, I can't stop.

When she is finally beside me, I lift the veil.

Stunning.

She's wearing the emerald earrings she was wearing when she arrived. I couldn't bear to allow Billy to keep one since they were sentimental and a reminder of her beloved grandmother, and so I gave him fifty pounds and arranged for him and his sister to move in with the Gibbs's. They're both here, seated with Marjorie and Harold and their other foster children, Norman—who Red and I liberated from the Nightingale's—Ronald, Deidre and Christine—who have also been rescued from the workhouse.

"You look incredible. Breathtaking," I tell Red. And she does. Her lashes appear darker, thicker somehow. Her cheeks are rouge, flushed like how they look after we make love. And her lips...

I lean down and press a kiss to her mouth. I am quite sure it is not the done thing, but I do not care and Red doesn't seem to mind at all, kissing me back with gusto. We only stop when we're ready, despite the coughs and clearing of throats from the crowd.

She looks sheepish as we conduct ourselves, ready for our vows.

"You weren't supposed to do that," she whispers while the pastor whittles on about God or something or other. I hold both her hands in mine and my heart races.

"I know, I couldn't help myself."

She grins wildly and I have to remind myself that I will get to taste her again soon.

Patience, Daniel.

We repeat the words back to the pastor and feel their power pulling us closer until I am sure we are almost one. The meaning of phrases such as sickness and health weigh heavily as I make a pact with God himself to just give us time. Now that we have each other, all we need is time. We deserve that, don't we?

Sliding the ring down onto Red's finger cements our promise, and I lift her hand and kiss it. I'm desperate to kiss every inch of her and claim her as my wife, but I keep myself still, waiting until I can get her alone.

"You may kiss your bride... *again,*" the pastor says only slightly admonishingly, and I waste no time, blocking out the chuckles of the crowd as I scoop my wife up into my arms and tell her, "You're mine now."

"And you are mine," she replies and the sweet sound of her declaration detonates a desire in me. Our lips meet as if for the first time, slow and tender. I close my eyes and allow the light tingle to travel straight to my heart. I dip my tongue in briefly to taste her and she lets out an appreciative mewl.

Once we have broken the kiss, I turn to the crowd and fist the air.

"I introduce you all to my wife!" I call, unable to keep the joy from spilling from my lips. "Thankfully and finally!" I wrap my arm around her waist and we walk the aisle as our guests congratulate us, and honestly, the world has never seen a happier man.

Chapter 46

Roseanna

Farewell

After our vows, we are ordered to stand in front of the house for photographs. The first one is of Danny and me, and I'm once again reminded that this is a different time by the enormity of the camera.

"Stand still for the Kodak," the photographer calls, and as he does Danny leans down and kisses me once again. It's like he can't get enough, and I am loving how happy he seems. After everything we have both been through, today is a reminder that love sometimes wins.

"Now, thee will pose for a photograph that doesn't belong on the cover of one of those smut books!" Ida hisses to Danny at the inappropriateness of kissing on camera and we both chuckle. I think Ida would throw a fit if she ever came by a modern device and had a scroll through *TikTok*.

Danny and I stand still, holding hands—which is apparently only barely acceptable by Ida's standards judging by the downward look she throws us over the rim of her spectacles—and pose for the second photo and then all of the guests are invited to come stand with us for the third.

I am delighted to see Beatrice and Verity here and assume Danny must have somehow found them after I told him how they got me through my jail time. Now I can arrange to see my friends again and maybe even visit Mags, though the thought of returning to Holloway fills me with dread. Strangely, they also mentioned that *The Daily Herald* reported that Ned's body was found floating in the Thames. Suicide, apparently.

"Please, can I have a photograph with my mother?" I ask Danny.

"Red, I'd capture you the moon if you asked for it," he replies and then orders everyone off the steps of the manor so I can have my picture taken with my mother.

"How long until I can have a copy?" I ask the photographer once he's done from behind the device that hides his head entirely.

"Three to four weeks," he replies.

"Oh," I say trying to keep the disappointment from my voice.

"What's the matter?" Mum asks, noting my glum face.

"I wanted you to have a copy to take back with you."

Mum smiles and squeezes my hand. "My darling, I think I can get to a printer and operate *Yahoo* still. I'll probably have a copy before you do." She winks and I laugh.

"You might want to try using *Google* to search the wedding. Yahoo isn't used for search functions so much anymore."

Mum throws me a questioning look. "There are still printers, though?"

"Yes, though you'll want to visit the library. Nanna didn't want wi-fi, she thought it was a fire risk."

"Wi-fi?" It's then I realise that my mother has as much as a learning curve ahead of her as I do, here in 1922.

"Modern things you'll soon get the hang of. As a modern woman, however, will I survive without them?" Though, as I stand here today, I can't say there are many modern conveniences I miss.

She glances at Danny. "Oh I think you will have quite enough delights to take your mind off them."

I elbow her jovially. "Mother! That's my husband you are talking about."

"And what a fine husband he is too." She kisses my cheek. "You're going to be so happy."

"Will you tell Nanna all about him, please."

"I will. She'll be so happy that she'll be dancing in her nightgown."

"Roseanna, over here!" Alice calls from near the side entrance to the house.

"Go to her. I'll come find you before I go."

We hug for a moment longer than it takes to say "goodbye for now." I don't want to let her go and wish we had more time, but then time has always dictated my path so I don't suppose I get to decide its course.

"Roseanna! Come on! Your dance." I look over to see Alice, but all I see is Danny, standing in the middle of the cleared floor, arms out, waiting for me.

**

Later, when everyone has eaten and danced until their feet hurt, I spot Agnes and Jimmy making out behind the makeshift bar. I thought he had softened recently and am pleased to see that a part of that is mostly because he has also found love.

I catch up with Beatrice and Verity and find out that baby Ozzy is thriving and Beatrice's popularity following the Holloway riots meant that she was awarded a favourable settlement in her divorce, and best of all, she is now free to follow her heart. She didn't confirm it, but a certain journalist, who shall not be named—in *The Daily Herald* at least—has moved near her new residence in Shropshire and they are quietly enjoying the company of one another.

As the sky darkens and my feet ache from all the dancing, I sit outside the steps of the manor and hold onto a quiet moment on what is the best day of my life, when Danny suddenly appears beside me. My mother is behind him.

"The fireworks are about to start. They're being set off behind the house. It should provide a good distraction, while you both say farewell." He pulls me up by my hand, wrapping his arms around me and whispers, "Please, don't get too close to the arch. Stand back, don't leave me, my love."

I graze my lips against his jaw and reply, "You're not getting rid of me that easily."

"I shall never want rid of you."

He kisses the tip of my head and then turns to my mother. "Ms Chapman, it has been an honour meeting you. Our door will always be open for you, particularly during the solstice."

My mother throws her arms around him and whispers something in his ear and he nods in a very serious manner.

"Come along, daughter. Walk me to my taxi." She holds out her hand, and I let go of Danny to escort her home while Danny calls the crowd to head around the back of the house for the display.

We walk slowly as though being pulled by magnets in the opposite direction.

As my feet move across the gravel, I ask her, "Where will you say you've been all this time? The authorities, the police and such will want answers. You've been listed as a missing person. There was some rather unpleasant media interest in you."

"I've been thinking about that a lot and my best explanation is a good bout of amnesia. In the future I have a birth certificate, National Insurance documentation. It'll all be filed in Nanna's house; it should make the transition easier. Thankfully your Nanna has never moved house, so I'll just rock up there. To Nanna, it might even seem like I was never away."

"I suppose if you can survive twenty years in Holloway prison, modern police enquiries will be a doddle."

She lets go of my hand and suddenly her arm is around me. "Exactly. You've no need to worry about me or your nanna. Life is for living, and that is what we must do."

"That reminds me." I pull the emerald earrings from my ears and give them to her. "Please give these to Nanna. They were from Grandad Leonard; I'd like her to have them back."

She deposits them into the pocket of her dress. "I will give them to her with your love. If I can find a photo of today when I get where I'm going, she'll be delighted you were wearing them." I find it comforting, knowing there may well be a piece of me in the future.

About ten metres from the arch, she pulls me to a stop and it starts to rain.

"It'll be raining. It always is," we both say in unison and then chuckle.

"This is where we must say goodbye."

Tears spring to my eyes and my mother wipes them away. "You can't cry on your wedding day. Your happiness is only just beginning."

"I know," I sniff. "But I just got you back and now I have to say goodbye."

"Not goodbye, farewell. We've always been connected. All these years, I've felt you right here in my heart, and I know I will continue to." She squeezes my hands tightly in hers. "It will be a mixed blessing the day I return to you." And I know she means my nanna's passing. "But for one life, others will then join the tapestry of our family. Besides, there are going to be some grandbabies I'm going to want to spoil."

She wipes away her own tears and then pulls me into a bone-crushing hug.

"I love you," she whispers into my ear and then walks towards the arch. I hug myself gently and watch as the rain now falls in earnest.

"I love you too," I call after her and she turns to face me as she becomes level with the arch and then, in a crack of lightning, she is suddenly gone.

Chapter 47

Roseanna

Time for Us

When the last person has gone home and the children are in bed, I begin to clean up when Danny's arm wrap around me from behind.

"Leave that. There is a team coming in the morning to clean." I can smell brandy on his breath and the scent is enticing. I turn in his arms and kiss his lips. "I have much less honourable plans for you."

Heat floods my core and I reply, "Is that so?"

He doesn't respond, instead swooping me up until I am lifted in his arms and he is taking the stairs two-by-two.

Inside our bedroom, he shuts the door and sets me down. Suddenly I feel nervous. He loosens his tie and walks to the window, glancing outside before turning to me.

"You looked perfect today. Utterly heart-stoppingly beautiful." He stalks towards me and my heart beats faster. "Waiting for you to walk down the aisle was torture. So many fears and yet, none at all. I knew you'd be there. I knew you loved me and wanted to marry me, and yet I was besieged by fear. I feel like that a lot lately."

I shake my head. "You have nothing to fear."

"I have everything to fear. I could lose everything in a heartbeat. Time, illness, accidents, risks. I have never paid them much mind before, but since I met you they play on my mind constantly."

I walk to him, taking hold of his hands in mine. "I feel that way too. But know this, I will never willingly leave you. You hold my beating heart in your hands. I cannot live without you."

His head dips down and he kisses me gently. "You are as much a part of me as the blood that runs through my veins. Without you, I am nothing more than flesh and bone. You make me a person who wants to live. A person who wants to do good."

He deepens our kiss and suddenly we are rampant with desire. Undoing one another's clothes as though they have done us harm, and sheer desperation causing us to shed them until we are gloriously naked in front of each other, hands and mouths everywhere.

Then he pulls away and takes a step back. His eyes rove across my body. "So fucking perfect." His finger trails across my breast and his gaze darkens. "I always want you. But today I have not been able to stop thinking about undressing you. Seeing you. Taking you. Taking my wife."

My fingers trail over his pec and down to his navel. "It has been a long day." My hand continues down. "The longest," I murmur just inches from his mouth.

His mouth clamps over mine and his chest presses against mine. An enticing sensation builds and a moan escapes my mouth which only serves to spur him on. In one swift movement, he lifts me and flips me up and back down onto the bed. A second later he is hovering over me, planting kisses and trailing his tongue down my body until he takes my aching core with his tongue. My hands are in his hair, begging him to stop and then begging him for more until I come apart.

Still, I want more of him.

This moment, everything we have been through apart and together, it feels like it has been building to a union of forever and I want to feel and experience all of it. Everything he has to offer.

He teases my entrance with his length, but I know he can no more deny the inevitable than I can and I buck my hips towards him.

"Eager tonight, Red?"

"I want you, Danny. I need you." My words are breathless. My body on fire with desire.

"Mine," he growls as he slips into me. "My fucking wife," he grins proudly.

"My fucking husband," I groan into his mouth and as his hips move and we become one, I know we were meant to be together. Destined somehow, for how could anything be so perfect if it were not written by fate itself?

My hands are gripping his shoulders and then his ass as our pleasure builds and I beg him not to stop, for I am on the very edge, and I can tell by the way his butt contracts and by the way he fills every part of me that he is too. We look into one another's eyes as we hover on the edge of bliss and then, with one last pump, we crash together and it feels so good I cry out that I love him.

We end up somehow side by side, sweat coating our bodies and he strokes my hair and tells me, "I'm going to take care of you. You'll want for nothing and no one will ever hurt you. My wife."

"And I will take care of you too." I stroke my thumb across his angular jaw. "This life was made for living, and I'm blessed to get to live my life with you."

He kisses my temple. "Sleep, my love. Tomorrow we're starting our adventure."

"Adventure? Our time has been nothing if not an adventure. I'm looking forward to the mundane and the ordinary, though I can't imagine life with you will ever be anything less than spectacular."

"This is an adventure I believe you will approve of."

"I'm intrigued." When he doesn't answer, I press. "What is it?"

"A surprise."

"A surprise?" He locks his lips as though with a key, and I tickle him until he lets out a belly laugh.

"Our honeymoon, and that is all I will say on the matter."

And so, I let him keep his secret because, the promise of a honeymoon with my husband is all the knowledge of the future I need.

Chapter 48

Roseanna

A Witch in our Midst

We sleep in, later than usual. For me, I'm still accustomed to Holloway early mornings, and Danny has never seemed to need very much sleep, but with him lying beside me, utterly spent and looking a vision of sheer perfection, I let him sleep, throw my robe on, and descend the stairs with the intention of making my husband breakfast.

It's still early and with the festivities yesterday, I'm certain the rest of the household are all still sleeping. Likely the only person awake is Ida, who believes the nonsense of evil penetrating the bodies of those who aren't working their fingers to the bone before dawn and such, but as I reach the lowest stair, I hear movement about the house and follow the sound, wondering if it is the team Danny mentioned who are coming by to clean.

I walk through the dining hall, passing the table that still houses various cakes and tarts all in a half-eaten state. I hear Ida's voice in the smaller sitting room in the east of the house and approach carefully as I always do when I enter this particular room—remembering the night Benny was murdered within it.

I may be home and safe, but I can't shake the foreboding feeling that all is not right. I approach with caution, allowing the door to provide cover as I did the night Benny was killed.

And then I hear his voice.

Frank.

"I'm telling you, she's a fucking witch!"

"You'll shush your mouth, Frank Alderman. I'll not have you waking the children from their beds with talk of such evil. Letting yourself inside this house like you own it. I don't know whatever possessed you, but you'll leave this once, before Danny wakes and puts a bullet inside of your brain," Ida hisses at him.

"I'm telling you, he'll want to know what I saw. Poof, she went, right into thin air!"

I creep closer, wondering what exactly he thinks he saw. So far as I know, there were no witch trials in these parts, not in this decade at least, but I wouldn't put it past Frank to try to initiate one.

"Have you been drinking, Frank? You're making no sense at all. Now put your pistol away and scarper, before the man of the house finds you here."

I pause at the mention of a pistol, wondering whether to stay put or risk running back to get Danny.

"Not had so much as a sip in months. Mum, I am telling you, Roseanna's a witch. It was pouring with rain and she hugged the woman, who looked just like her but older. Like she was her older twin sister, from another time, it looked like. And then she shouted something and the lightening fired right over head and then poof she was gone! A spell I reckon. Mum, you got to believe me. I saw it!"

"You've gone mad, more like it. Look at the state of thee. You've holes in your shirt and you look like you haven't washed in a month. Now, put your pistol away and let's be having you out the door."

The floorboards creak in the room beyond the door I hide behind. Then I hear Ida say, "You'd shoot your own mother?"

"I don't want to Mum, but I saw what I saw. There is evil under this roof. I knew it the second I laid eyes on Roseanna Chapman, she's trouble. It's why I tried to rid you all of her, but she got out of Holloway. Not even prison could keep her wickedness away for long."

"No. And it couldn't keep yours away either."

When I hear a hard slap, I burst inside the room in time to see Ida cowering from Frank.

"Get out of here, now. Danny is dressing and he'll be down here in just a moment," I say.

"Good. I want him to know what sort of sorceress he's gone and married!"

Frank points his gun at me while Ida peers at me too closely to make me believe she is not immune to Frank's allegations.

"It's nonsense. The man is clearly mad," I tell Ida.

"Where did your mother go last night? She was here and then suddenly she wasn't."

"What? Ida, you can't seriously believe—"

"I know what I saw," Frank spits out, "and you magicked her away in a spell of evil! And the only way to rid ourselves of evil is to destroy it!" His gun is pointed right at my head.

"I—"

Ida interrupts. "You're right, son. I always knew it. The second I saw her, there was a glint of the devil beneath that fair skin of hers. She's been worming her way in ever since she arrived. She's got them all under her spell, but I could see her for what she was, right from the start. Son, we'll rid this place of her. We will. We need to get this place back to how it was, like when you was the lord and master of the manor."

"What? Ida, he's clearly—"

"You'll quieten thee tongue or I shall take the pistol on thee meself." She eyes me with a bitter glare and my back stiffens. Just when I finally thought Ida and I had turned a corner, she convinces herself, with the help of her batshit crazy son, that I am a witch. I try to appeal to Frank, hoping I can get through to him. "I know it probably looked quite strange last night. The rain was coming down fast and there was lightning, which had a strobe-like effect, but my mother had a driver on the other side of the arch waiting for her. I'm not a witch!"

"She's a witch all right, I can see it in her eyes. Thank the Lord you came when you did, son, or else we could have all have been charged by the devil and made to do his bidding in no time at all. And with those innocent babies sleeping upstairs in their beds. Have you no shame?" Ida snarls at me then turns to Frank. "Son, you're shaking. Are thee all right? Let me get thee some sustenance. You're looking as meek as a mouse. Bet you've been sleeping rough and barely eating, while this loathsome louse swans about the manor like lady muck herself." Then she turns back to me. "The presence of evil has that effect on the good folk of this world."

Ida shoulders past me and into the dining hall where she fills a plate with cake and then returns. "Sit. You'll need your strength for what is ahead of us." Frank, looking lordly and full of himself, sits in the small winged back chair beside the fireplace and starts snaffling down cake as though he hasn't eaten in a month.

"I'm glad you are finally seeing the truth of it, Mum, and it be about time you start listening to me again proper. Now, we'll tell Danny she ran off. Boy won't understand about witches and evil and such. Too stupid and lured in by her feminine ways." He takes another giant bite, filling his disgusting gob with Ida's fruit cake. Dried fruit and crumbs sully the frayed lapel of his jacket. Besides the disgust at looking at him, I am horrified at what is happening. It shouldn't surprise me that Ida is supporting her son. I'd seen her do it before when Frank came here, and she'd kept that secret from Danny. Still, I have to try to appeal to their sense of family.

"You'd hurt your own son in such a way?" I ask Frank, but from the way he sneers at me, instead choosing to fill his mouth with food, I know his answer. So, I turn to Ida. "And you, you'd nigh on kill your own grandson? Because that's what it will do, he'd be devastated to find me gone."

Ida peers at me over her glasses, piercing me with a hard glare. "I will do whatever it takes to keep those innocents upstairs safe. I've been around much longer than you have, and the longer I have been around, the more I have come to know that that is the Lord's purpose for me."

"Then if you think I'm evil, I'll go. You'll never see me again. I'll get Danny and we'll leave or he can stay if he chooses. I don't mind, but give him a choice."

"This is the boy's home. Without Danny there is no Alderman Manor." Frank pierces her with a glare.

"I'm sorry, Frank, but it's true. Everything is in his name and the children's. I'm an old lady. Me hip won't carry me much longer, and I've always liked it here, you know I have. I'll keel over if I have to go work in the liver house again."

"Ida, you can't be serious. You can't stay here with Frank, he's a selfish monster." Unable to believe what is happening, I beg. "Ida. You can't go along with this crazy plan!" Tears are springing to my eyes.

"It's done." Frank smiles at me, standing from the chair, brushing the crumbs of the cake down onto the floor and adjusting the gun in his hand until he seems to have it angled right in my face.

I laugh bitterly. It isn't time or Holloway that's going to end me. The love of my life's own bloodline will. "Danny will never forgive you."

He nods. "He'll never find out. See my boy, since he found love, he's become more forgiving. He'd have shot me soon as look at me for what I done, but that night in the King's Head when he wanted to kill me but wouldn't because he thought you'd think less of him, I saw, he'd changed and not for the better. He used to be a ruthless son of a bitch. I was proud of him. And now I hear that he's letting people off, letting them think he's gone soft! But I knew. I knew once I came to me ma with news of your witchery, she'd see you for what you are. And she'll help me persuade Danny to give me another shot, just as soon as you're out of the way. Now come on, outside and don't make a fuss or I'll shoot you right here and you'll die just like Benny."

From the corner of my eye, I catch Ida wince at his callous reference of Benny.

Frank coughs, loudly and deeply, bashing the centre of his chest like the crumbs of the cake are choking him—and I hope they are.

His face pinks up until it is angry and red. I watch the pistol sway from left to right as he tries to purge whatever is caught in his throat. I want to snatch it from his hand, but he still seems in enough control of himself to shoot me if I try.

"Thought you'd enjoy your favourite loaf cake, son," Ida says, and I am utterly stupefied and in shock at her support for her wayward son.

"Might not be much of a cook, Mum, but you could always bake a decent loaf," Frank says winking at her while trying to catch his breath.

"What sort of grandmother are you?! Taking the side of that evil bastard over your own grandson. Alice, Henry, Clifford! Even Harriet and the baby! I thought you loved them."

She gently shrugs. Her eyes looking saddened. "I've brought up those kids and gone without. I love them but I'm old—"

"You'll be all right with me, Mum," Frank says, then coughs again as though a piece of cake is still lodged in his windpipe.

Ida stands as though to go and tap his back but stops herself and holds still, watching him over the rim of her half-moon spectacles.

Frank coughs again. His meaty hand, the one that's not clutching the gun, goes to his heart. His eyes are watery and his face turns an even angrier reddish-purple colour. He tries to speak but his tongue seems to be swelling right inside his mouth.

At that moment, Danny bursts into the room, his pistol in his hand. But as he enters the threshold, his father falls to the floor and his body starts to shudder.

"Dear boy," Ida says, crouching at Frank's side, "looks like you're having one of your reactions. I do hope the cake you had didn't contain nuts."

I shake my head, not understanding what's going on.

Ida continues, "Terrible if there was almonds in that cake mix, what with you having an allergy to them and all. Especially after that time you nearly died as a child and the doctor said that even a sniff of a peanut could kill you."

Frank's feet are twitching but his eyes are solidly fixed on Ida.

"I prayed you'd come good. I defended you and stuck by you, but I won't have you take what belongs to those kids, no I won't." Ida strokes his head as the last heaves of life sink from Frank's body; then she closes his eyes. "You'll have to say your piece to the Lord himself now, child. I'll pray that he forgives you." Ida's face becomes wretchedly sombre and she adds, "And I'll pray he forgives me too."

And with that, Frank dies soundlessly on the rug on the living room floor with his mother by his side.

Chapter 49

Roseanna

What's Done is Done

"We'll need to dispose of his body. Can't lift him on my own," Ida says, acting as though it's business as usual even though she just killed her only child.

I go to her, holding both of her arms and standing in front of her. "You did that? To save me?"

Ida straightens her long neck. Her throat bobbing with her swallow is the only sign that she is in anyway shaken. "I gave him every chance, but I won't have him turning up here and taking the food out of those children's mouths like he did before. It ain't right and it ain't proper." Ida shakes her head and I notice the tiniest watery glint on her eyes.

I turn to Danny, he's staring at his dead father with a look of loathing. "He couldn't just stay away and let us be happy."

"We do what we must for those we love," Ida says.

Danny looks up, his eyes focusing on me, then he nods, as if in agreement to Ida's rationale.

"Come on then, let's get him moved before the children wake. They were late to bed, so they'll be languishing in their pits awhile longer but we won't have long."

"I'll go dig the hole," Danny says.

"I'll help you," I offer, placing my hand on his bicep but Danny shakes his head.

"I need to lay him and his ghosts to rest alone."

"I understand," I whisper though it breaks my heart to see his emotions torn this way.

"Beneath the oak tree," Ida calls after Danny. "He once climbed a tree like that on a day trip down at Southend. He'll like it there."

Danny agrees but looks at Ida strangely. She's acting as though she didn't just end her son's life. Ida stares down at the crumbs from the nut-laced cake on the floor and then stops the clock on the mantel. She looks around, looking everywhere except where her son's body lay on the floor, and so I lead her into the kitchen under the guise of sheets that must be washed. She seems dithery, in shock. As she boils water in one of the enormous, cast-iron pans she talks like we are planning a funeral. "We'll put him under the tree and when I go to town, I'll fetch him some nice fresh flowers. Yellow, he liked yellow." She brushes imaginary crumbs from her apron and stares down at it.

"You did what you needed to," I say.

Ida stops fussing with her apron, unties it and then dumps it in the pan to be boil washed.

"You think I'll go to hell?"

I don't answer immediately. Ida has done a terrible thing, but it was the right decision. "Frank was on a path of destruction and he had lost all sense of family, only operating for his own means. You didn't put a gun to his head, he chose this. So no, I don't think you'll go to hell. In fact, for what it's worth, I think you'll all have richer lives without him."

"Always was trouble. His father through and through." She begins placing plates from last night's party into the sink and then says, as though an afterthought, "I wouldn't have let him kill you. You might be a witch, but I know there's good in that there heart of yours."

My mouth pops open.

"I saw your mother disappear. It was then I knew, whether it was God himself that had sent you to save this family, you did. You saved us all. For if you hadn't come when you did, my darling Danny would have become his own undoing and heaven knows what that'd have meant for the rest of us. The Lord moves in mysterious ways. I know that more than most." And with that, she asks, "Tea?"

Chapter 50

Danny

Honeymoon Time

"You ready?" I ask. We're both standing six feet in front of the arch.

I shake my head. "You still want to go?"

The sun, high in the sky, beats down on my head. "You have been the most special thing in my life. You're smile alone has lit up all my darkness. It's time we stepped into the light, for a while at least."

"But I still don't know where we're going."

I wrap my arms around the absolute love of my life and turn her to face the family who are on the steps of the manor ready to wave us off.

A shiver runs through me as a cloud passes over the sun and it starts to rain.

"We're going to Blackpool. A little house and a sandy beach just me and you for a week. It's not the future, but it kind of is."

Red looks up at the arch and then down at the Alderman motorcar that's parked before us and the sky crackles before spits of rain begin to fall.

"I remember Nanna saying, 'It'll be raining. It always is...,' and now I wonder if she meant that it has to rain before we can fully appreciate the sun."

I move closer until her head is almost tucked beneath my chin and look down into her bright green eyes. "Kiss me?"

She reaches up onto her toes until her lips meet mine. Passionate, her lips caress mine until we are melded as one. Her kiss is everything and my body and mind are screaming that we are meant to be together. I crave her touch like I crave air, feeling starved without it. And I want her. At all costs I need her.

Her arms pull me in tighter. We spend seconds or minutes wrapped in each other, savouring every taste, allowing passion to fill us, until I am falling in love with her all over again. The feel of her around me, her scent, it is home no matter where we are in this world. Time is inconsequential, and all is right with the world so long as we are together.

When we break apart, Roseanna looks up at me with her big green eyes, expressive and mesmerising as ever and says, "Let's go, husband. Our future awaits us."

Thank you for reading.

If you enjoyed this novel and would like to see more in this series then please leave a review on Amazon. I read all my reviews and am so very grateful for your support.

A note from the author

Hi!

Thank you for reading Captive Songbird. I hope you have enjoyed spending time with these characters as much as I have loved writing them.

In my research of the roaring twenties, I have read harrowing tales of poverty, injustice, and difficulties, but also, I've been comforted by the sense of community and family that isn't always so prominent in our time.

I have tried throughout this book to stay true to the 1920's but I have had to use some creative license in order to bring forward the tale you hold in your hands. I hope any errors or omissions found in this story are received in the good faith they were intended and that they didn't in any way spoil your enjoyment of the story.

Kindest regards

Ophelia

Acknowledgements

Special thanks to my editor and friend, Randie Creamer. This lady has been with me since the start of my crazy publishing journey and without her this book (and many others) would not exist. She is my saviour and confidante and also the most kind and gracious that human nature has to offer. Randie, I salute you! (I'm still working on the damehood for you!)

To Ellen Montoya, a calm voice in a crazy world. This lady's empathy and sheer goodness is beyond compare. I am blessed to have found a friend in you and look forward to sharing drinks on a beach someplace soon!

Thank you to Ana Rita Clemente. You are a book wizard and special friend. I adore you!

To Christina Gamboa, I love our chats! Thank you for your friendship and support.

To Laurie Dunlap, from one crazy dog lady to another—it has been a pleasure getting to know you and Chilli. Thank you for all your help!

To Jacqui Buckley, fellow warrior and listening ear. Thank you! I appreciate you more and more with every passing year.

To all my readers, thank you for reading my work and in doing so making my dreams come true!

About the Author

Ophelia Lockheart lives in south England with her two dogs, husband and three children.

She's a huge fan of powerful, cranky men with hearts-of-gold and chivalrous values who'll do anything for the sassy, independent women who own their hearts.

With plenty of suspense, swoon-worthy storylines, and enough sizzle to set your hearts on fire, you can rest assured that if you're reading one of Ophelia's books, you're putting your time into just the right tale!

Follow her on FB: https://www.facebook.com/OpheliaLockheartAuthor

Message her on email: ophelialockheart.author@gmail.com

~~

Ophelia also writes romantic comedy using the pen name: Emily James which are available on Amazon.

Made in United States
North Haven, CT
08 May 2023